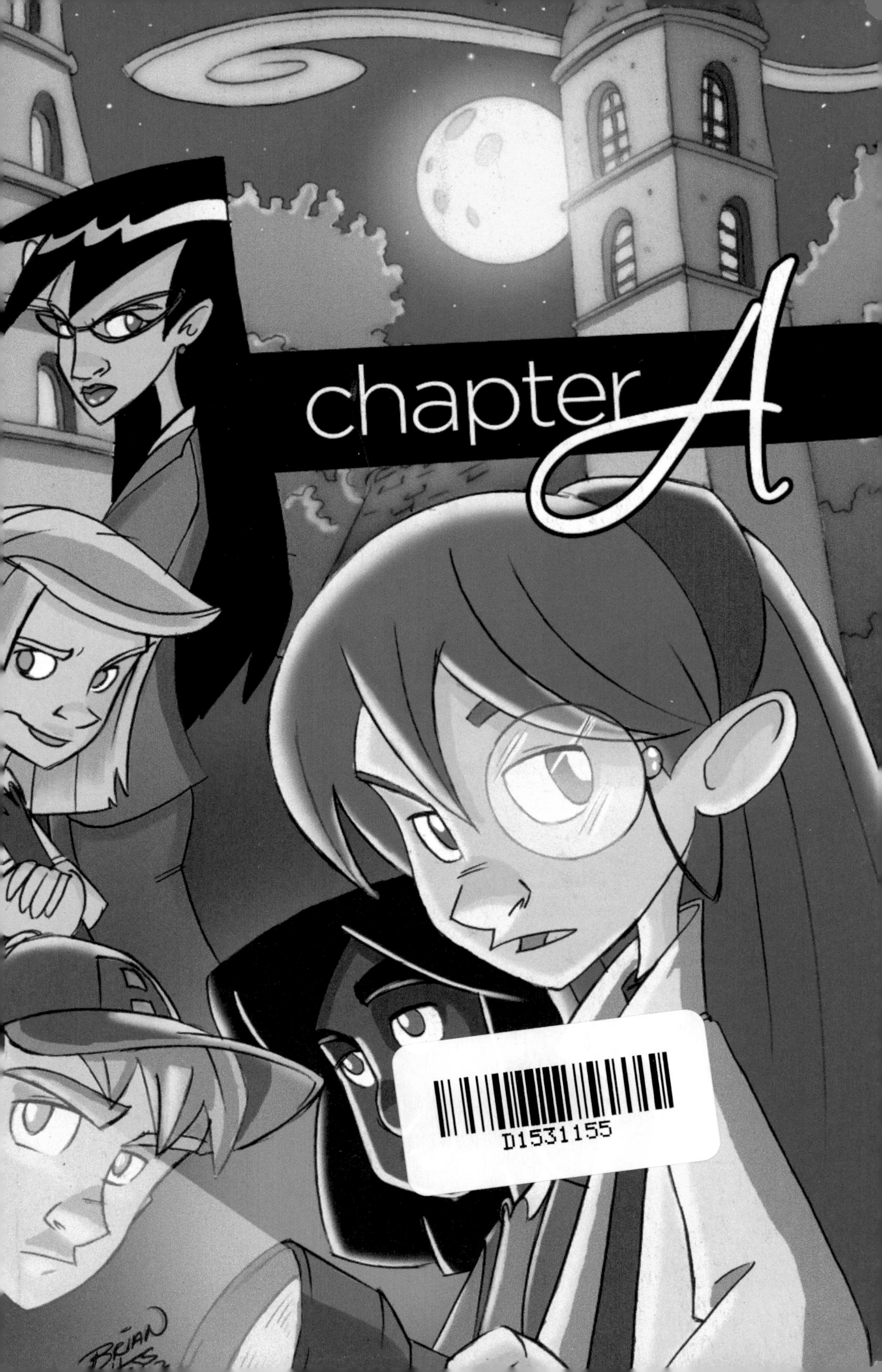
chapter A

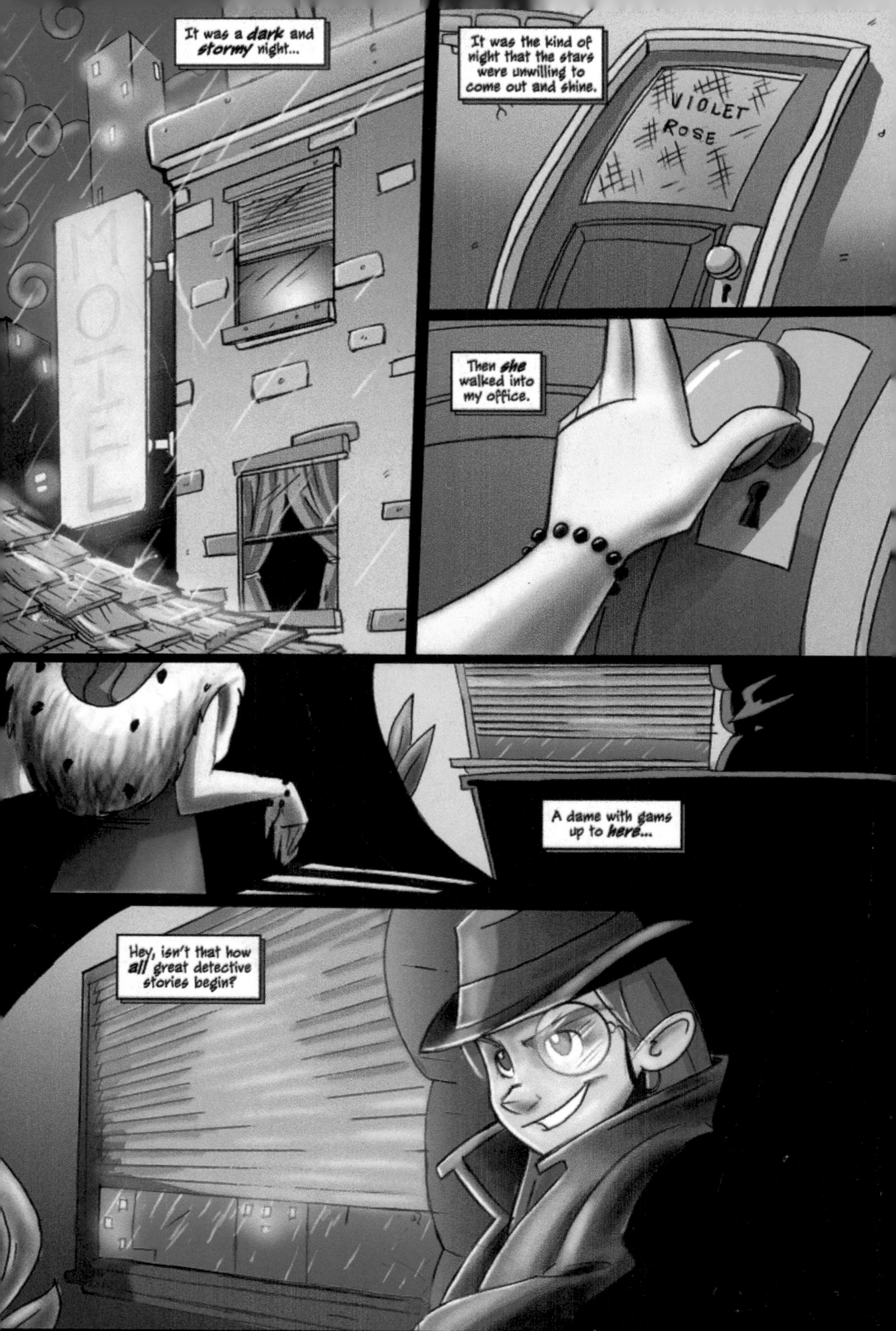
It was a *dark* and *stormy* night...
MOTEL
It was the kind of night that the stars were unwilling to come out and shine.
VIOLET ROSE
Then *she* walked into my office.
A dame with gams up to *here*...
Hey, isn't that how *all* great detective stories begin?

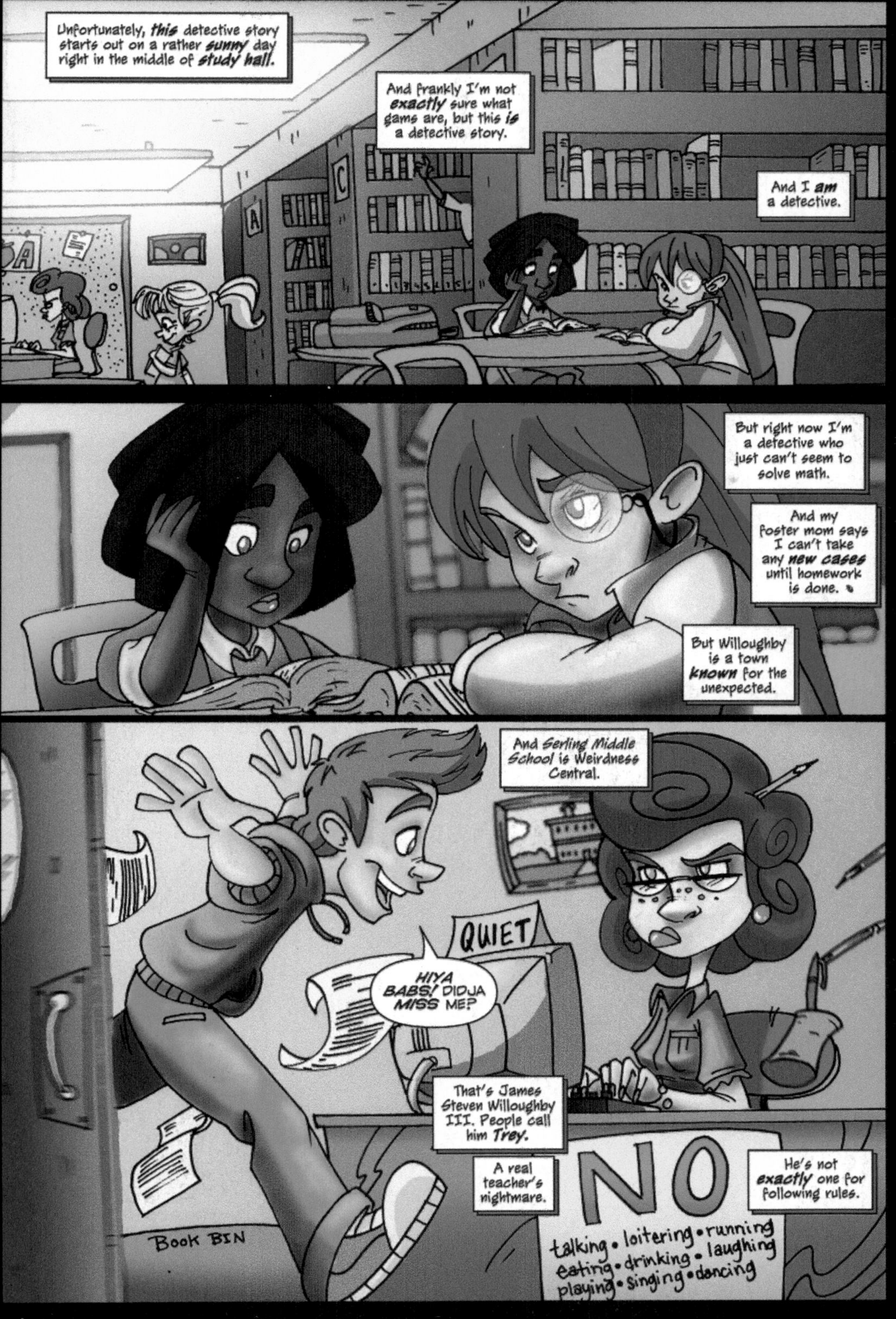

Unfortunately, this detective story starts out on a rather sunny day right in the middle of study hall.
And frankly I'm not exactly sure what gams are, but this is a detective story.
And I am a detective.
But right now I'm a detective who just can't seem to solve math.
And my foster mom says I can't take any new cases until homework is done.
But Willoughby is a town known for the unexpected.
And Serling Middle School is Weirdness Central.
QUIET
HIYA BABS! DIDJA MISS ME?
That's James Steven Willoughby III. People call him Trey.
A real teacher's nightmare.
He's not exactly one for following rules.
NO
talking • loitering • running
eating • drinking • laughing
playing • singing • dancing
BOOK BIN

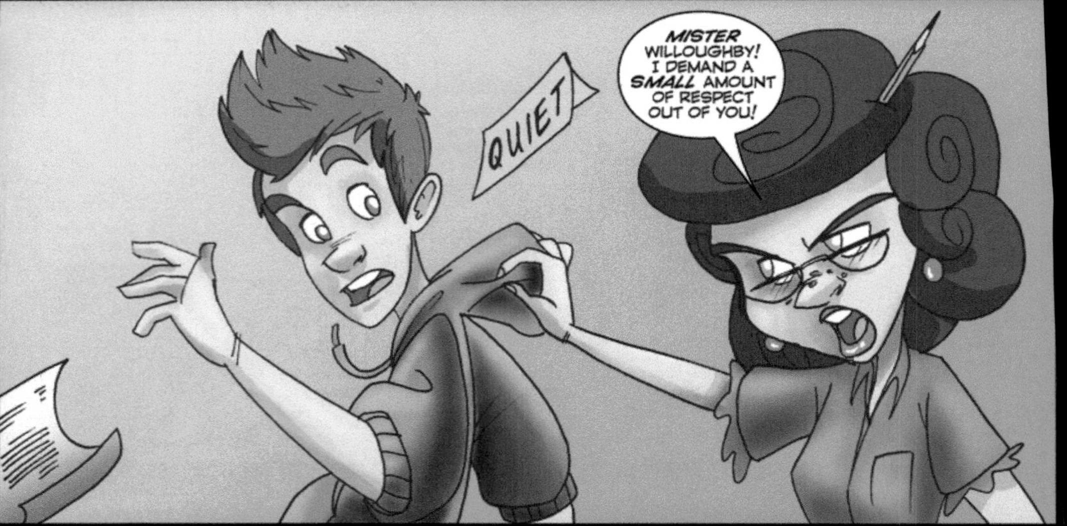
QUIET
MISTER WILLOUGHBY! I DEMAND A SMALL AMOUNT OF RESPECT OUT OF YOU!

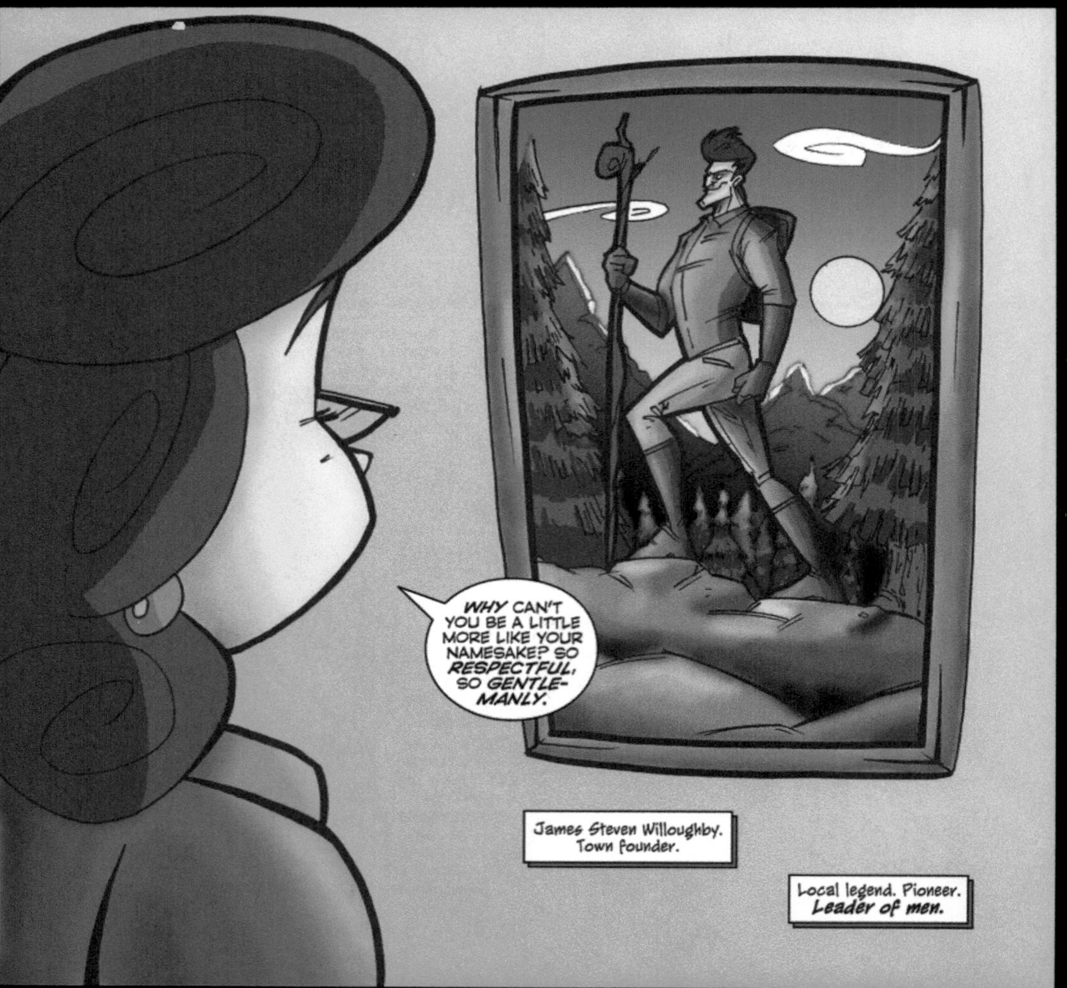
WHY CAN'T YOU BE A LITTLE MORE LIKE YOUR NAMESAKE? SO RESPECTFUL, SO GENTLE-MANLY.
James Steven Willoughby. Town founder.
Local legend. Pioneer. Leader of men.

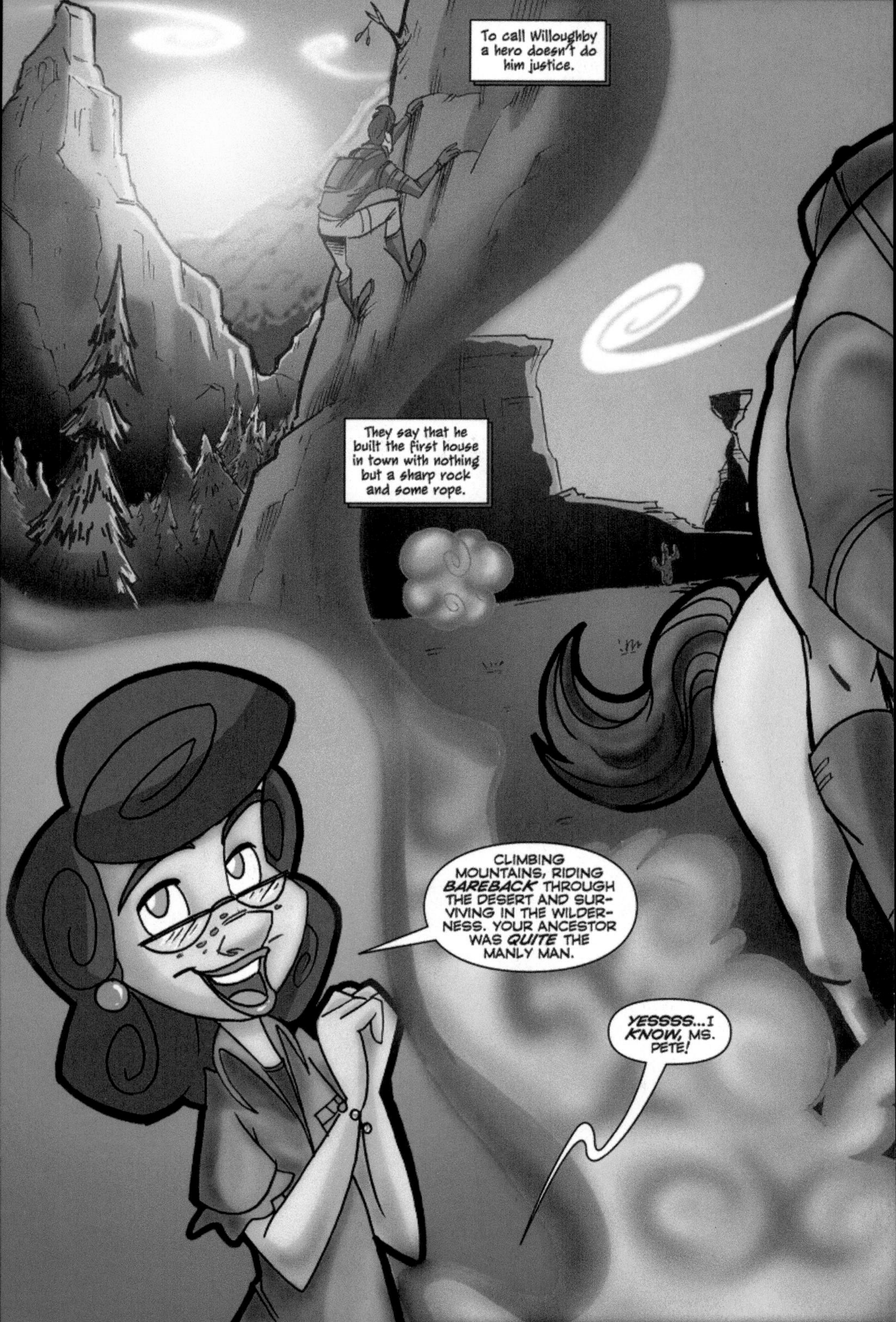

To call Willoughby a hero doesn't do him justice.
They say that he built the first house in town with nothing but a sharp rock and some rope.
CLIMBING MOUNTAINS, RIDING *BAREBACK* THROUGH THE DESERT AND SURVIVING IN THE WILDERNESS. YOUR ANCESTOR WAS *QUITE* THE MANLY MAN.
YESSSS...I KNOW, MS. PETE!

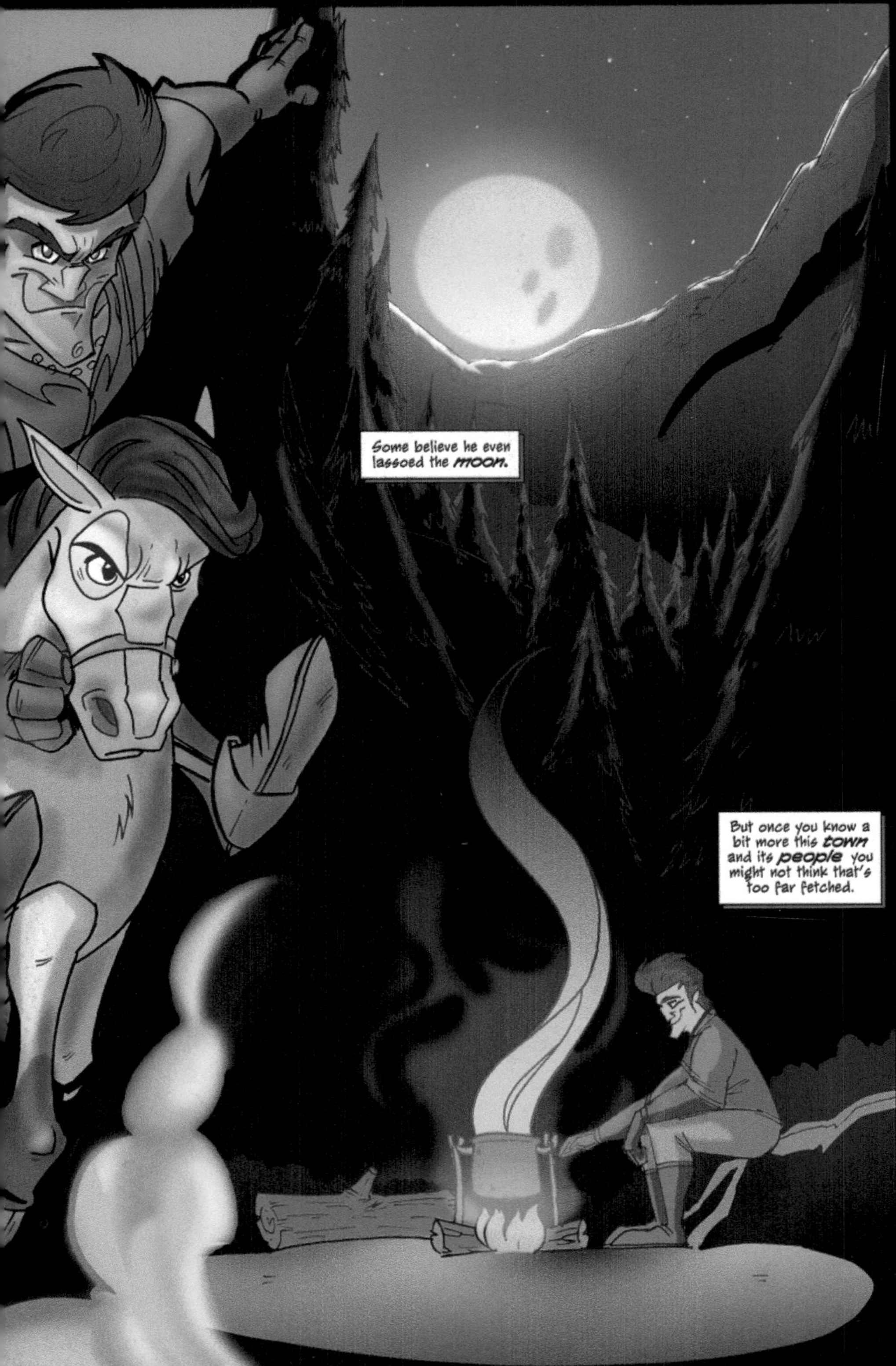
Some believe he even lassoed the *moon.*
But once you know a bit more this *town* and its *people* you might not think that's too far fetched.

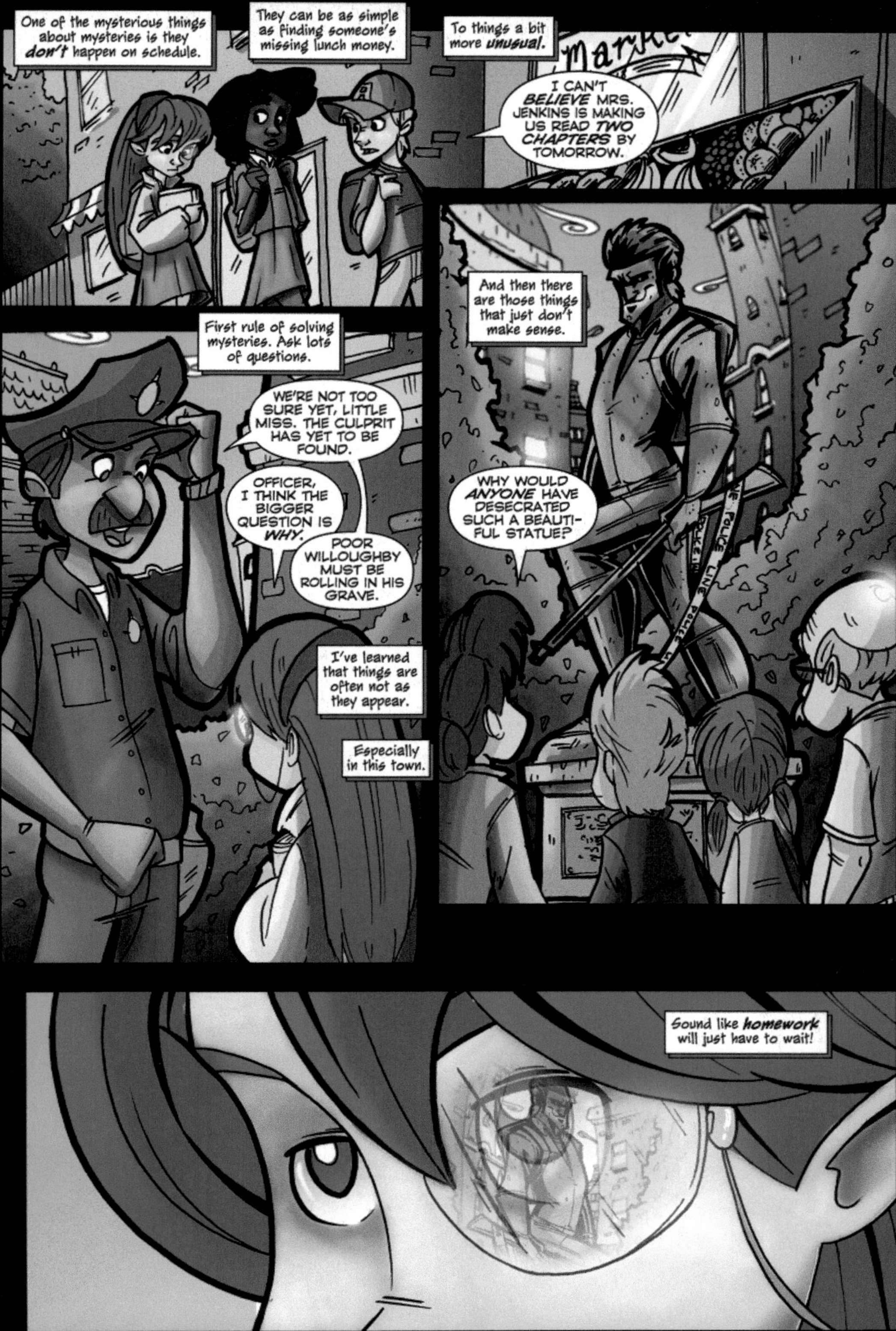
One of the mysterious things about mysteries is they *don't* happen on schedule.
They can be as simple as finding someone's missing lunch money.
To things a bit more *unusual*.
Market
I CAN'T *BELIEVE* MRS. JENKINS IS MAKING US READ *TWO CHAPTERS* BY TOMORROW.
And then there are those things that just don't make sense.
WHY WOULD *ANYONE* HAVE DESECRATED SUCH A BEAUTI-FUL STATUE?
POLICE LINE
First rule of solving mysteries. Ask lots of questions.
WE'RE NOT TOO SURE YET, LITTLE MISS. THE CULPRIT HAS YET TO BE FOUND.
OFFICER, I THINK THE BIGGER QUESTION IS *WHY.*
POOR WILLOUGHBY MUST BE ROLLING IN HIS GRAVE.
I've learned that things are often not as they appear.
Especially in this town.
Sound like *homework* will just have to wait!

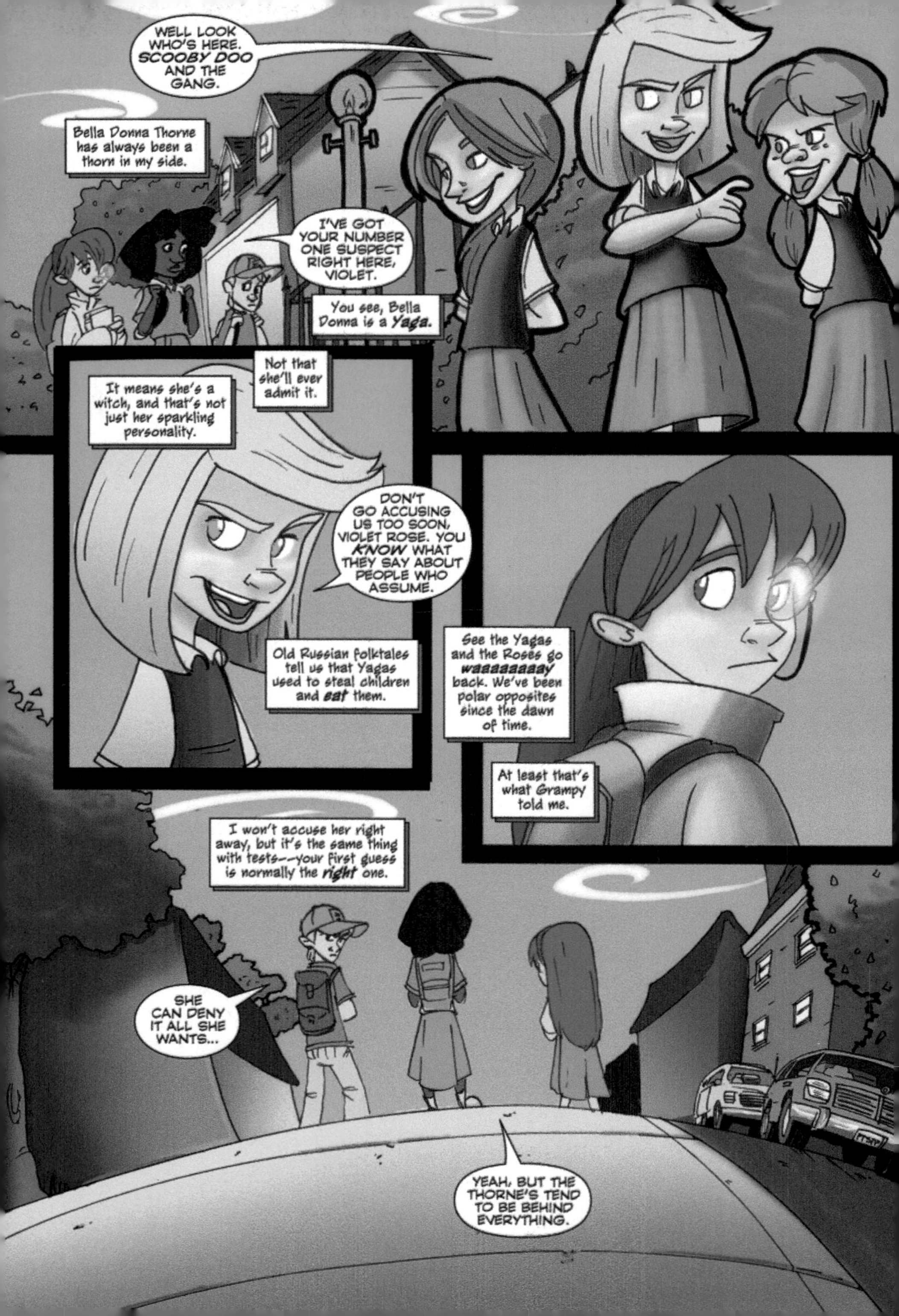
WELL LOOK WHO'S HERE. SCOOBY DOO AND THE GANG.
Bella Donna Thorne has always been a thorn in my side.
I'VE GOT YOUR NUMBER ONE SUSPECT RIGHT HERE, VIOLET.
You see, Bella Donna is a Yaga.
It means she's a witch, and that's not just her sparkling personality.
Not that she'll ever admit it.
DON'T GO ACCUSING US TOO SOON, VIOLET ROSE. YOU KNOW WHAT THEY SAY ABOUT PEOPLE WHO ASSUME.
Old Russian folktales tell us that Yagas used to steal children and eat them.
See the Yagas and the Roses go waaaaaaaay back. We've been polar opposites since the dawn of time.
At least that's what Grampy told me.
I won't accuse her right away, but it's the same thing with tests--your first guess is normally the right one.
SHE CAN DENY IT ALL SHE WANTS...
YEAH, BUT THE THORNE'S TEND TO BE BEHIND EVERYTHING.

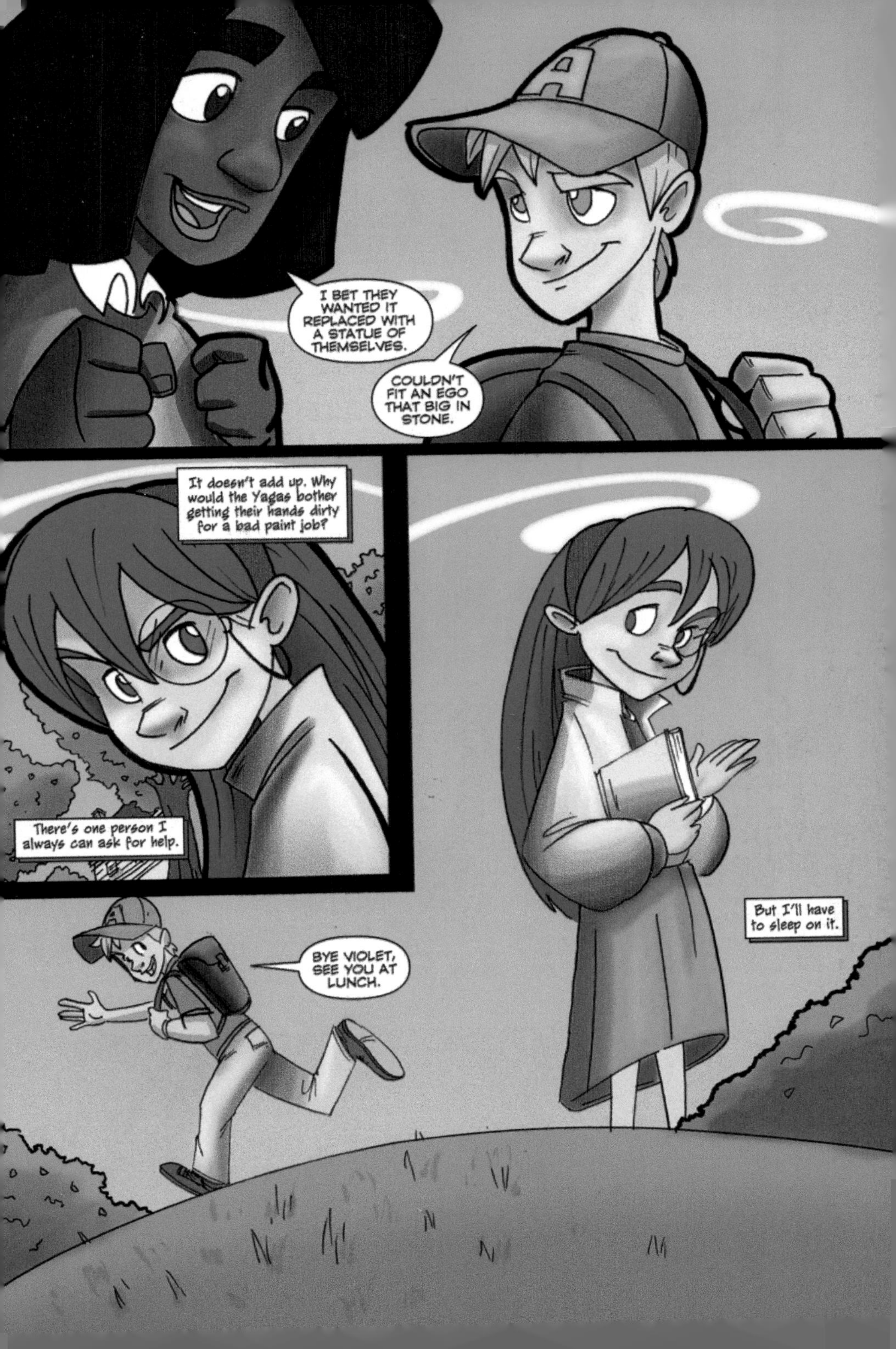
I BET THEY WANTED IT REPLACED WITH A STATUE OF THEMSELVES.
COULDN'T FIT AN EGO THAT BIG IN STONE.
It doesn't add up. Why would the Yagas bother getting their hands dirty for a bad paint job?
There's one person I always can ask for help.
But I'll have to sleep on it.
BYE VIOLET, SEE YOU AT LUNCH.

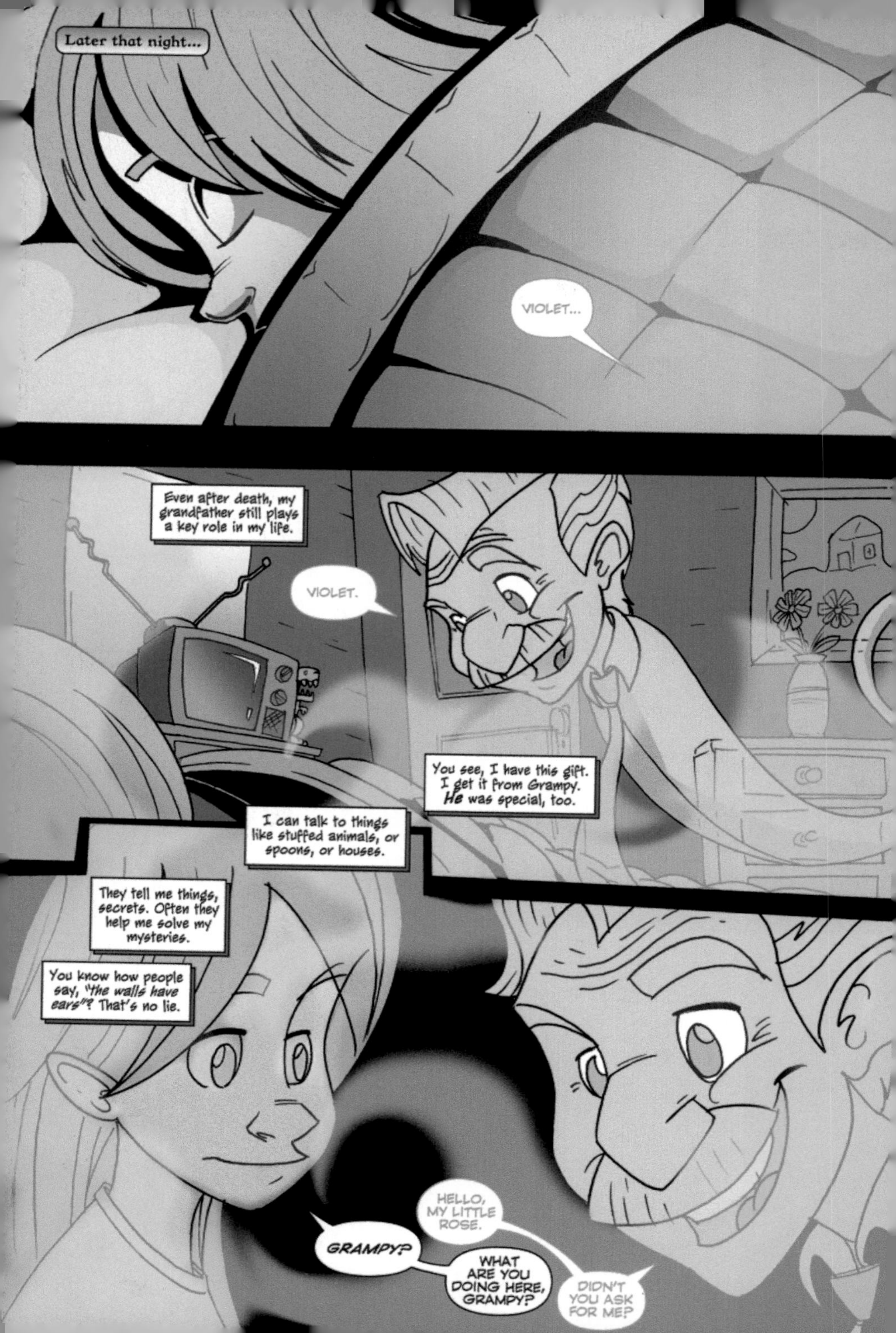

Later that night...
VIOLET...
Even after death, my grandfather still plays a key role in my life.
VIOLET.
You see, I have this gift. I get it from Grampy. He was special, too.
I can talk to things like stuffed animals, or spoons, or houses.
They tell me things, secrets. Often they help me solve my mysteries.
You know how people say, "the walls have ears"? That's no lie.
HELLO, MY LITTLE ROSE.
GRAMPY?
WHAT ARE YOU DOING HERE, GRAMPY?
DIDN'T YOU ASK FOR ME?

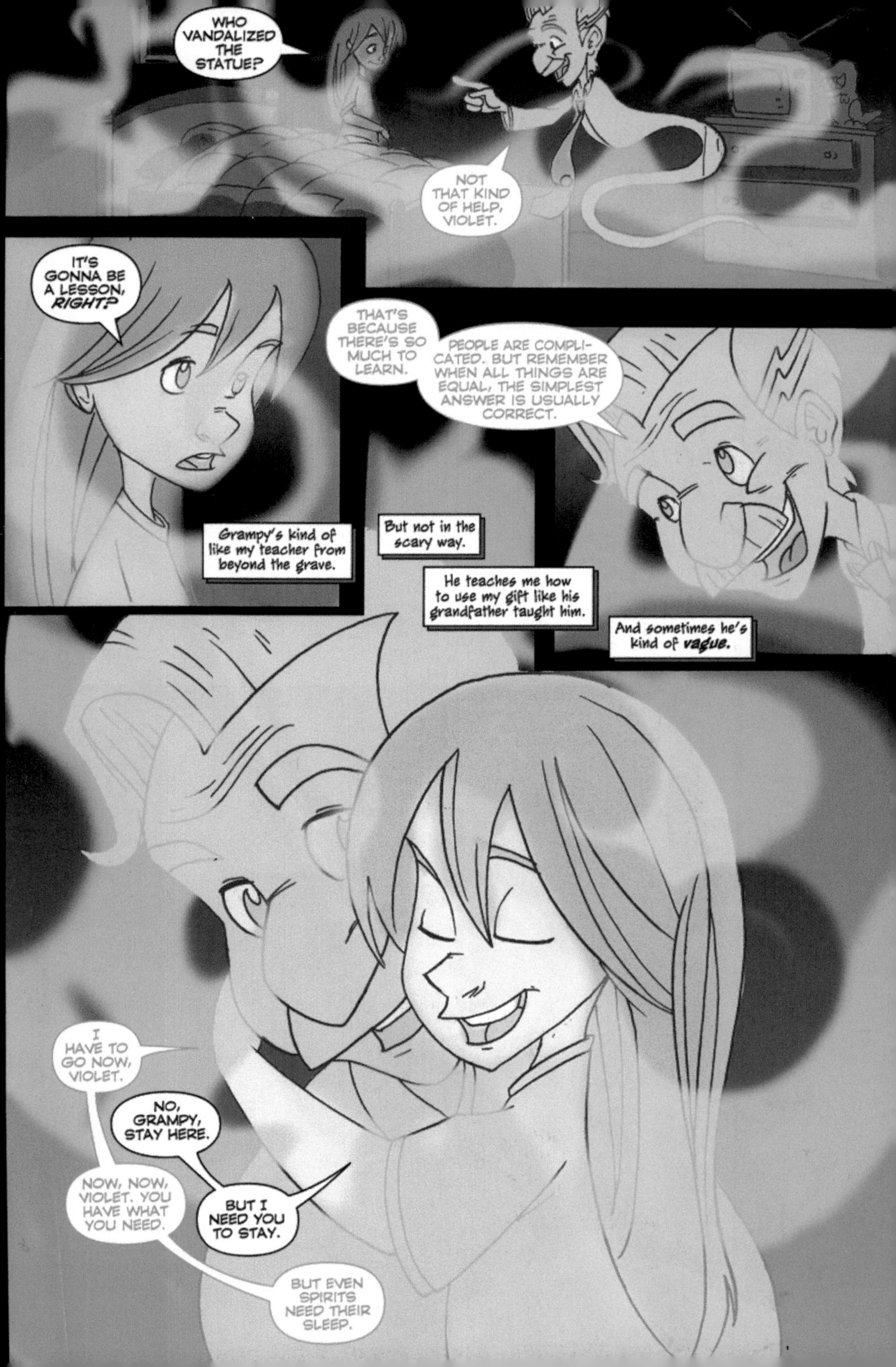
WHO VANDALIZED THE STATUE?
NOT THAT KIND OF HELP, VIOLET.
IT'S GONNA BE A LESSON, *RIGHT?*
THAT'S BECAUSE THERE'S SO MUCH TO LEARN.
PEOPLE ARE COMPLICATED. BUT REMEMBER WHEN ALL THINGS ARE EQUAL, THE SIMPLEST ANSWER IS USUALLY CORRECT.
Grampy's kind of like my teacher from beyond the grave.
But not in the scary way.
He teaches me how to use my gift like his grandfather taught him.
And sometimes he's kind of *vague.*
I HAVE TO GO NOW, VIOLET.
NO, GRAMPY, STAY HERE.
NOW, NOW, VIOLET. YOU HAVE WHAT YOU NEED.
BUT I NEED YOU TO STAY.
BUT EVEN SPIRITS NEED THEIR SLEEP.

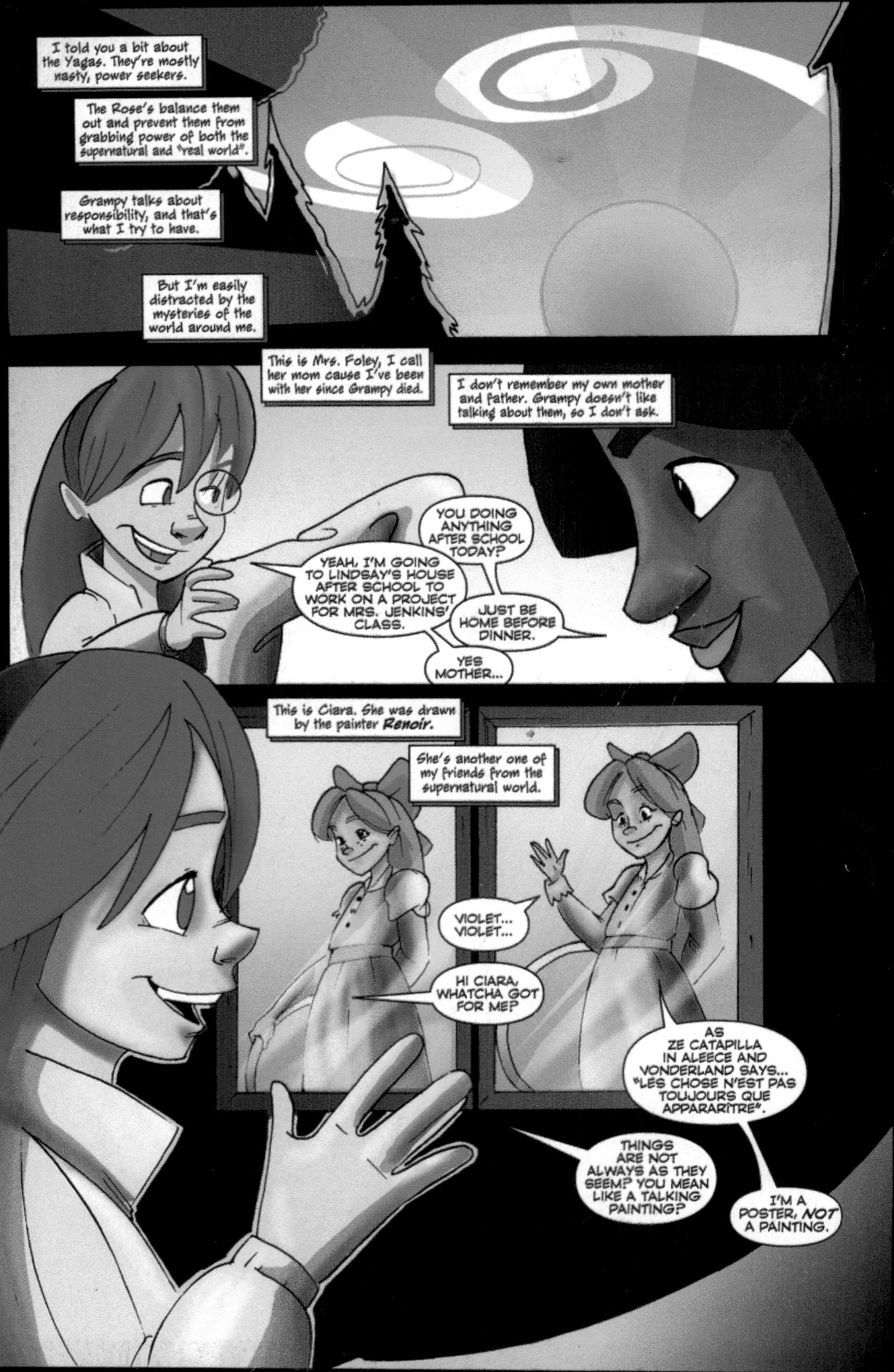
I told you a bit about the Yagas. They're mostly nasty, power seekers.
The Rose's balance them out and prevent them from grabbing power of both the supernatural and "real world".
Grampy talks about responsibility, and that's what I try to have.
But I'm easily distracted by the mysteries of the world around me.
This is Mrs. Foley, I call her mom cause I've been with her since Grampy died.
I don't remember my own mother and father. Grampy doesn't like talking about them, so I don't ask.
YOU DOING ANYTHING AFTER SCHOOL TODAY?
YEAH, I'M GOING TO LINDSAY'S HOUSE AFTER SCHOOL TO WORK ON A PROJECT FOR MRS. JENKINS' CLASS.
JUST BE HOME BEFORE DINNER.
YES MOTHER...
This is Ciara. She was drawn by the painter Renoir.
She's another one of my friends from the supernatural world.
VIOLET... VIOLET...
HI CIARA, WHATCHA GOT FOR ME?
AS ZE CATAPILLA IN ALEECE AND VONDERLAND SAYS... "LES CHOSE N'EST PAS TOUJOURS QUE APPARARITRE".
THINGS ARE NOT ALWAYS AS THEY SEEM? YOU MEAN LIKE A TALKING PAINTING?
I'M A POSTER, NOT A PAINTING.

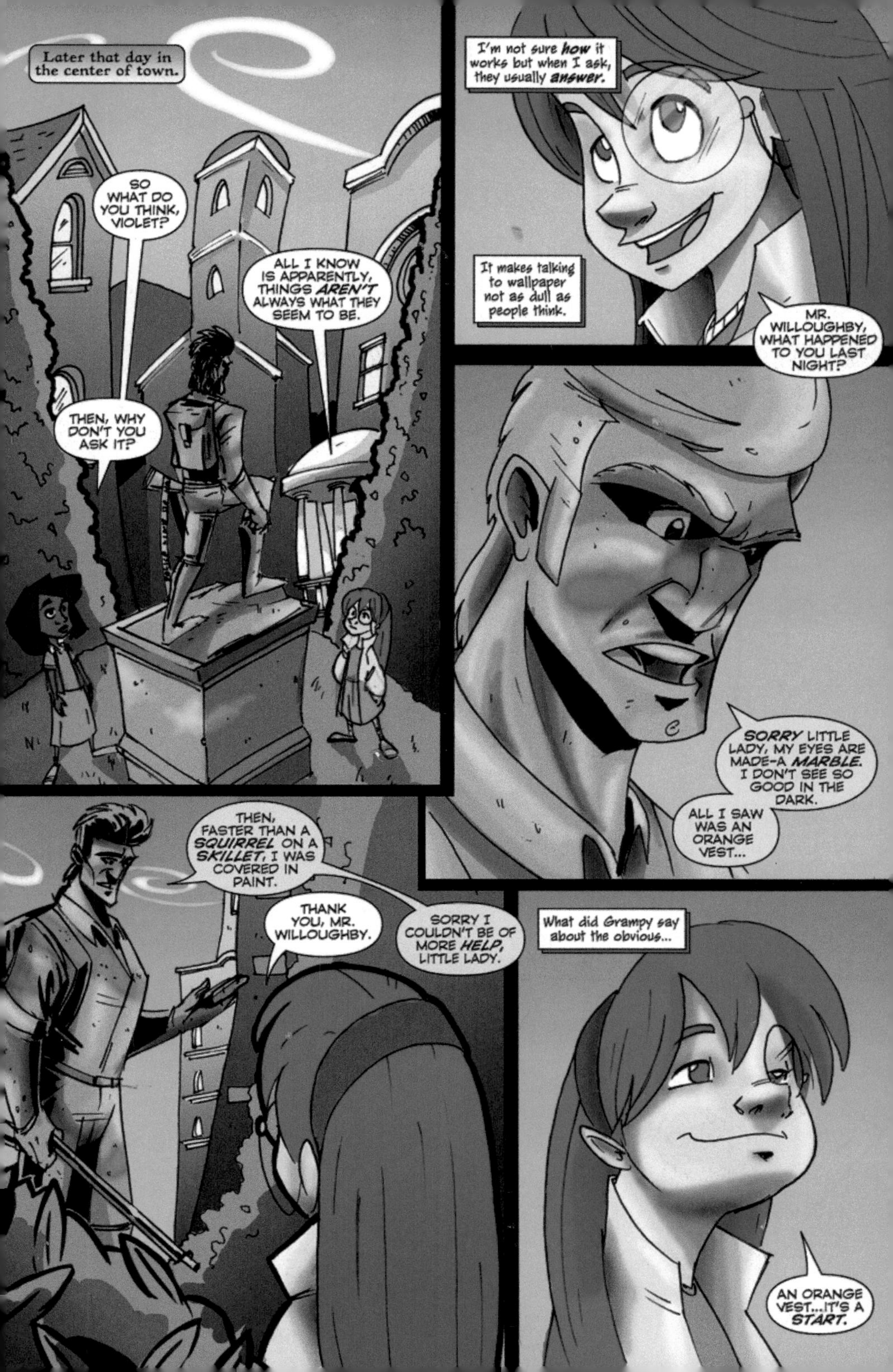
Later that day in the center of town.
SO WHAT DO YOU THINK, VIOLET?
ALL I KNOW IS APPARENTLY, THINGS AREN'T ALWAYS WHAT THEY SEEM TO BE.
THEN, WHY DON'T YOU ASK IT?
I'm not sure how it works but when I ask, they usually answer.
It makes talking to wallpaper not as dull as people think.
MR. WILLOUGHBY, WHAT HAPPENED TO YOU LAST NIGHT?
SORRY LITTLE LADY, MY EYES ARE MADE-A MARBLE. I DON'T SEE SO GOOD IN THE DARK.
ALL I SAW WAS AN ORANGE VEST...
THEN, FASTER THAN A SQUIRREL ON A SKILLET, I WAS COVERED IN PAINT.
THANK YOU, MR. WILLOUGHBY.
SORRY I COULDN'T BE OF MORE HELP, LITTLE LADY.
What did Grampy say about the obvious...
AN ORANGE VEST...IT'S A START.

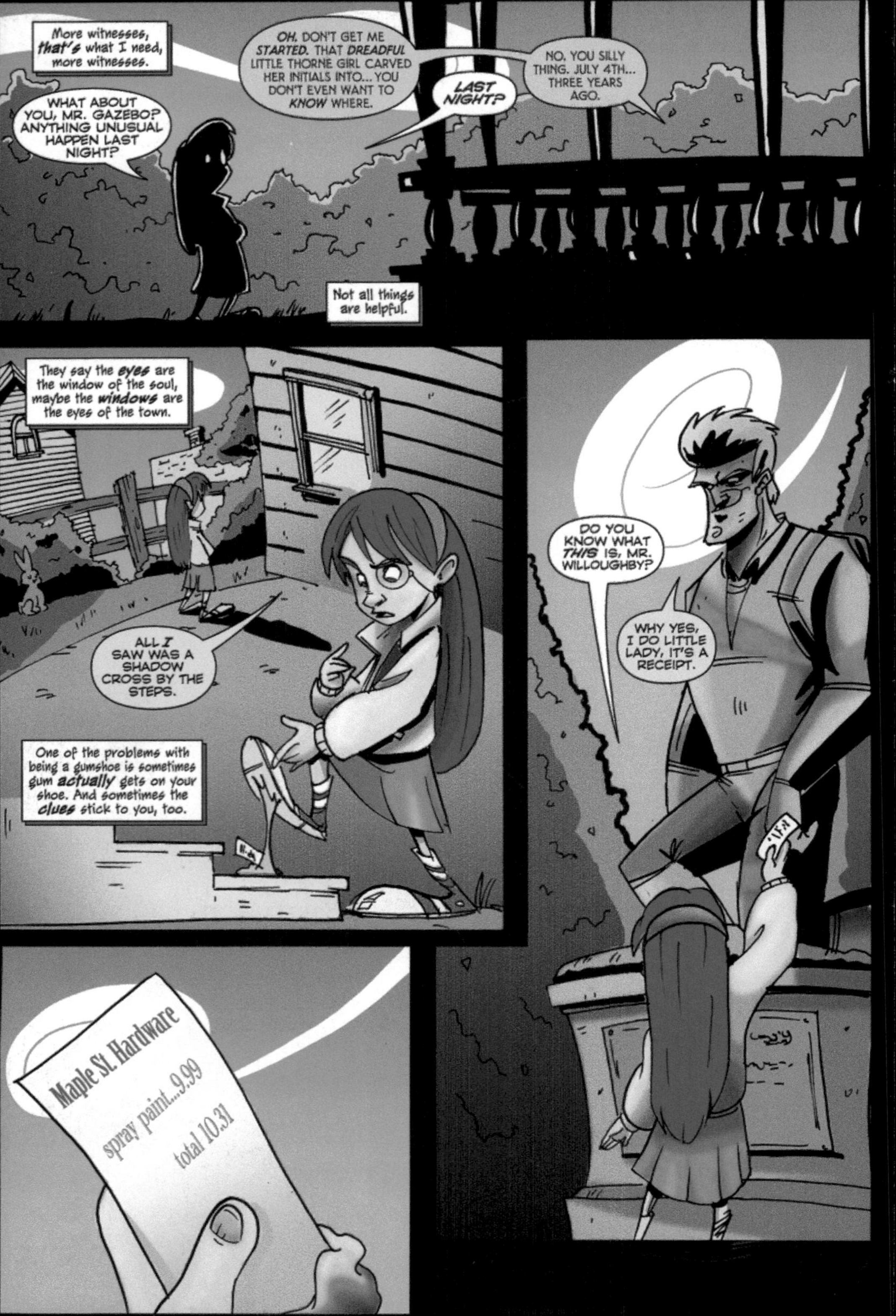
More witnesses, that's what I need, more witnesses.
WHAT ABOUT YOU, MR. GAZEBO? ANYTHING UNUSUAL HAPPEN LAST NIGHT?
OH. DON'T GET ME STARTED. THAT DREADFUL LITTLE THORNE GIRL CARVED HER INITIALS INTO... YOU DON'T EVEN WANT TO KNOW WHERE.
LAST NIGHT?
NO, YOU SILLY THING. JULY 4TH... THREE YEARS AGO.
Not all things are helpful.
They say the eyes are the window of the soul, maybe the windows are the eyes of the town.
ALL I SAW WAS A SHADOW CROSS BY THE STEPS.
One of the problems with being a gumshoe is sometimes gum actually gets on your shoe. And sometimes the clues stick to you, too.
DO YOU KNOW WHAT THIS IS, MR. WILLOUGHBY?
WHY YES, I DO LITTLE LADY, IT'S A RECEIPT.
Maple St. Hardware
spray paint...9.99
total 10.31

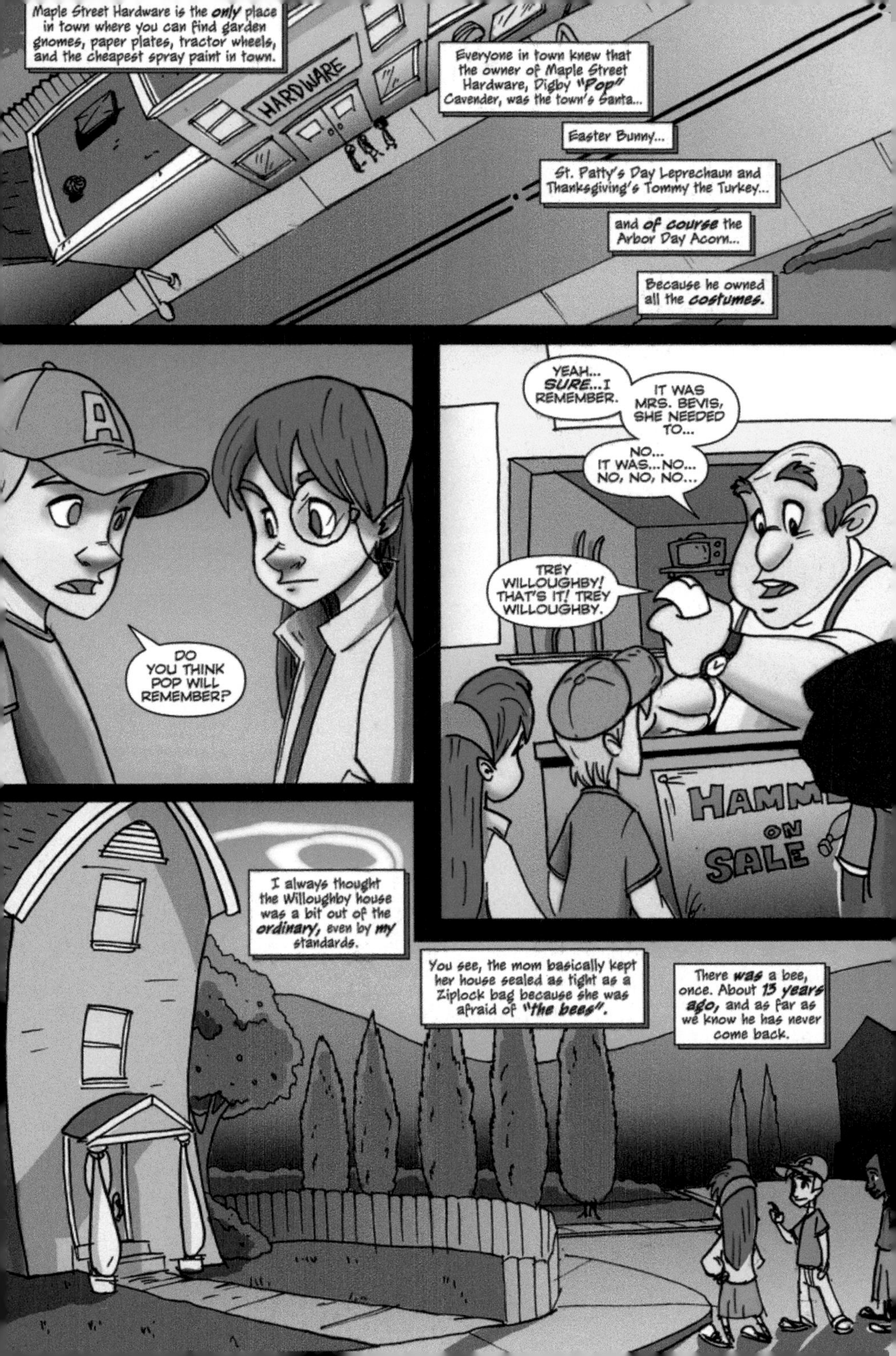
Maple Street Hardware is the *only* place in town where you can find garden gnomes, paper plates, tractor wheels, and the cheapest spray paint in town.
HARDWARE
Everyone in town knew that the owner of Maple Street Hardware, Digby *"Pop"* Cavender, was the town's Santa...
Easter Bunny...
St. Patty's Day Leprechaun and Thanksgiving's Tommy the Turkey...
and *of course* the Arbor Day Acorn...
Because he owned all the *costumes.*
DO YOU THINK POP WILL REMEMBER?
YEAH... *SURE*...I REMEMBER.
IT WAS MRS. BEVIS, SHE NEEDED TO...
NO... IT WAS...NO... NO, NO, NO...
TREY WILLOUGHBY! THAT'S IT! TREY WILLOUGHBY.
HAMM
ON SALE
I always thought the Willoughby house was a bit out of the *ordinary,* even by *my* standards.
You see, the mom basically kept her house sealed as tight as a Ziplock bag because she was afraid of *"the bees".*
There *was* a bee, once. About *13 years ago,* and as far as we know he has never come back.

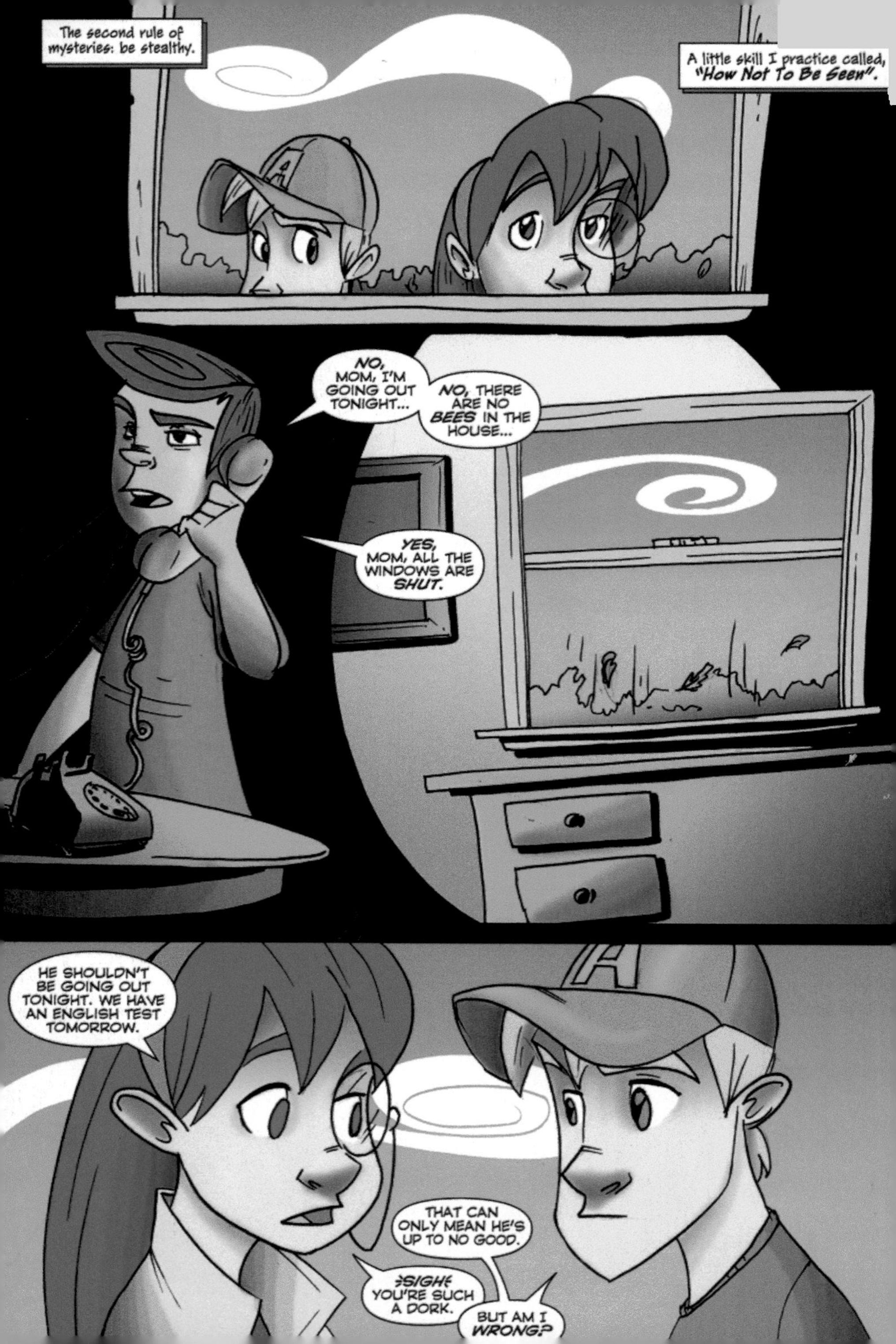
The second rule of mysteries: be stealthy.
A little skill I practice called, "How Not To Be Seen".
NO, MOM, I'M GOING OUT TONIGHT...
NO, THERE ARE NO BEES IN THE HOUSE...
YES, MOM, ALL THE WINDOWS ARE SHUT.
HE SHOULDN'T BE GOING OUT TONIGHT. WE HAVE AN ENGLISH TEST TOMORROW.
THAT CAN ONLY MEAN HE'S UP TO NO GOOD.
SIGH YOU'RE SUCH A DORK.
BUT AM I WRONG?

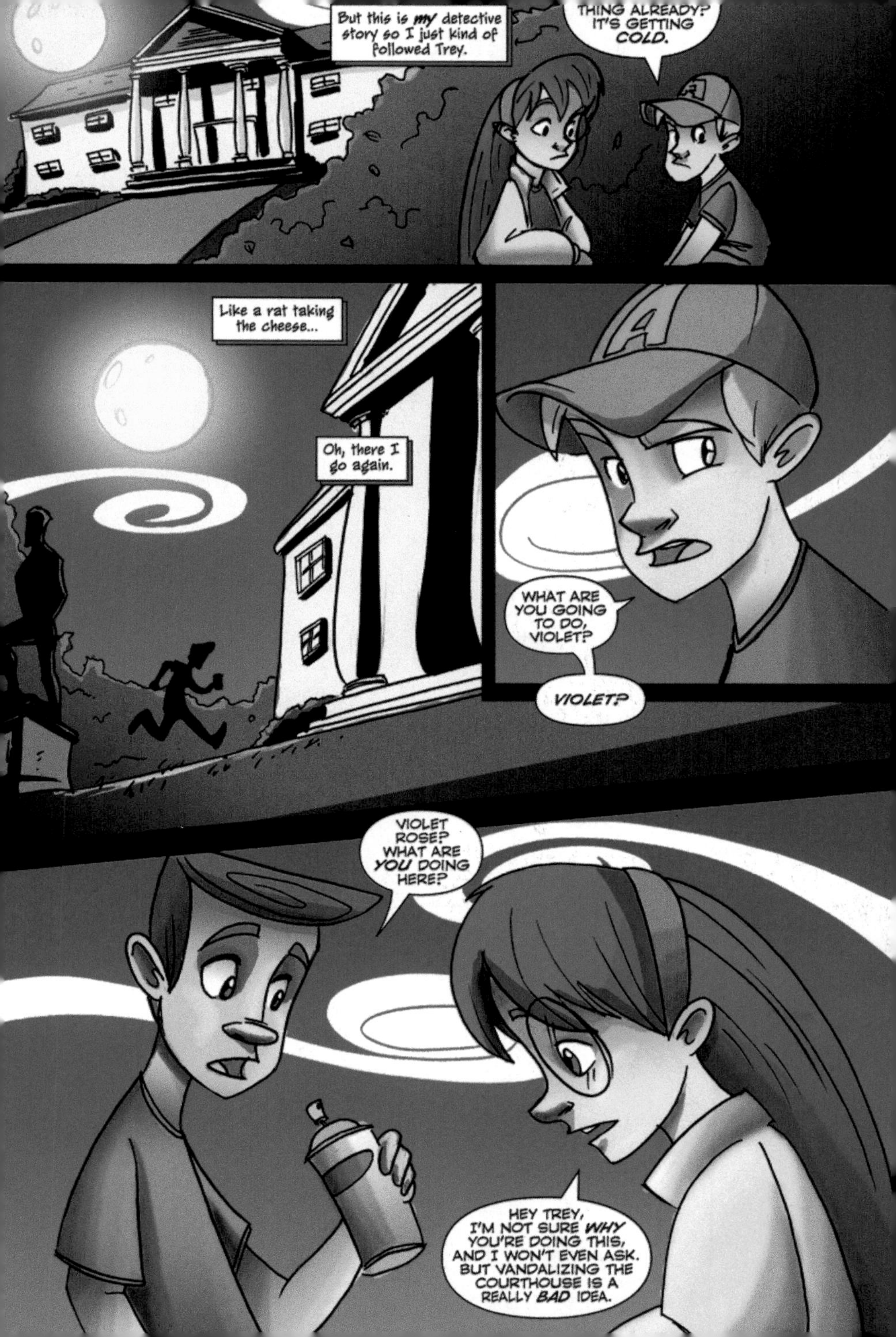
But this is *my* detective story so I just kind of followed Trey.
THING ALREADY? IT'S GETTING *COLD.*
Like a rat taking the cheese...
Oh, there I go again.
WHAT ARE YOU GOING TO DO, VIOLET?
VIOLET?
VIOLET ROSE? WHAT ARE *YOU* DOING HERE?
HEY TREY, I'M NOT SURE *WHY* YOU'RE DOING THIS, AND I WON'T EVEN ASK. BUT VANDALIZING THE COURTHOUSE IS A REALLY *BAD* IDEA.

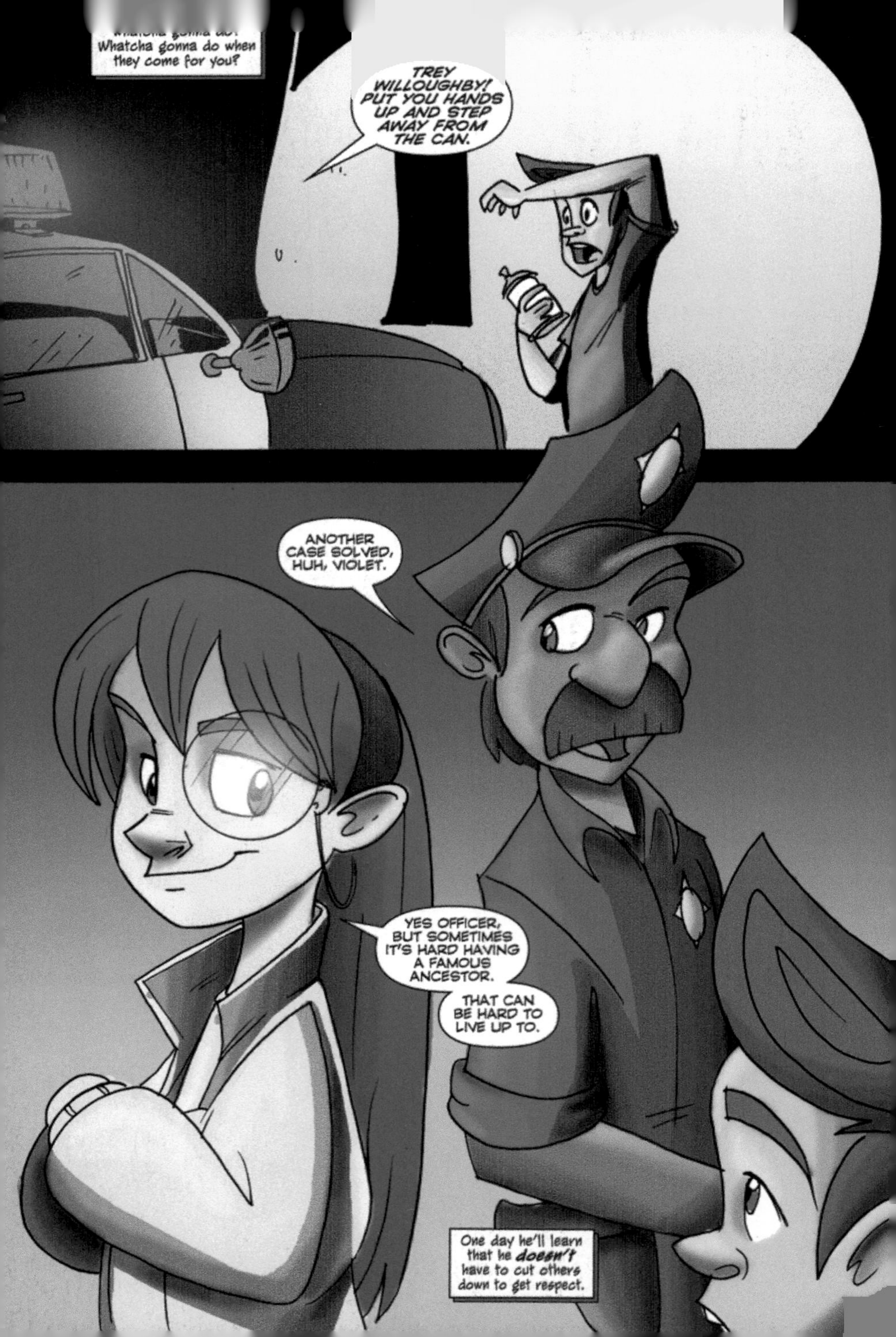
Whatcha gonna do when they come for you?
TREY WILLOUGHBY! PUT YOU HANDS UP AND STEP AWAY FROM THE CAN.
ANOTHER CASE SOLVED, HUH, VIOLET.
YES OFFICER, BUT SOMETIMES IT'S HARD HAVING A FAMOUS ANCESTOR.
THAT CAN BE HARD TO LIVE UP TO.
One day he'll learn that he *doesn't* have to cut others down to get respect.

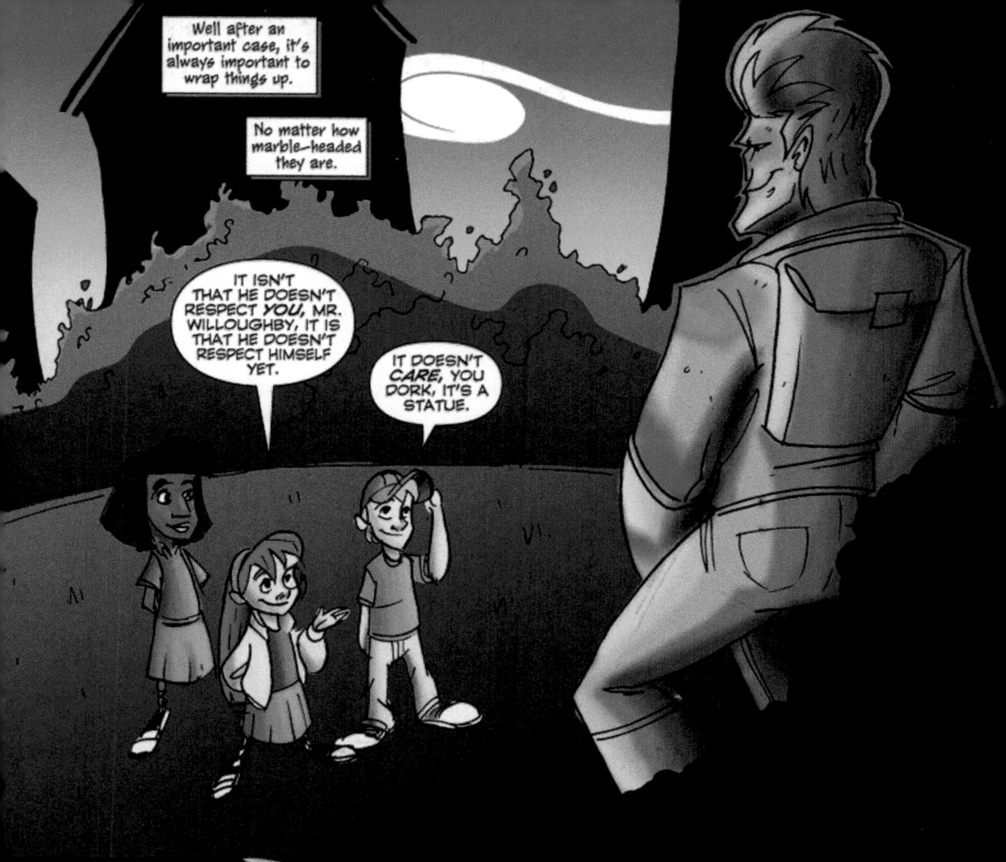
Well after an important case, it's always important to wrap things up.
No matter how marble-headed they are.
IT ISN'T THAT HE DOESN'T RESPECT YOU, MR. WILLOUGHBY, IT IS THAT HE DOESN'T RESPECT HIMSELF YET.
IT DOESN'T CARE, YOU DORK, IT'S A STATUE.

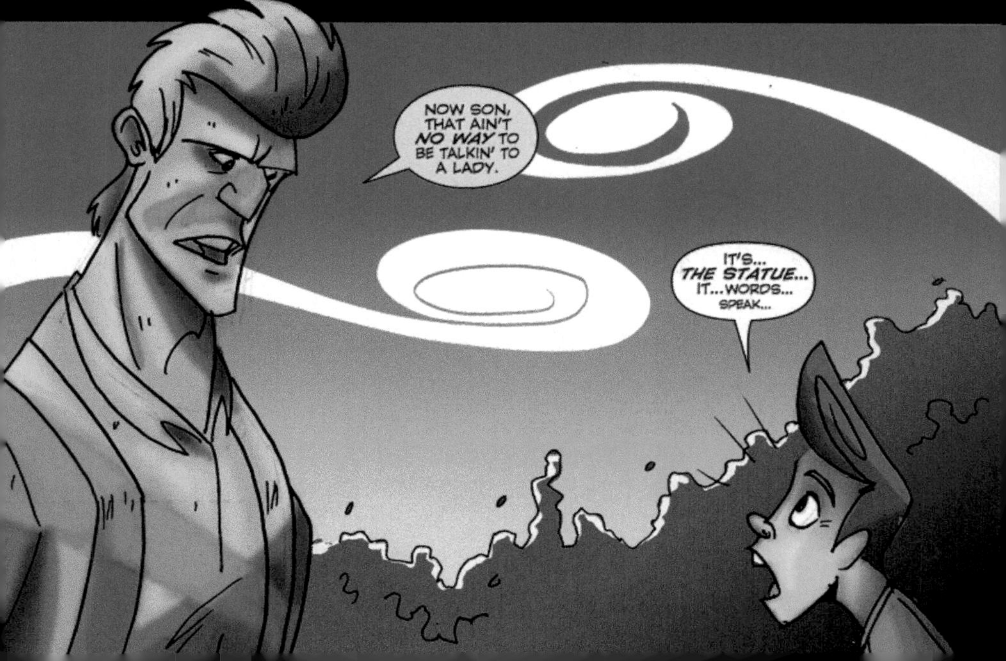
NOW SON, THAT AIN'T NO WAY TO BE TALKIN' TO A LADY.
IT'S... THE STATUE... IT...WORDS... SPEAK...

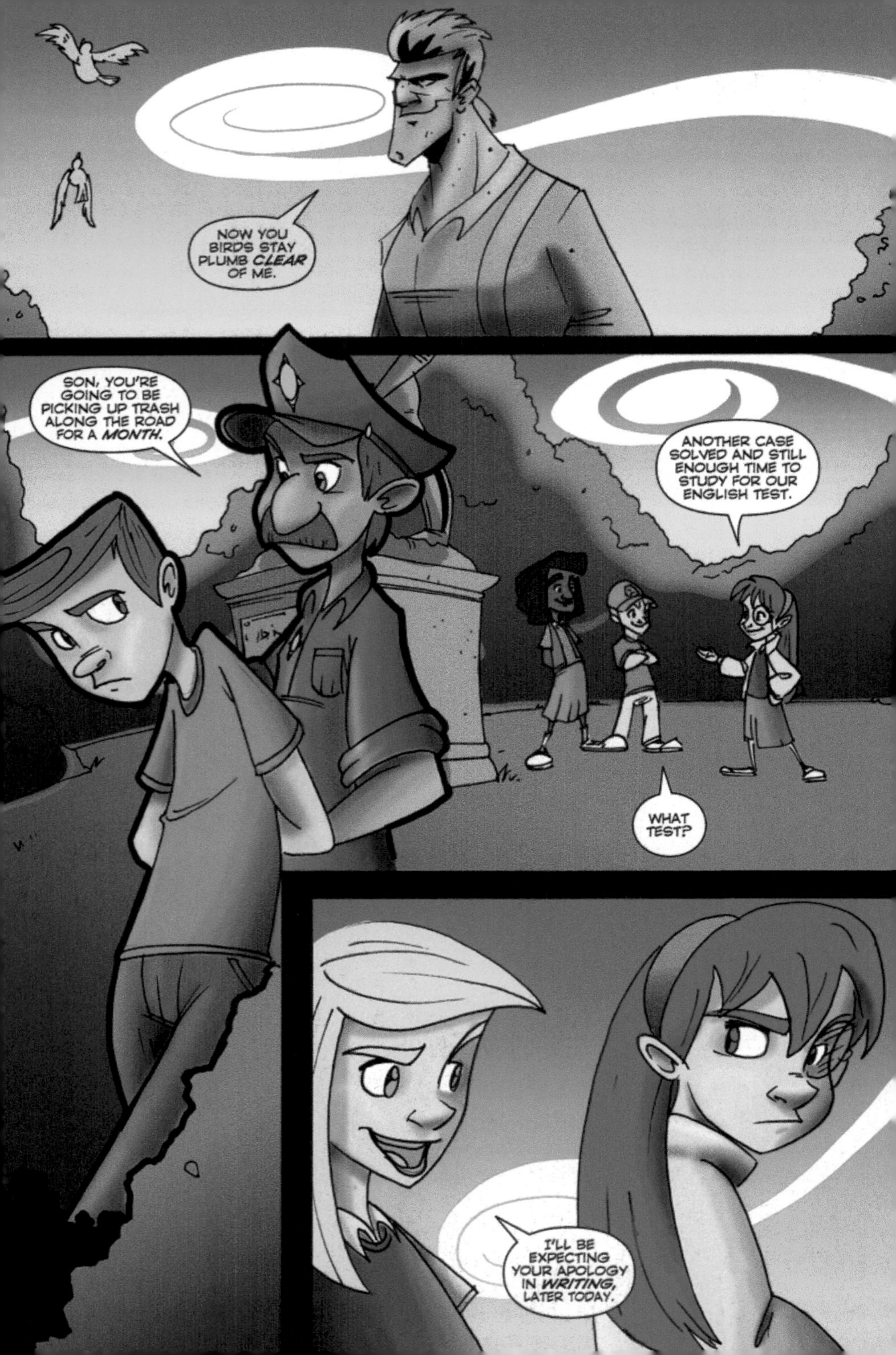
NOW YOU BIRDS STAY PLUMB CLEAR OF ME.
SON, YOU'RE GOING TO BE PICKING UP TRASH ALONG THE ROAD FOR A MONTH.
ANOTHER CASE SOLVED AND STILL ENOUGH TIME TO STUDY FOR OUR ENGLISH TEST.
WHAT TEST?
I'LL BE EXPECTING YOUR APOLOGY IN WRITING, LATER TODAY.

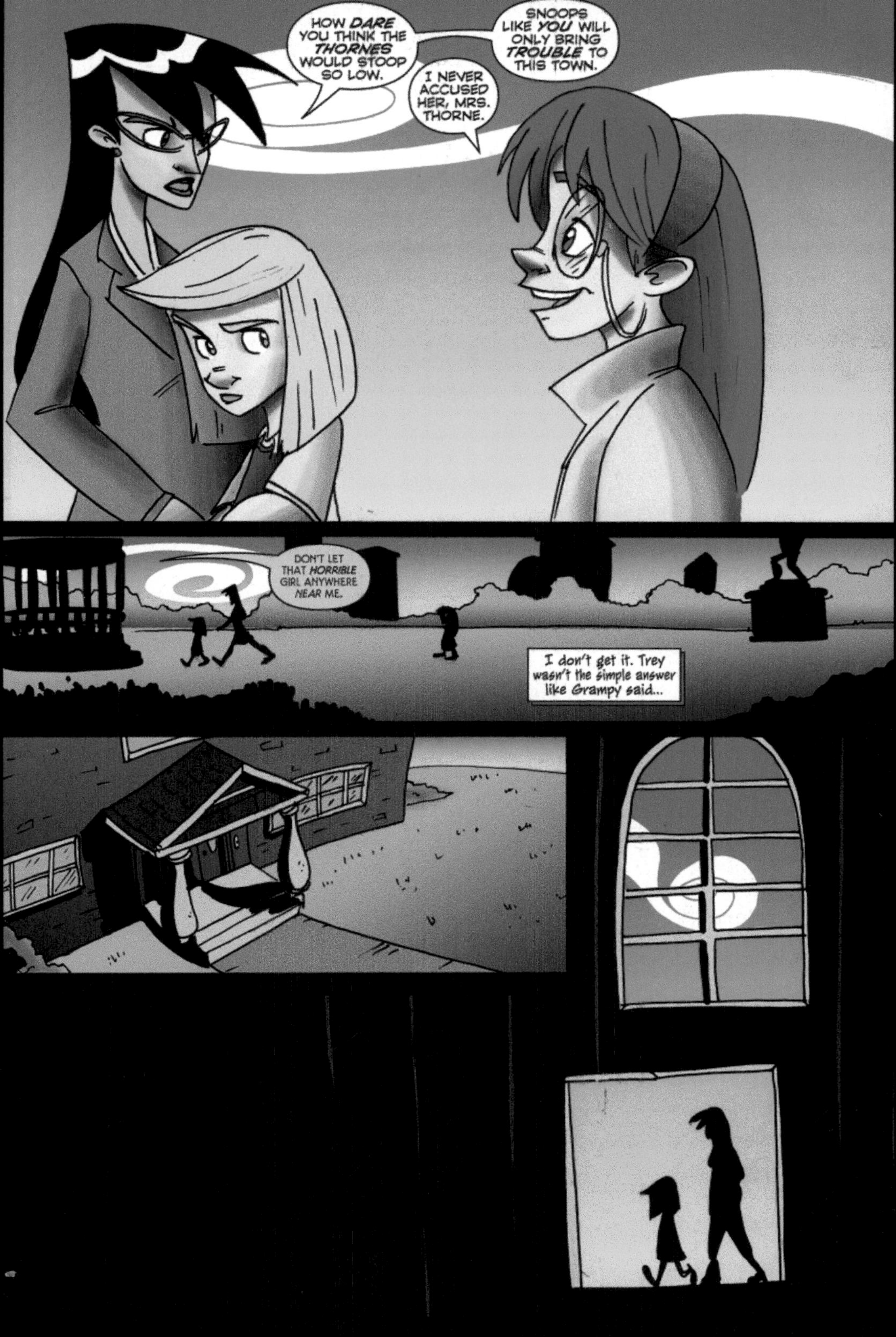
HOW DARE YOU THINK THE THORNES WOULD STOOP SO LOW.
SNOOPS LIKE YOU WILL ONLY BRING TROUBLE TO THIS TOWN.
I NEVER ACCUSED HER, MRS. THORNE.
DON'T LET THAT HORRIBLE GIRL ANYWHERE NEAR ME.
I don't get it. Trey wasn't the simple answer like Grampy said...

Once the advisor for Ivan the Terrible

and the mentor of *Rasputin.*

Valerya Thorne is ready to unite the worlds of *"reality"* and *supernatural.*

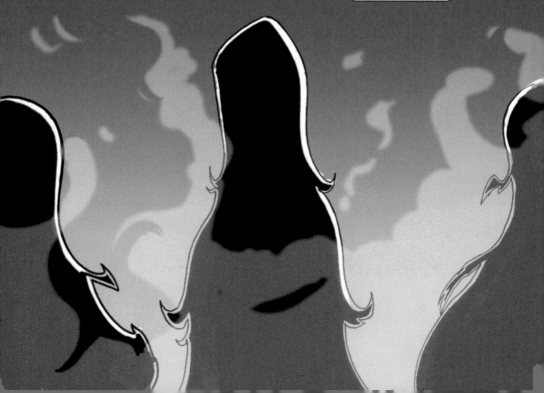

And rule them *both.*

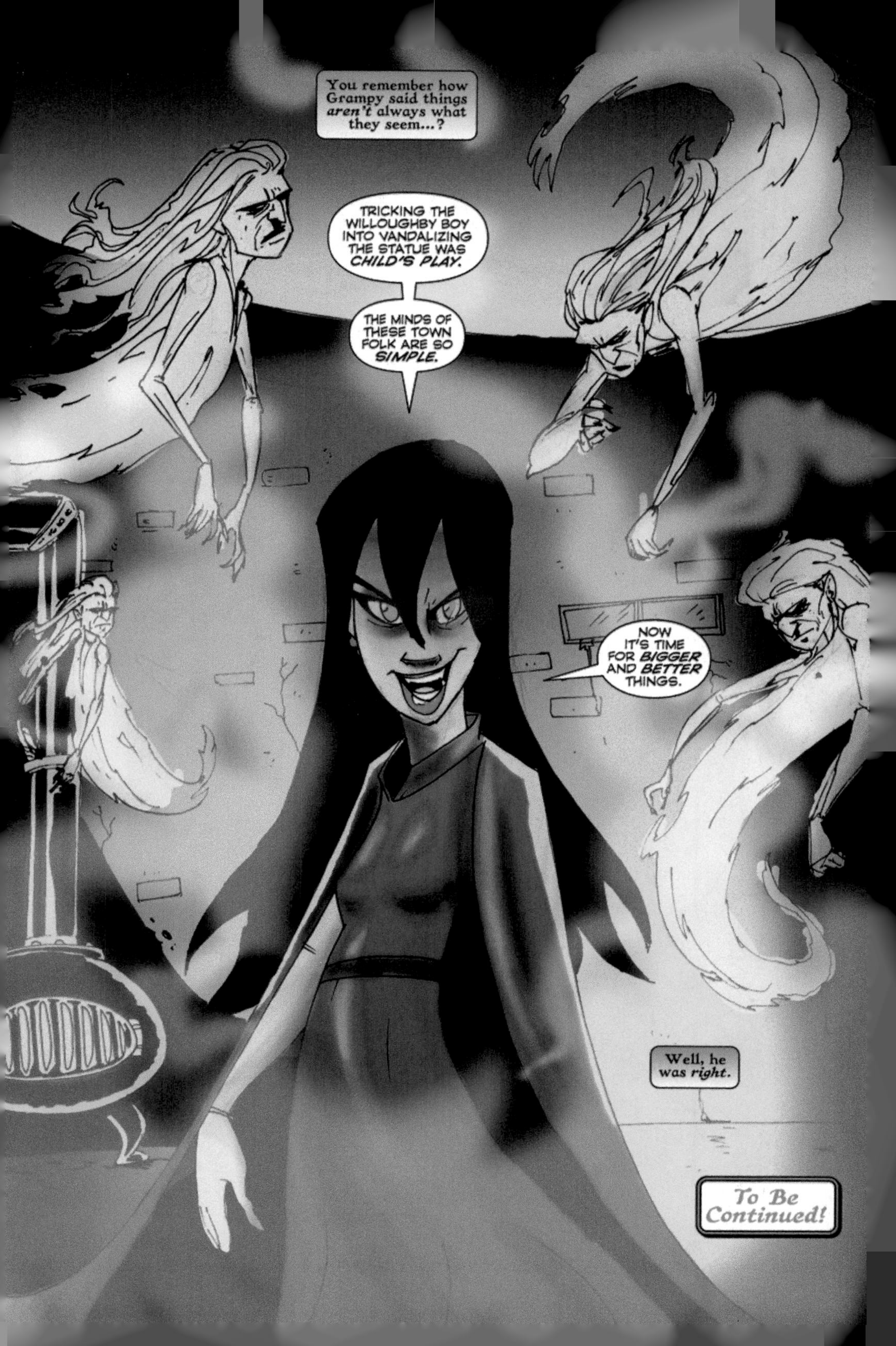
You remember how Grampy said things *aren't* always what they seem...?
TRICKING THE WILLOUGHBY BOY INTO VANDALIZING THE STATUE WAS *CHILD'S PLAY.*
THE MINDS OF THESE TOWN FOLK ARE SO *SIMPLE.*
NOW IT'S TIME FOR *BIGGER* AND *BETTER* THINGS.
Well, he was *right.*
To Be Continued!

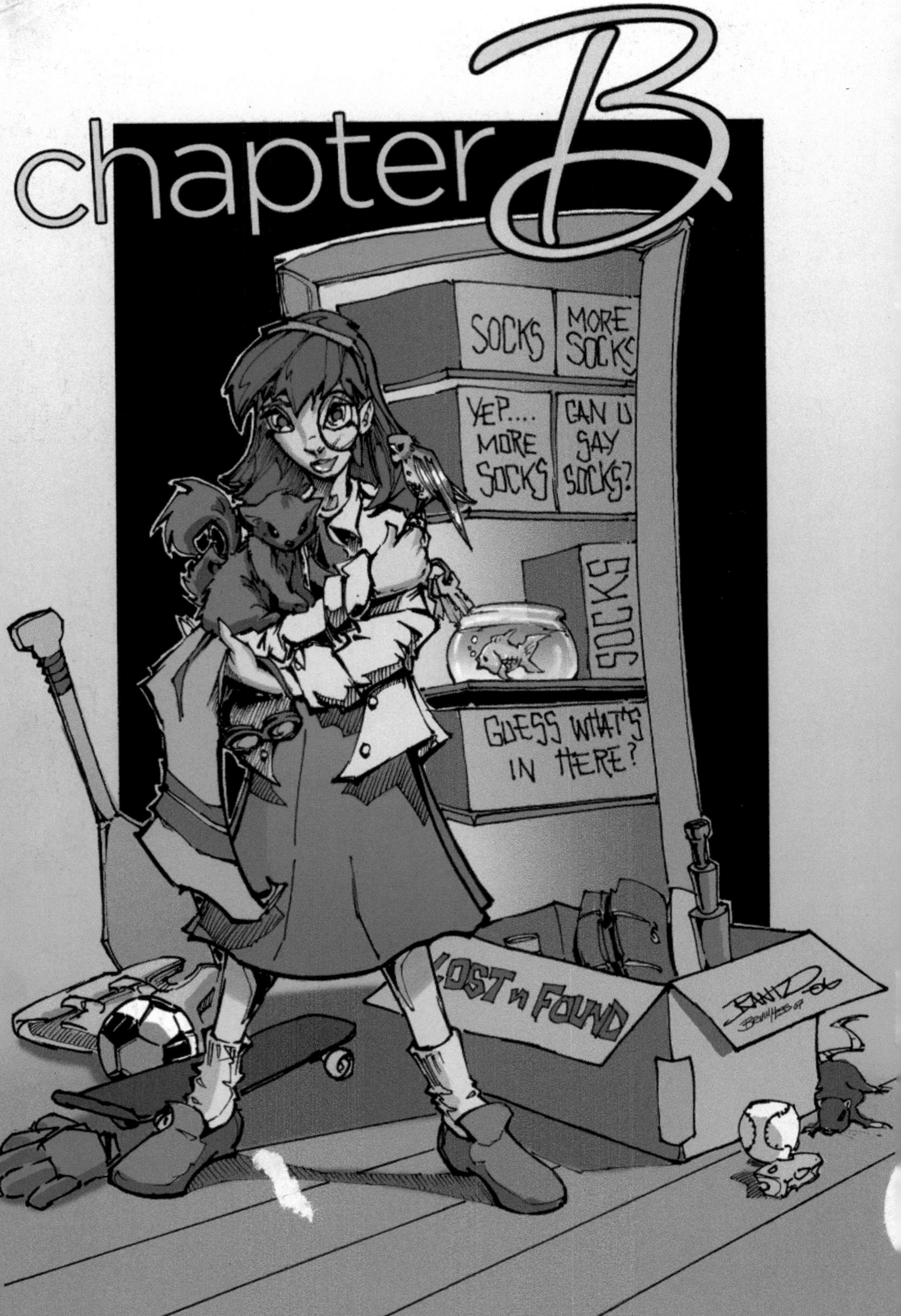
chapter B
SOCKS
MORE SOCKS
YEP..... MORE SOCKS
CAN U SAY SOCKS?
SOCKS
GUESS WHAT'S IN HERE?
LOST n FOUND

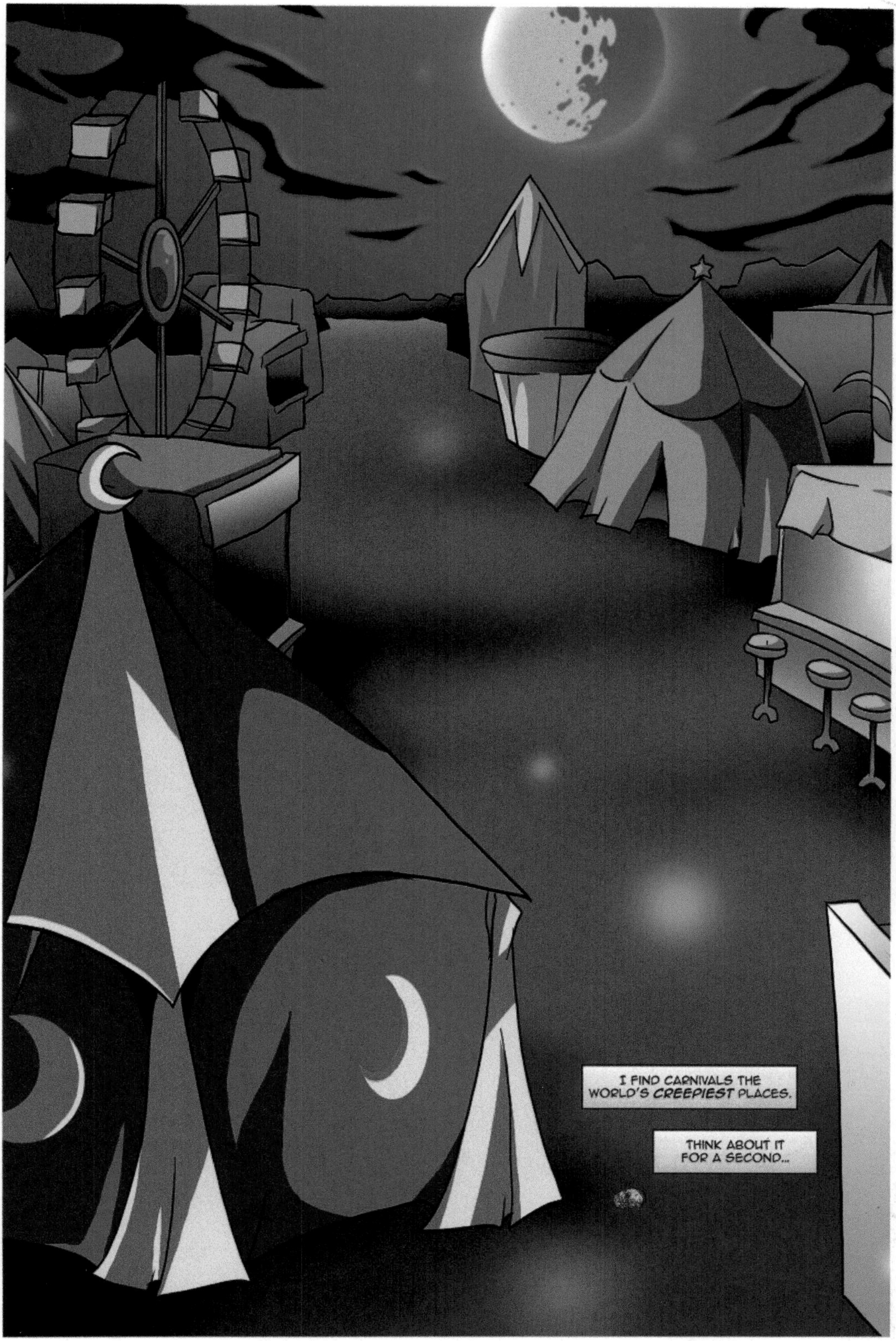
I FIND CARNIVALS THE WORLD'S *CREEPIEST* PLACES.
THINK ABOUT IT FOR A SECOND...

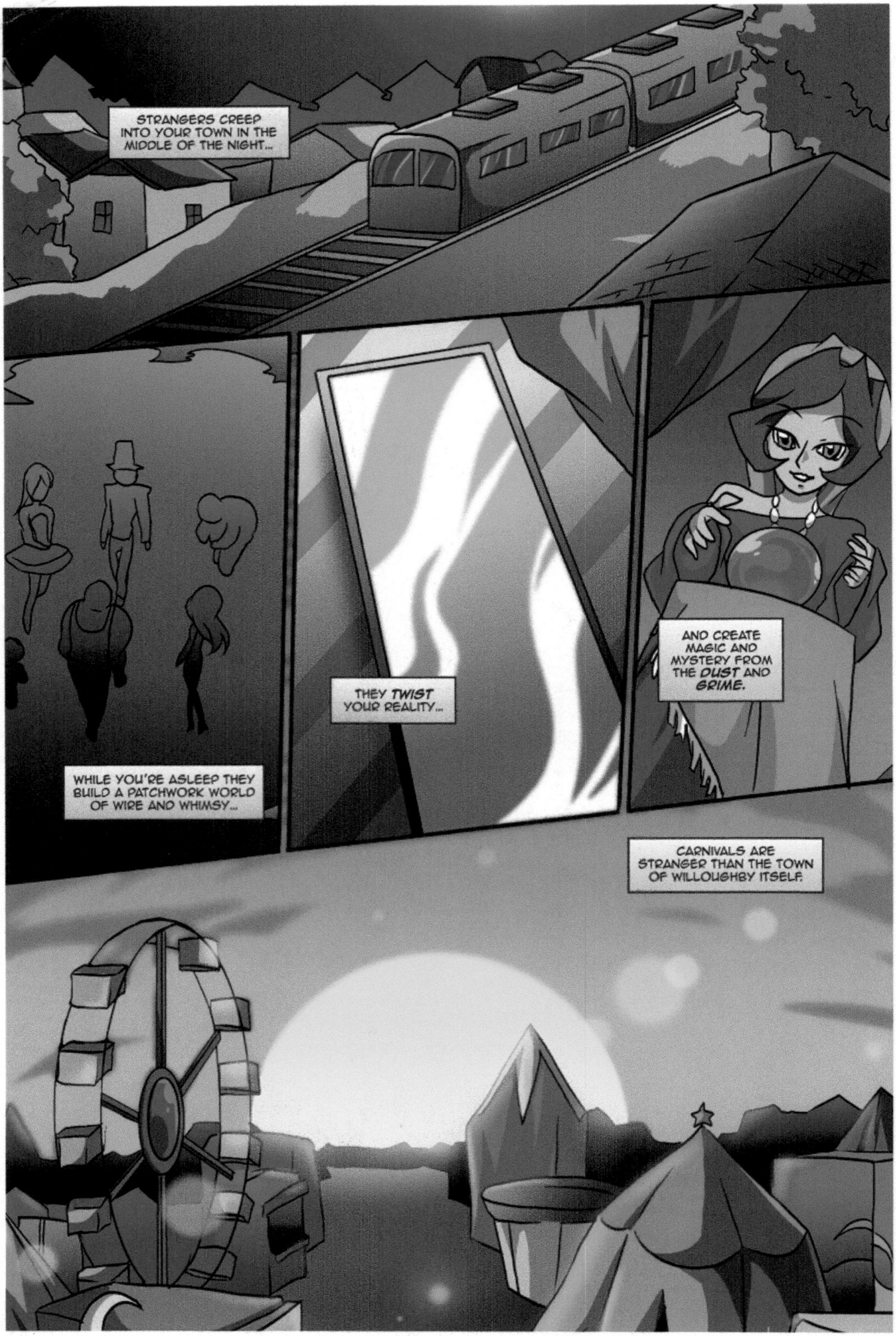
STRANGERS CREEP INTO YOUR TOWN IN THE MIDDLE OF THE NIGHT...
WHILE YOU'RE ASLEEP THEY BUILD A PATCHWORK WORLD OF WIRE AND WHIMSY...
THEY *TWIST* YOUR REALITY...
AND CREATE MAGIC AND MYSTERY FROM THE *DUST* AND *GRIME.*
CARNIVALS ARE STRANGER THAN THE TOWN OF WILLOUGHBY ITSELF.

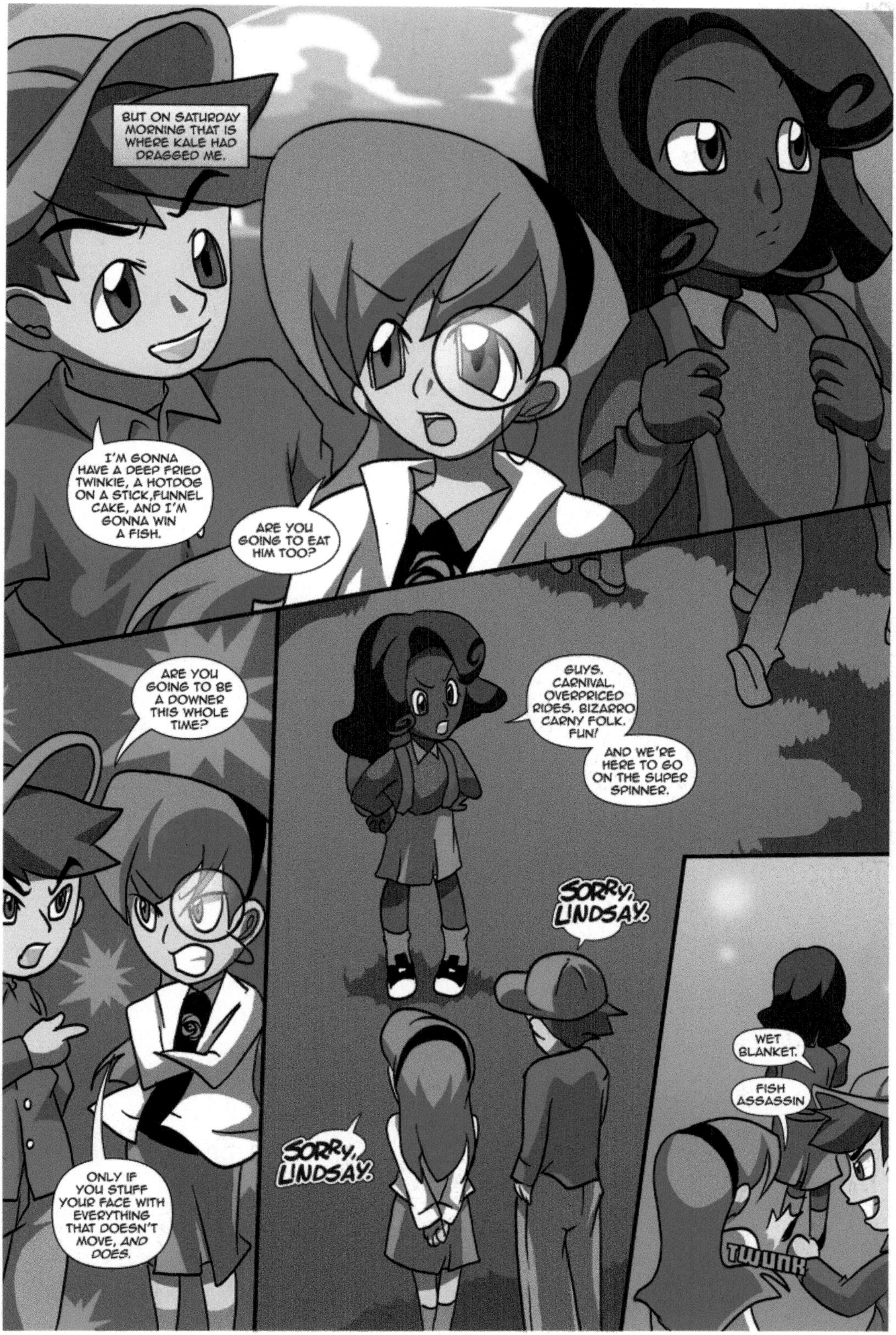

BUT ON SATURDAY MORNING THAT IS WHERE KALE HAD DRAGGED ME.
I'M GONNA HAVE A DEEP FRIED TWINKIE, A HOTDOG ON A STICK,FUNNEL CAKE, AND I'M GONNA WIN A FISH.
ARE YOU GOING TO EAT HIM TOO?
ARE YOU GOING TO BE A DOWNER THIS WHOLE TIME?
ONLY IF YOU STUFF YOUR FACE WITH EVERYTHING THAT DOESN'T MOVE, AND DOES.
GUYS. CARNIVAL. OVERPRICED RIDES. BIZARRO CARNY FOLK. FUN!
AND WE'RE HERE TO GO ON THE SUPER SPINNER.
SORRY, LINDSAY.
SORRY, LINDSAY.
WET BLANKET.
FISH ASSASSIN
TWUNK

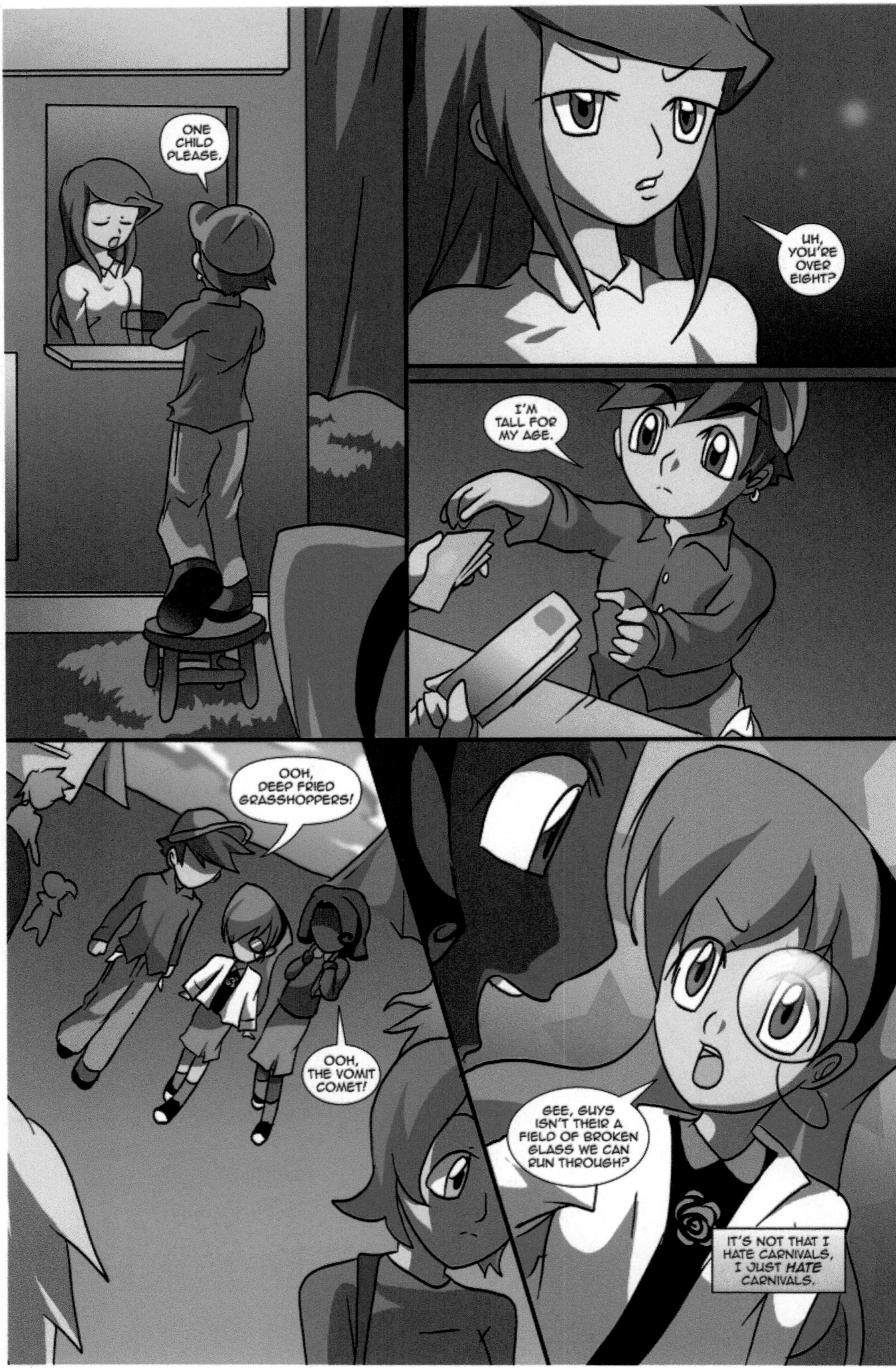
ONE CHILD PLEASE.
UH, YOU'RE OVER EIGHT?
I'M TALL FOR MY AGE.
OOH, DEEP FRIED GRASSHOPPERS!
OOH, THE VOMIT COMET!
GEE, GUYS ISN'T THEIR A FIELD OF BROKEN GLASS WE CAN RUN THROUGH?
IT'S NOT THAT I HATE CARNIVALS, I JUST *HATE* CARNIVALS.

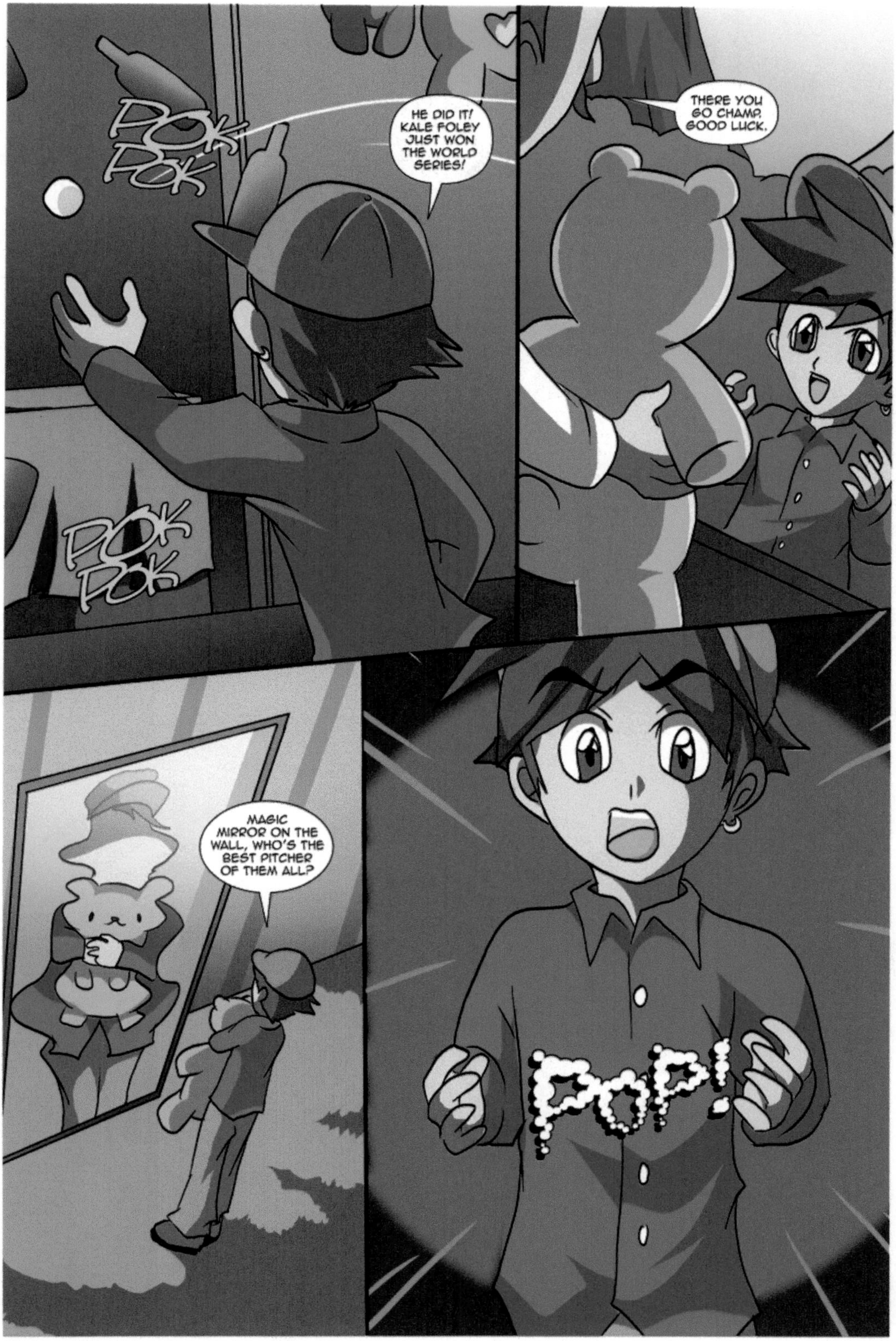

POK POK
HE DID IT! KALE FOLEY JUST WON THE WORLD SERIES!
POK POK
THERE YOU GO CHAMP. GOOD LUCK.
MAGIC MIRROR ON THE WALL, WHO'S THE BEST PITCHER OF THEM ALL?
POP!

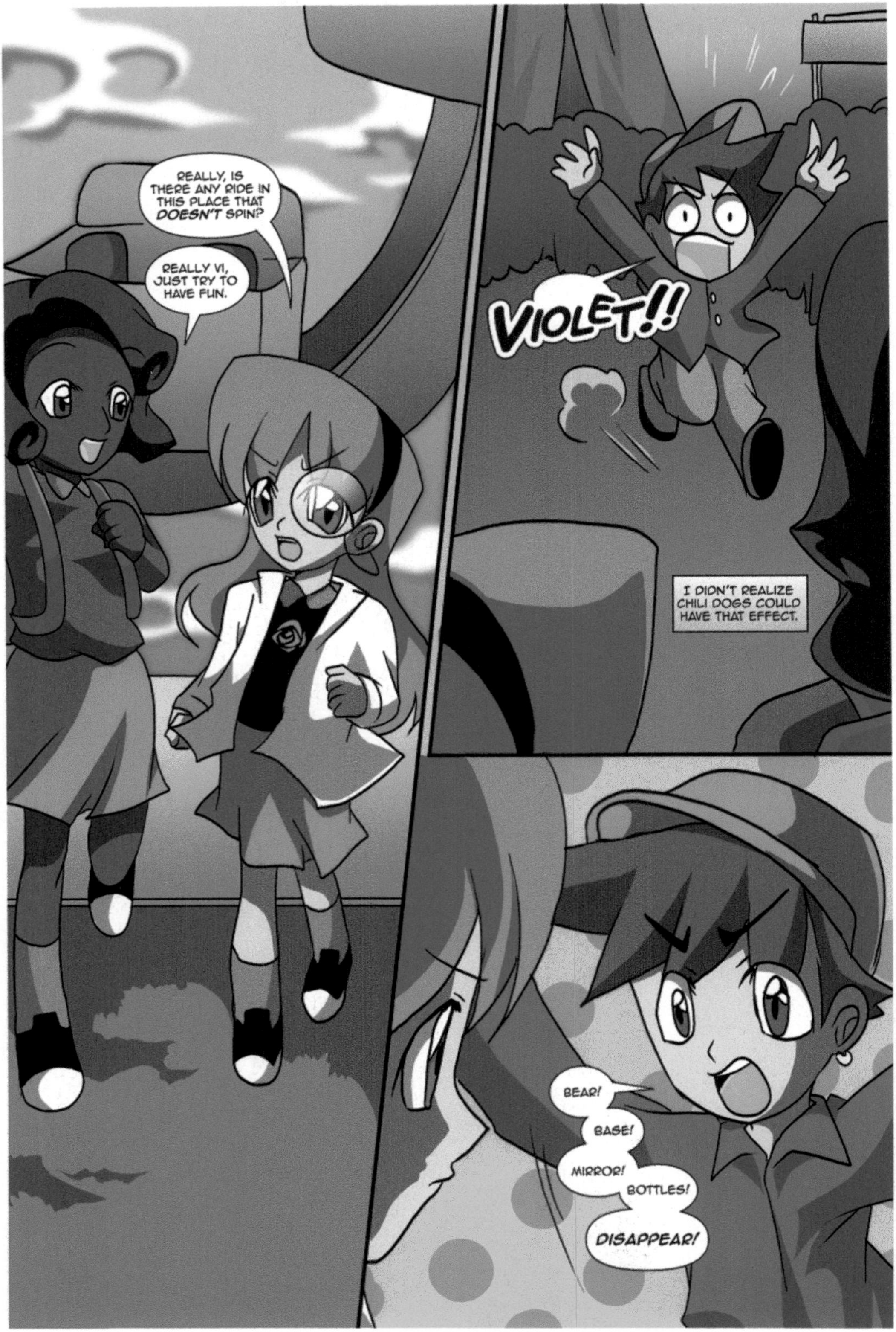
REALLY, IS THERE ANY RIDE IN THIS PLACE THAT DOESN'T SPIN?
REALLY VI, JUST TRY TO HAVE FUN.
VIOLET!!
I DIDN'T REALIZE CHILI DOGS COULD HAVE THAT EFFECT.
BEAR!
BASE!
MIRROR!
BOTTLES!
DISAPPEAR!

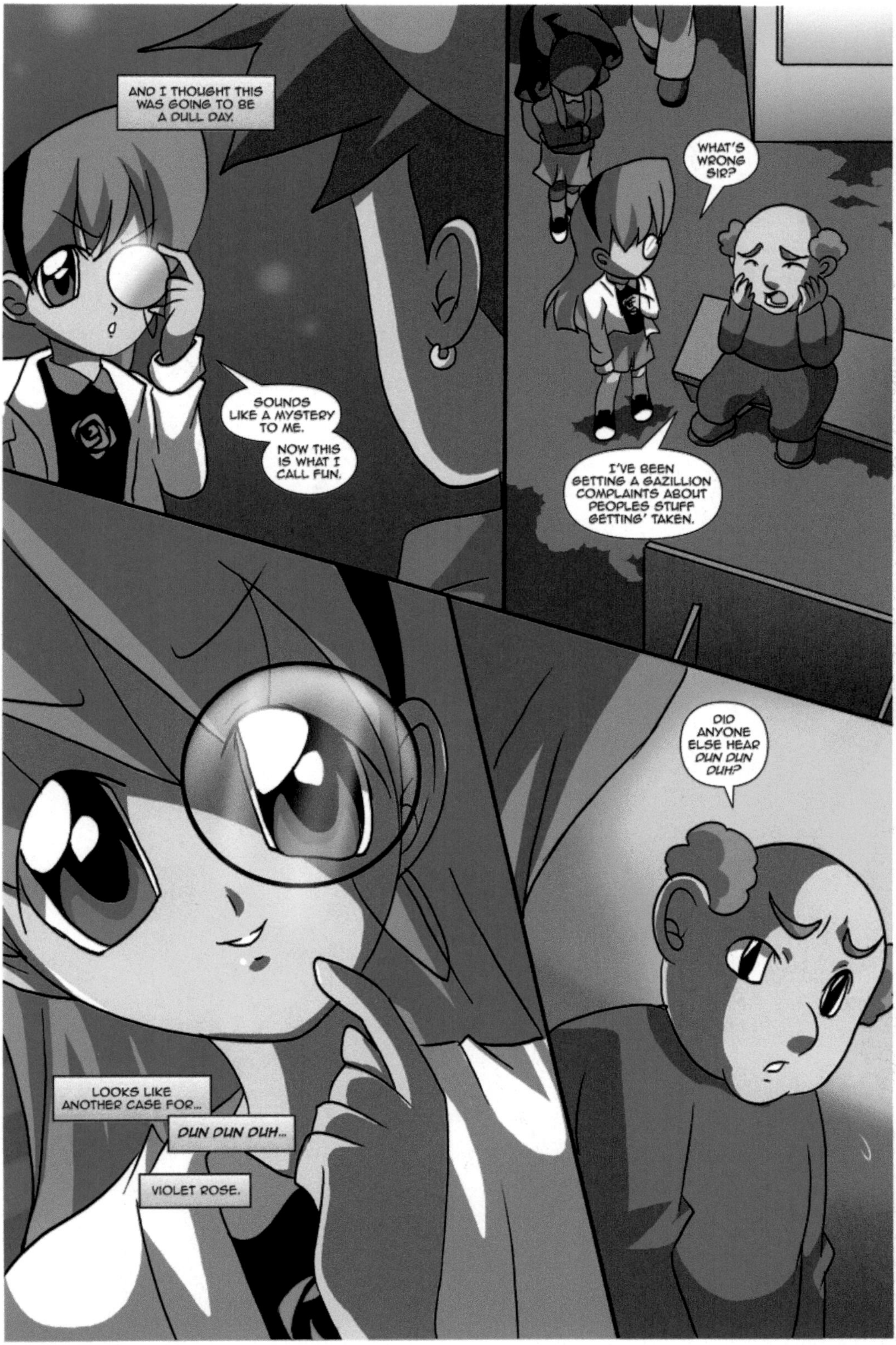
AND I THOUGHT THIS WAS GOING TO BE A DULL DAY.
SOUNDS LIKE A MYSTERY TO ME.
NOW THIS IS WHAT I CALL FUN.
WHAT'S WRONG SIR?
I'VE BEEN GETTING A GAZILLION COMPLAINTS ABOUT PEOPLES STUFF GETTING' TAKEN.
LOOKS LIKE ANOTHER CASE FOR...
DUN DUN DUH...
VIOLET ROSE.
DID ANYONE ELSE HEAR *DUN DUN DUH*?

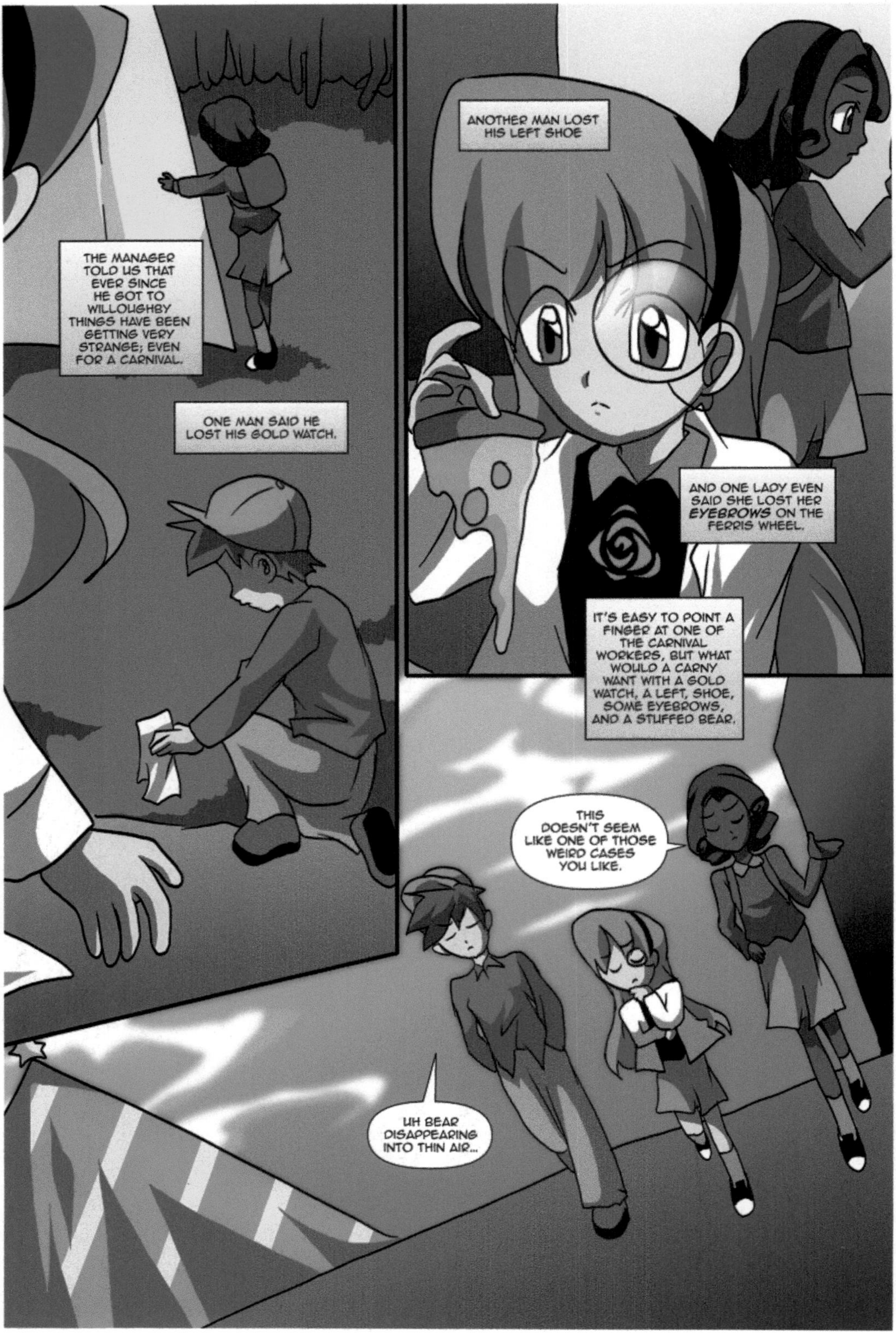
THE MANAGER TOLD US THAT EVER SINCE HE GOT TO WILLOUGHBY THINGS HAVE BEEN GETTING VERY STRANGE; EVEN FOR A CARNIVAL.
ONE MAN SAID HE LOST HIS GOLD WATCH.
ANOTHER MAN LOST HIS LEFT SHOE
AND ONE LADY EVEN SAID SHE LOST HER EYEBROWS ON THE FERRIS WHEEL.
IT'S EASY TO POINT A FINGER AT ONE OF THE CARNIVAL WORKERS, BUT WHAT WOULD A CARNY WANT WITH A GOLD WATCH, A LEFT, SHOE, SOME EYEBROWS, AND A STUFFED BEAR.
THIS DOESN'T SEEM LIKE ONE OF THOSE WEIRD CASES YOU LIKE.
UH BEAR DISAPPEARING INTO THIN AIR...

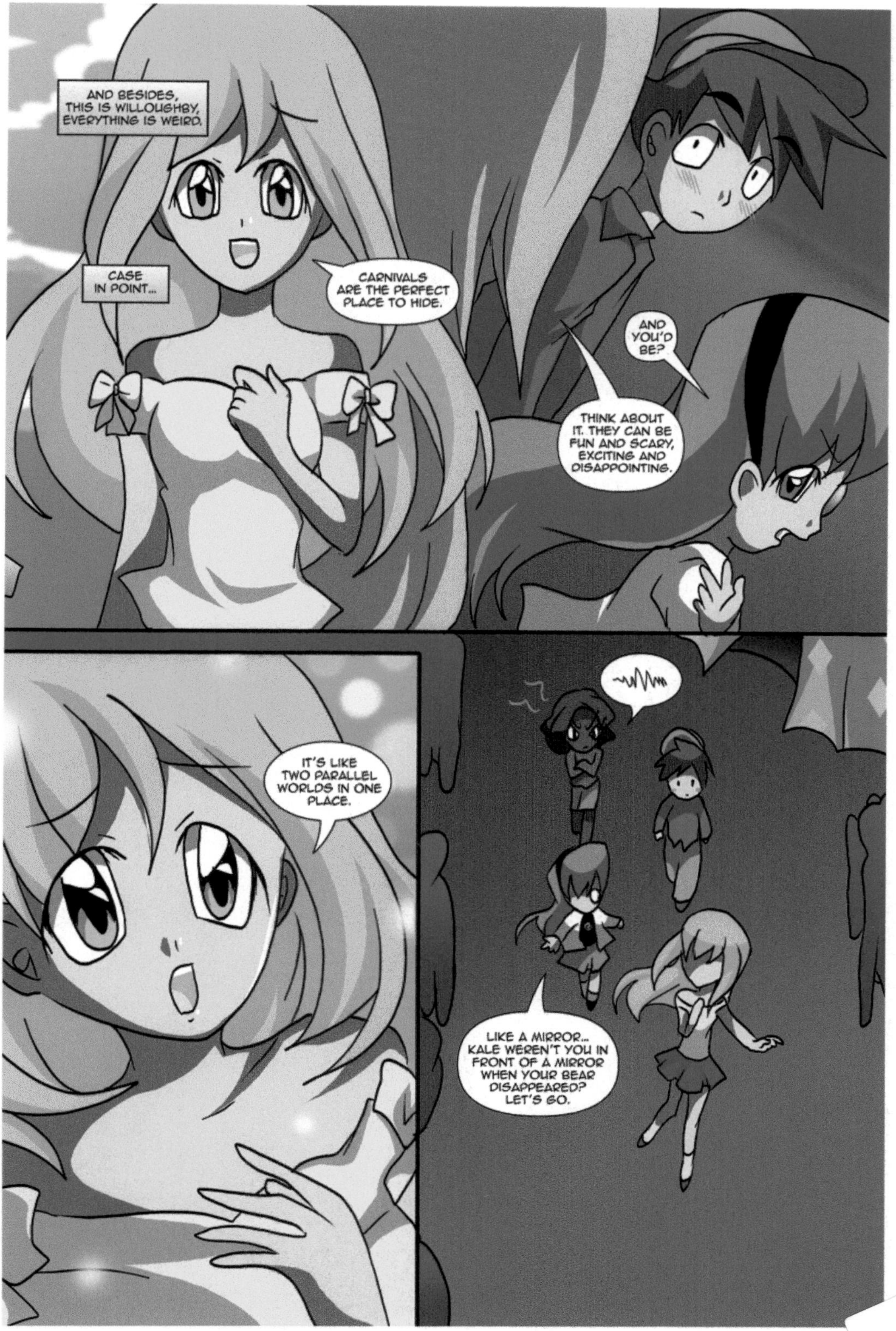
AND BESIDES, THIS IS WILLOUGHBY, EVERYTHING IS WEIRD.
CASE IN POINT...
CARNIVALS ARE THE PERFECT PLACE TO HIDE.
AND YOU'D BE?
THINK ABOUT IT. THEY CAN BE FUN AND SCARY, EXCITING AND DISAPPOINTING.
IT'S LIKE TWO PARALLEL WORLDS IN ONE PLACE.
LIKE A MIRROR... KALE WEREN'T YOU IN FRONT OF A MIRROR WHEN YOUR BEAR DISAPPEARED? LET'S GO.

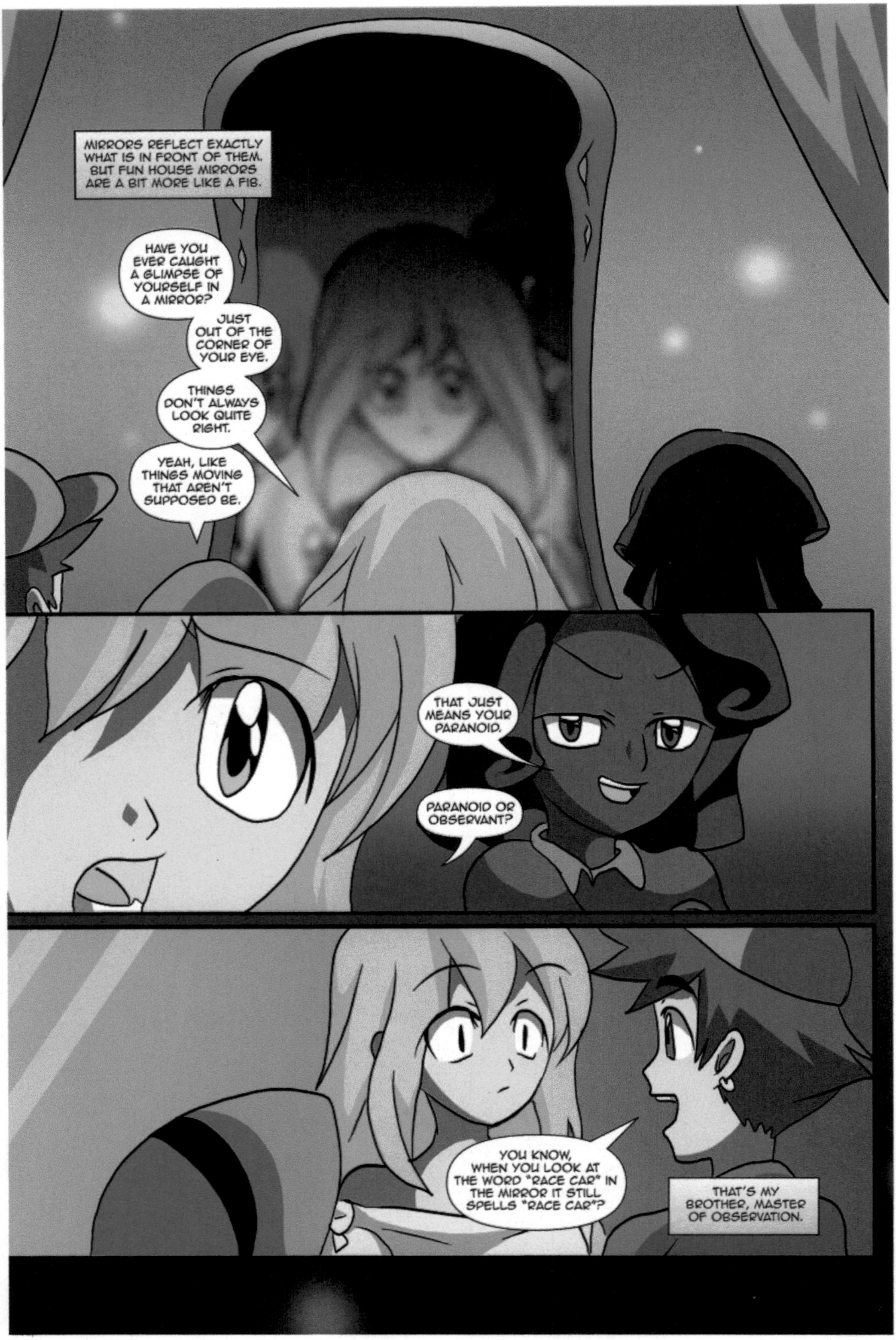

MIRRORS REFLECT EXACTLY WHAT IS IN FRONT OF THEM. BUT FUN HOUSE MIRRORS ARE A BIT MORE LIKE A FIB.
HAVE YOU EVER CAUGHT A GLIMPSE OF YOURSELF IN A MIRROR?
JUST OUT OF THE CORNER OF YOUR EYE.
THINGS DON'T ALWAYS LOOK QUITE RIGHT.
YEAH, LIKE THINGS MOVING THAT AREN'T SUPPOSED BE.
THAT JUST MEANS YOUR PARANOID.
PARANOID OR OBSERVANT?
YOU KNOW, WHEN YOU LOOK AT THE WORD "RACE CAR" IN THE MIRROR IT STILL SPELLS "RACE CAR"?
THAT'S MY BROTHER, MASTER OF OBSERVATION.

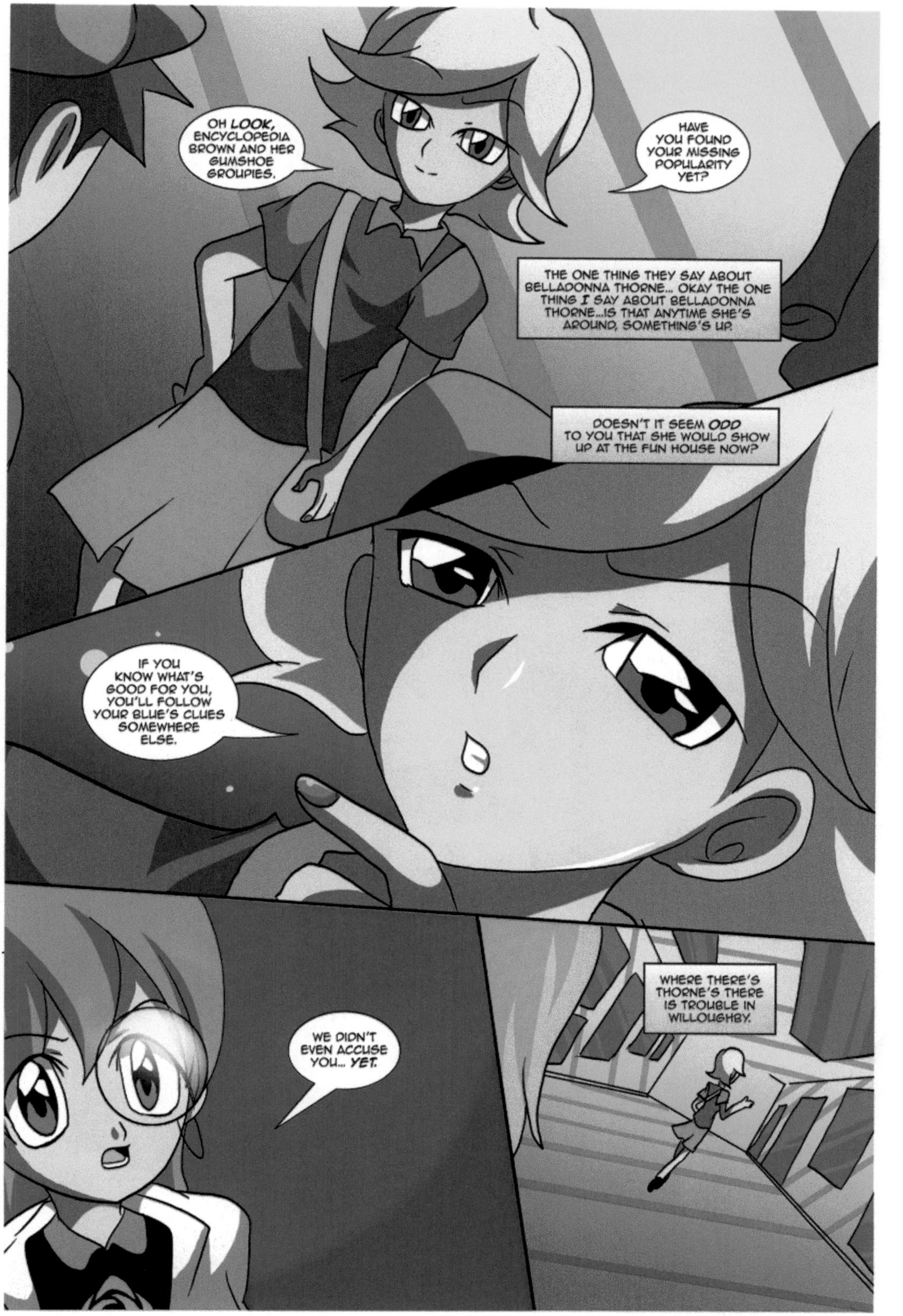
OH LOOK, ENCYCLOPEDIA BROWN AND HER GUMSHOE GROUPIES.
HAVE YOU FOUND YOUR MISSING POPULARITY YET?
THE ONE THING THEY SAY ABOUT BELLADONNA THORNE... OKAY THE ONE THING I SAY ABOUT BELLADONNA THORNE...IS THAT ANYTIME SHE'S AROUND, SOMETHING'S UP.
DOESN'T IT SEEM ODD TO YOU THAT SHE WOULD SHOW UP AT THE FUN HOUSE NOW?
IF YOU KNOW WHAT'S GOOD FOR YOU, YOU'LL FOLLOW YOUR BLUE'S CLUES SOMEWHERE ELSE.
WE DIDN'T EVEN ACCUSE YOU... YET.
WHERE THERE'S THORNE'S THERE IS TROUBLE IN WILLOUGHBY.

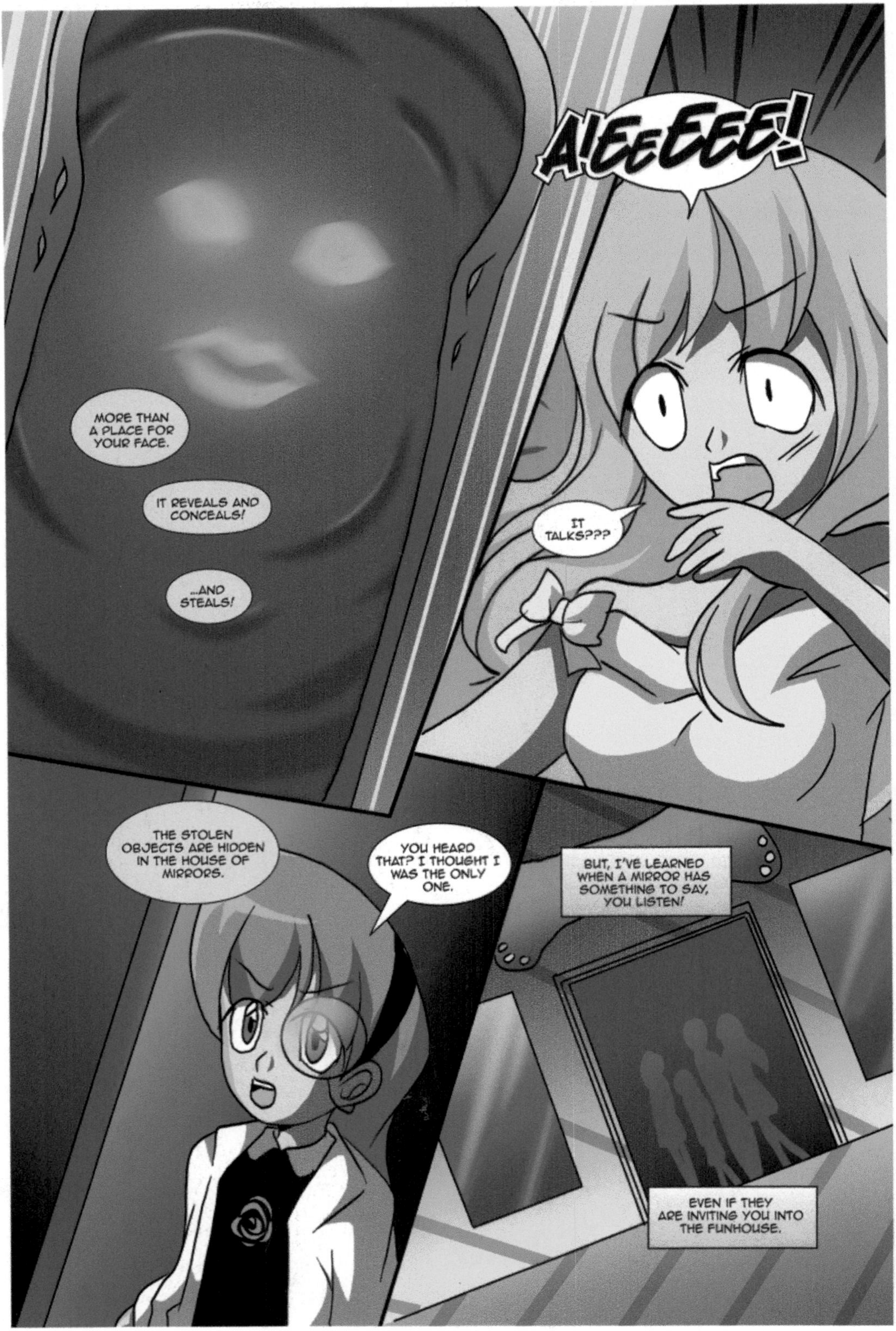
AIEEEEE!
MORE THAN A PLACE FOR YOUR FACE.
IT REVEALS AND CONCEALS!
...AND STEALS!
IT TALKS???
THE STOLEN OBJECTS ARE HIDDEN IN THE HOUSE OF MIRRORS.
YOU HEARD THAT? I THOUGHT I WAS THE ONLY ONE.
BUT, I'VE LEARNED WHEN A MIRROR HAS SOMETHING TO SAY, YOU LISTEN!
EVEN IF THEY ARE INVITING YOU INTO THE FUNHOUSE.

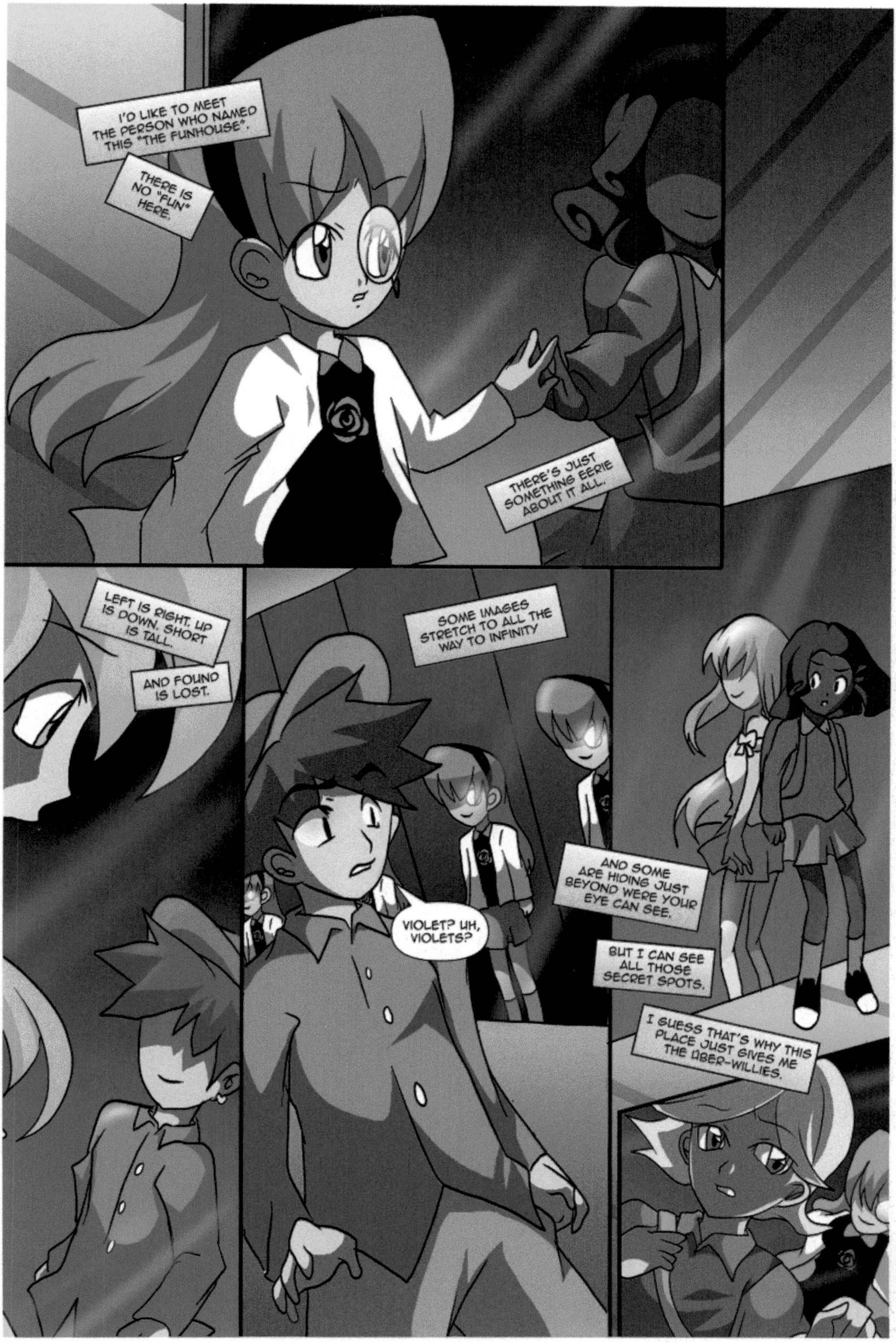
I'D LIKE TO MEET THE PERSON WHO NAMED THIS "THE FUNHOUSE".
THERE IS NO "FUN" HERE.
THERE'S JUST SOMETHING EERIE ABOUT IT ALL.
LEFT IS RIGHT, UP IS DOWN, SHORT IS TALL.
AND FOUND IS LOST.
SOME IMAGES STRETCH TO ALL THE WAY TO INFINITY
VIOLET? UH, VIOLETS?
AND SOME ARE HIDING JUST BEYOND WERE YOUR EYE CAN SEE.
BUT I CAN SEE ALL THOSE SECRET SPOTS.
I GUESS THAT'S WHY THIS PLACE JUST GIVES ME THE ÜBER-WILLIES.

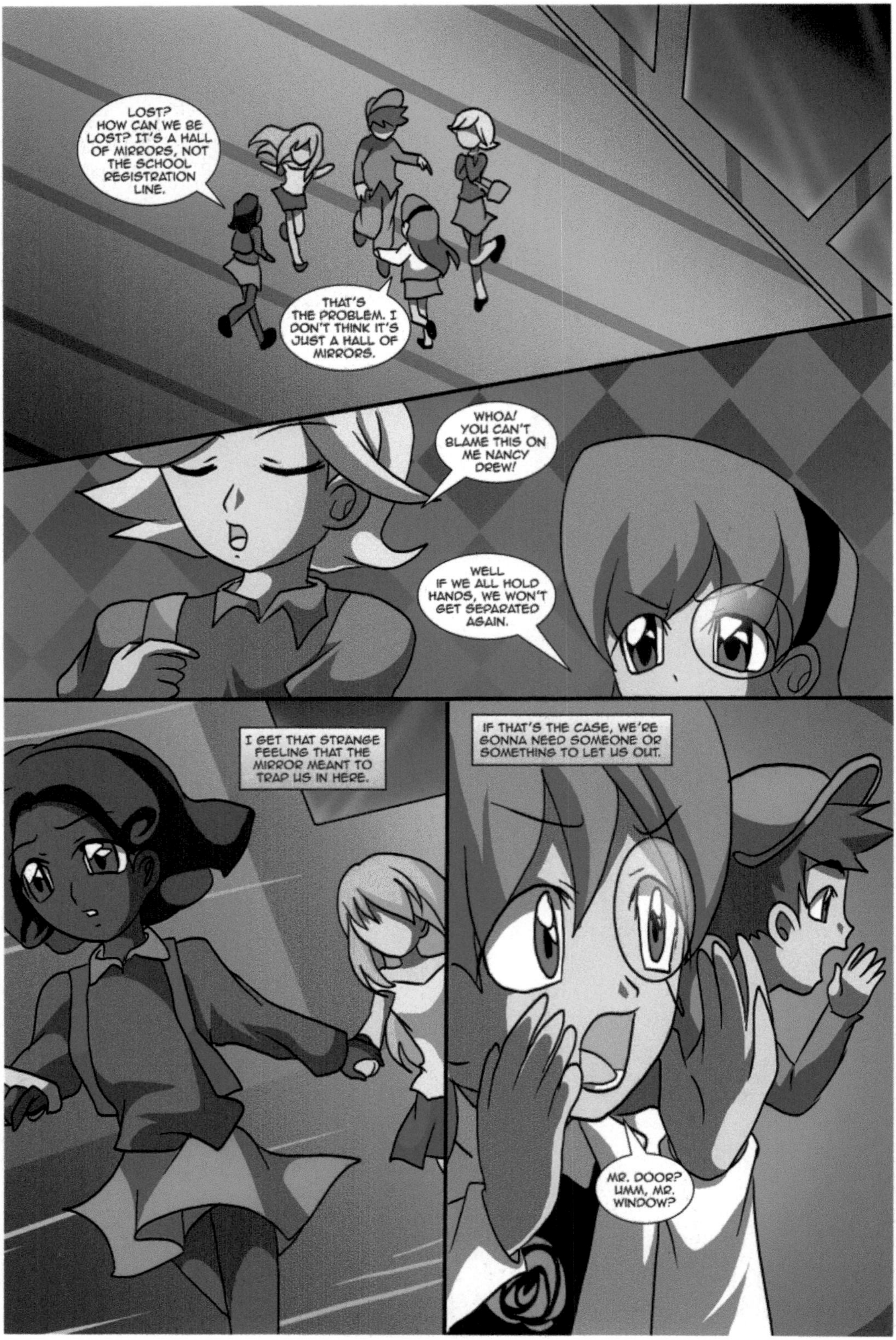
LOST? HOW CAN WE BE LOST? IT'S A HALL OF MIRRORS, NOT THE SCHOOL REGISTRATION LINE.
THAT'S THE PROBLEM. I DON'T THINK IT'S JUST A HALL OF MIRRORS.
WHOA! YOU CAN'T BLAME THIS ON ME NANCY DREW!
WELL IF WE ALL HOLD HANDS, WE WON'T GET SEPARATED AGAIN.
I GET THAT STRANGE FEELING THAT THE MIRROR MEANT TO TRAP US IN HERE.
IF THAT'S THE CASE, WE'RE GONNA NEED SOMEONE OR SOMETHING TO LET US OUT.
MR. DOOR? UMM, MR. WINDOW?

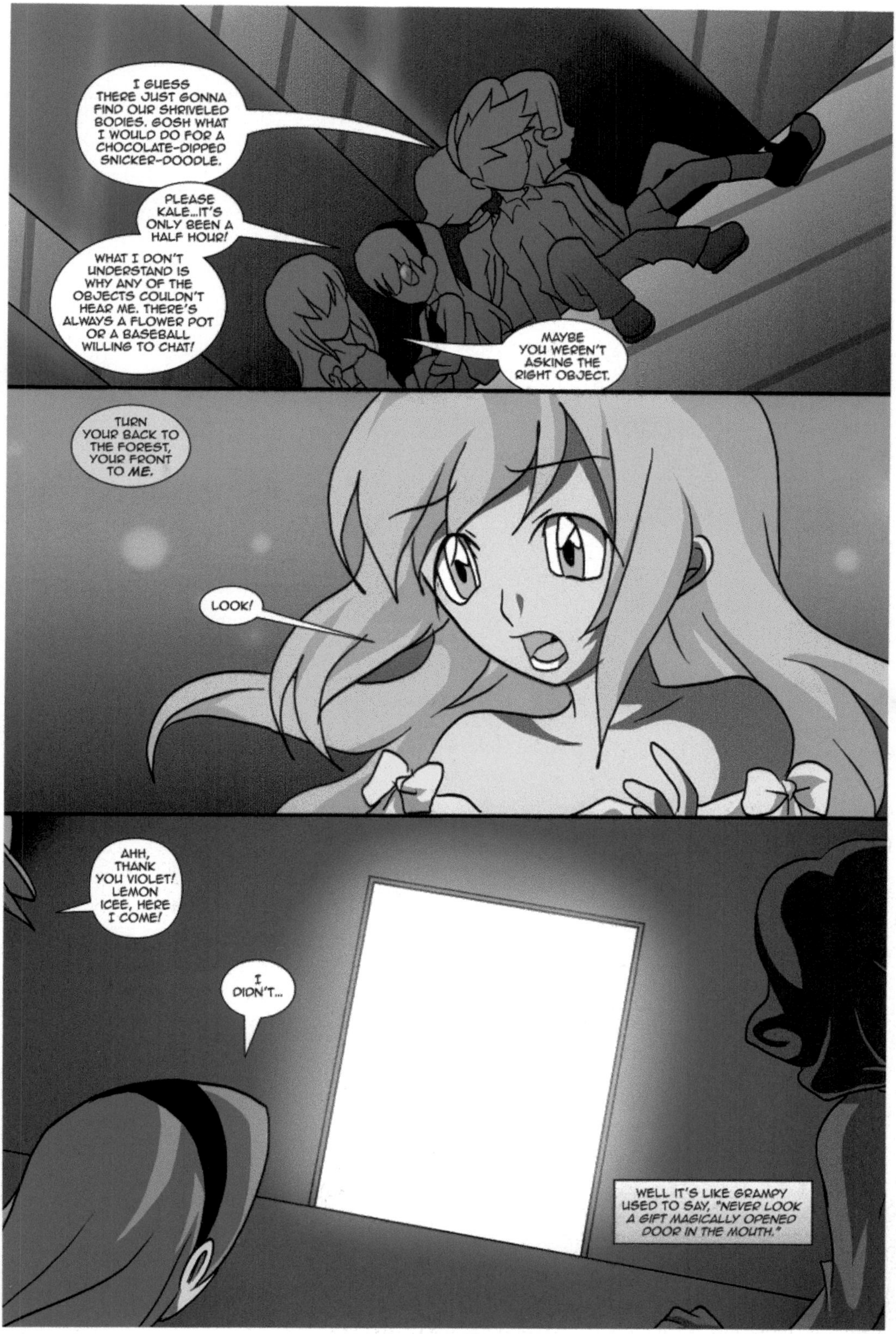
I GUESS THERE JUST GONNA FIND OUR SHRIVELED BODIES. GOSH WHAT I WOULD DO FOR A CHOCOLATE-DIPPED SNICKER-DOODLE.
PLEASE KALE...IT'S ONLY BEEN A HALF HOUR!
WHAT I DON'T UNDERSTAND IS WHY ANY OF THE OBJECTS COULDN'T HEAR ME. THERE'S ALWAYS A FLOWER POT OR A BASEBALL WILLING TO CHAT!
MAYBE YOU WEREN'T ASKING THE RIGHT OBJECT.
TURN YOUR BACK TO THE FOREST, YOUR FRONT TO *ME*.
LOOK!
AHH, THANK YOU VIOLET! LEMON ICEE, HERE I COME!
I DIDN'T...
WELL IT'S LIKE GRAMPY USED TO SAY, *"NEVER LOOK A GIFT MAGICALLY OPENED DOOR IN THE MOUTH."*

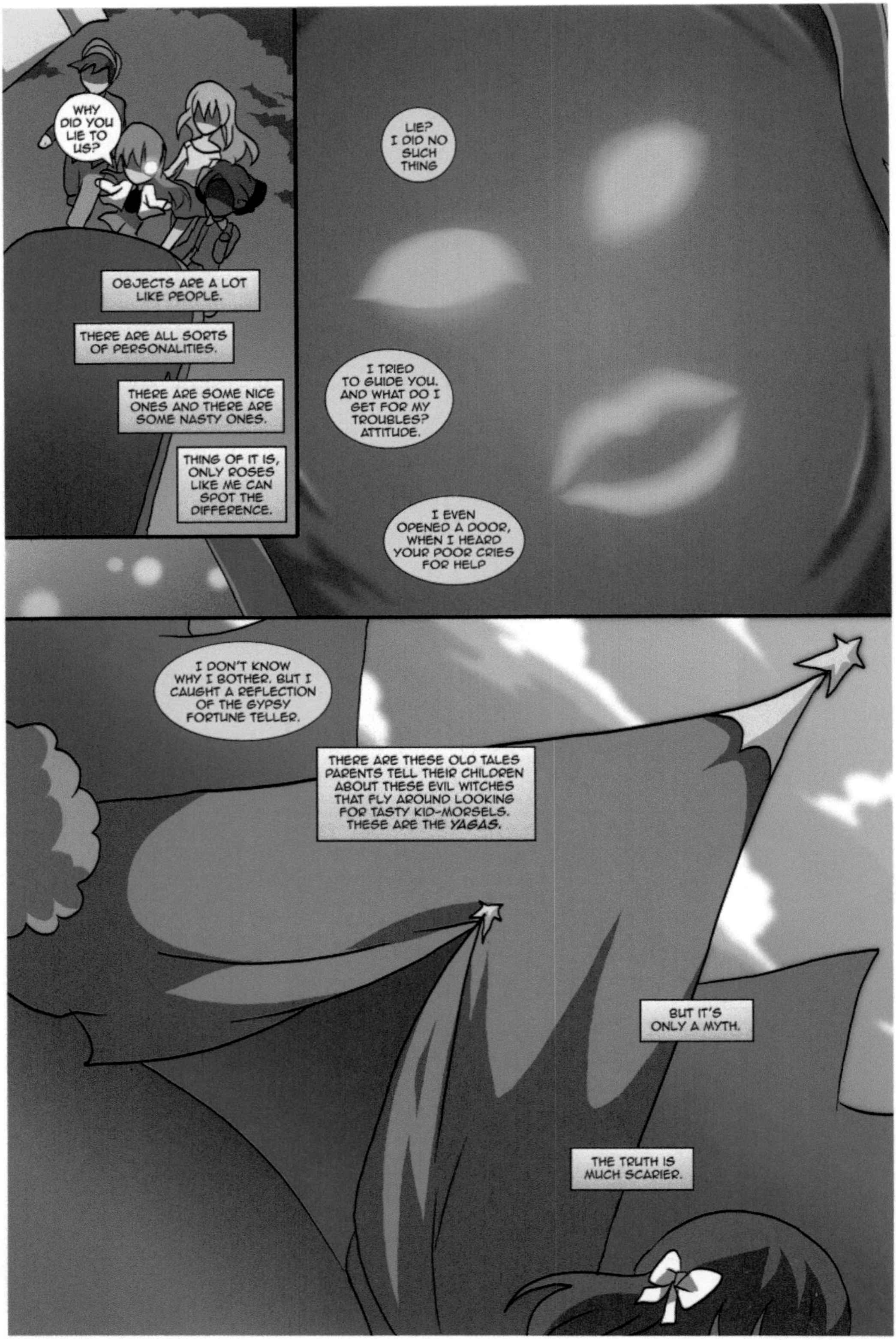
WHY DID YOU LIE TO US?
OBJECTS ARE A LOT LIKE PEOPLE.
THERE ARE ALL SORTS OF PERSONALITIES.
THERE ARE SOME NICE ONES AND THERE ARE SOME NASTY ONES.
THING OF IT IS, ONLY ROSES LIKE ME CAN SPOT THE DIFFERENCE.
LIE? I DID NO SUCH THING
I TRIED TO GUIDE YOU. AND WHAT DO I GET FOR MY TROUBLES? ATTITUDE.
I EVEN OPENED A DOOR, WHEN I HEARD YOUR POOR CRIES FOR HELP
I DON'T KNOW WHY I BOTHER. BUT I CAUGHT A REFLECTION OF THE GYPSY FORTUNE TELLER.
THERE ARE THESE OLD TALES PARENTS TELL THEIR CHILDREN ABOUT THESE EVIL WITCHES THAT FLY AROUND LOOKING FOR TASTY KID-MORSELS. THESE ARE THE *YAGAS*.
BUT IT'S ONLY A MYTH.
THE TRUTH IS MUCH SCARIER.

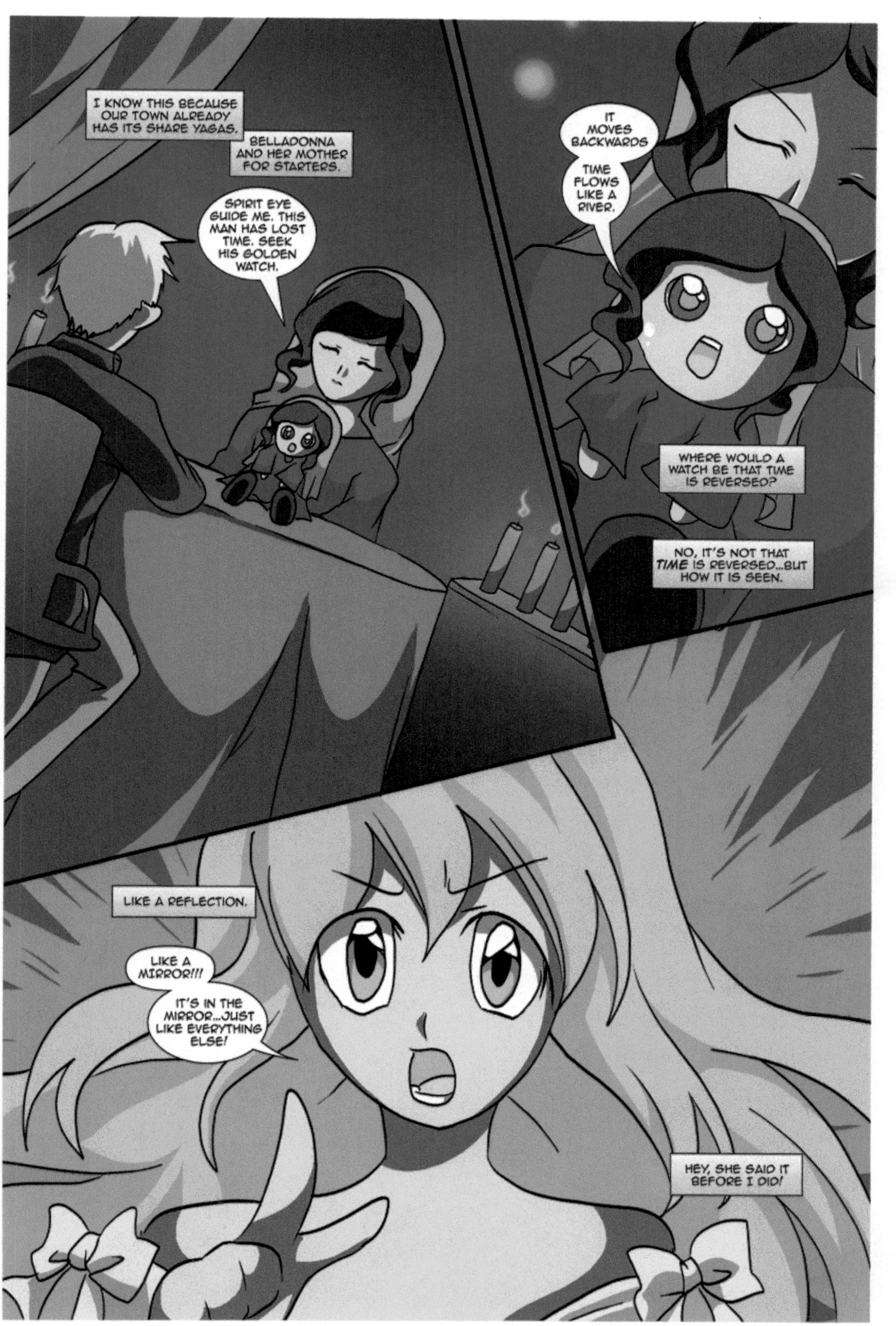
I KNOW THIS BECAUSE OUR TOWN ALREADY HAS ITS SHARE YAGAS.
BELLADONNA AND HER MOTHER FOR STARTERS.
SPIRIT EYE GUIDE ME. THIS MAN HAS LOST TIME. SEEK HIS GOLDEN WATCH.
IT MOVES BACKWARDS
TIME FLOWS LIKE A RIVER.
WHERE WOULD A WATCH BE THAT TIME IS REVERSED?
NO, IT'S NOT THAT *TIME* IS REVERSED...BUT HOW IT IS SEEN.
LIKE A REFLECTION.
LIKE A MIRROR!!!
IT'S IN THE MIRROR...JUST LIKE EVERYTHING ELSE!
HEY, SHE SAID IT BEFORE I DID!

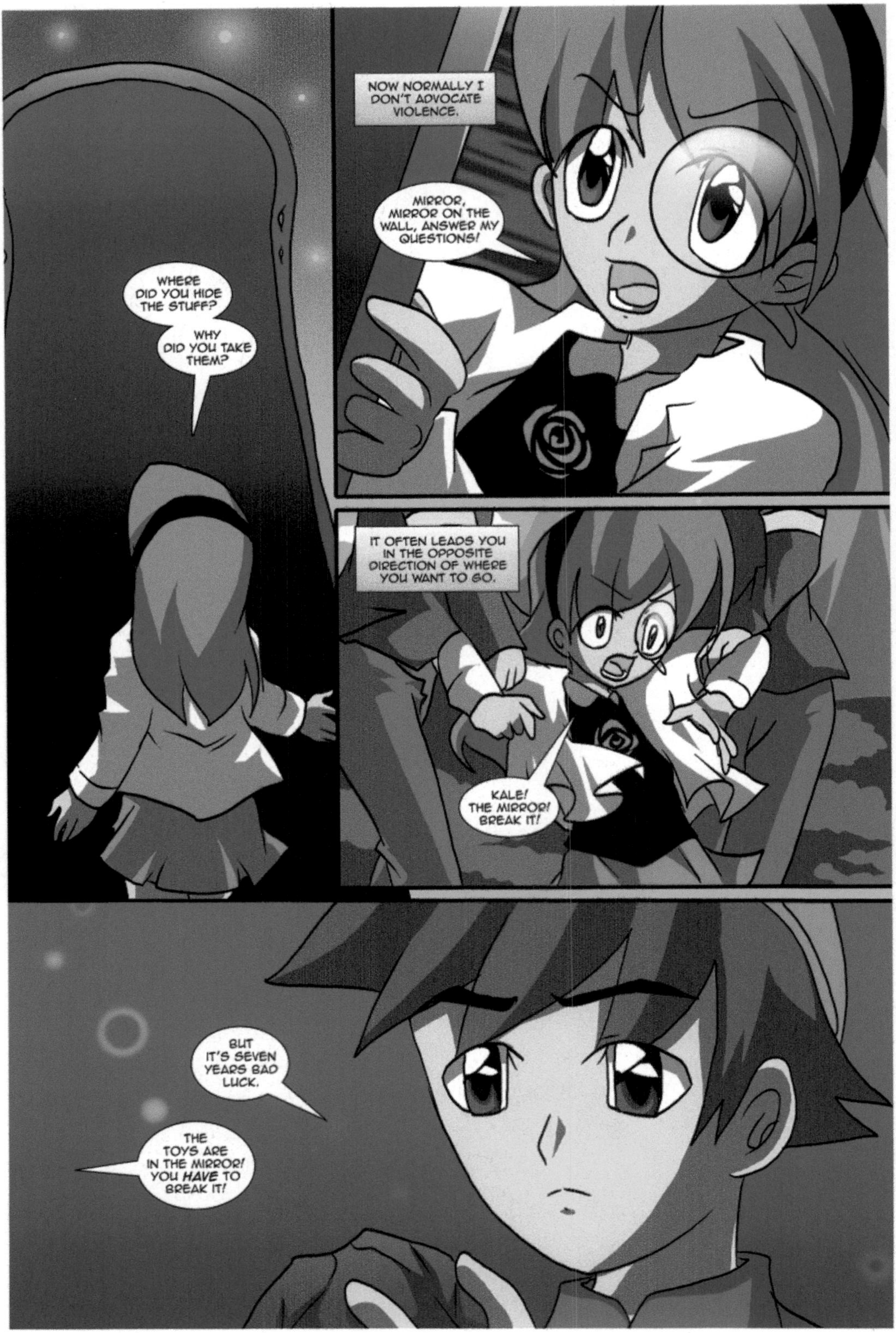
NOW NORMALLY I DON'T ADVOCATE VIOLENCE.
MIRROR, MIRROR ON THE WALL, ANSWER MY QUESTIONS!
WHERE DID YOU HIDE THE STUFF?
WHY DID YOU TAKE THEM?
IT OFTEN LEADS YOU IN THE OPPOSITE DIRECTION OF WHERE YOU WANT TO GO.
KALE! THE MIRROR! BREAK IT!
BUT IT'S SEVEN YEARS BAD LUCK.
THE TOYS ARE IN THE MIRROR! YOU *HAVE* TO BREAK IT!

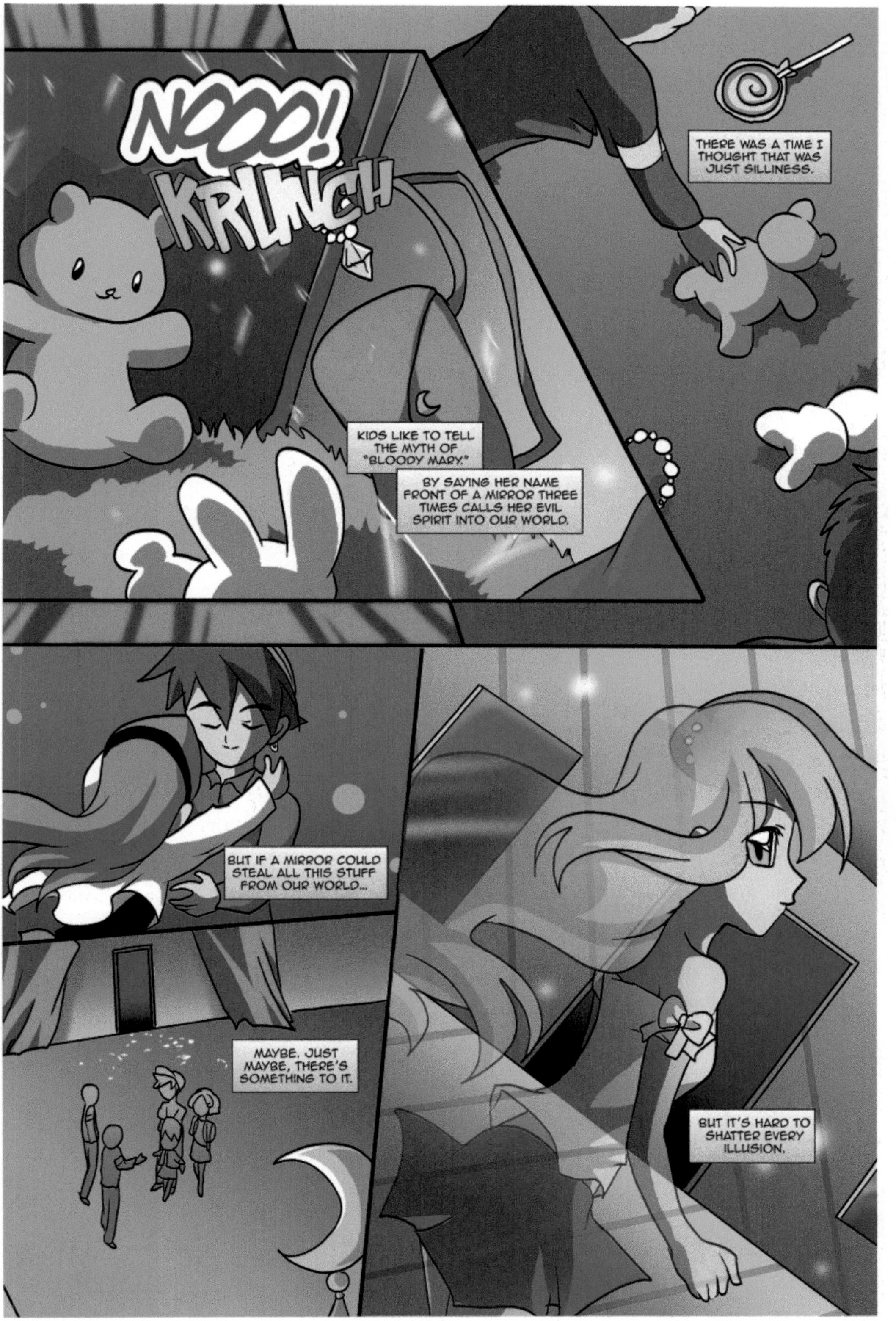
NOOO!
KRUNCH
KIDS LIKE TO TELL THE MYTH OF "BLOODY MARY."
BY SAYING HER NAME FRONT OF A MIRROR THREE TIMES CALLS HER EVIL SPIRIT INTO OUR WORLD.
THERE WAS A TIME I THOUGHT THAT WAS JUST SILLINESS.
BUT IF A MIRROR COULD STEAL ALL THIS STUFF FROM OUR WORLD...
MAYBE. JUST MAYBE, THERE'S SOMETHING TO IT.
BUT IT'S HARD TO SHATTER EVERY ILLUSION.

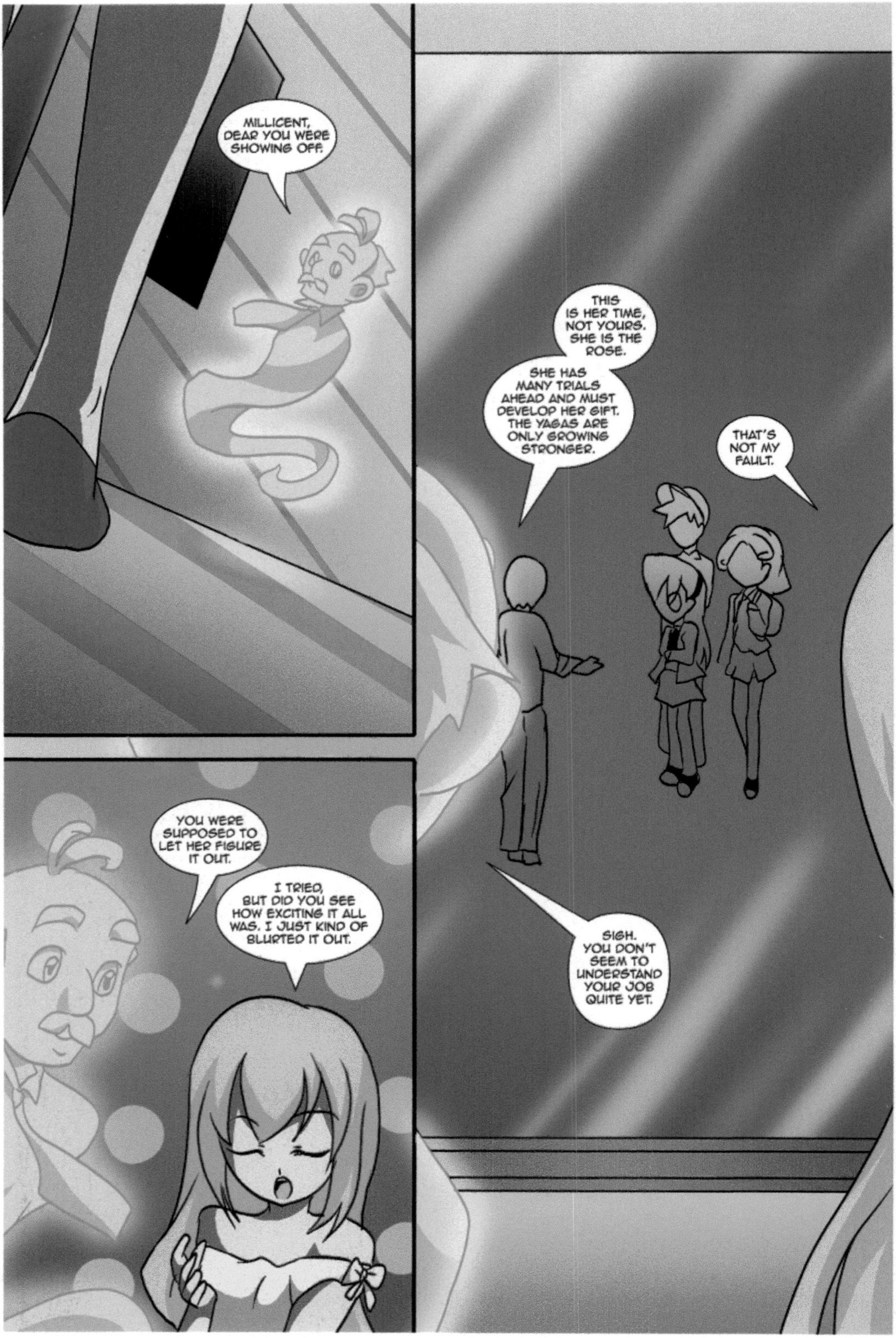
MILLICENT, DEAR YOU WERE SHOWING OFF.
THIS IS HER TIME, NOT YOURS. SHE IS THE ROSE.
SHE HAS MANY TRIALS AHEAD AND MUST DEVELOP HER GIFT. THE YAGAS ARE ONLY GROWING STRONGER.
THAT'S NOT MY FAULT.
YOU WERE SUPPOSED TO LET HER FIGURE IT OUT.
I TRIED, BUT DID YOU SEE HOW EXCITING IT ALL WAS. I JUST KIND OF BLURTED IT OUT.
SIGH. YOU DON'T SEEM TO UNDERSTAND YOUR JOB QUITE YET.

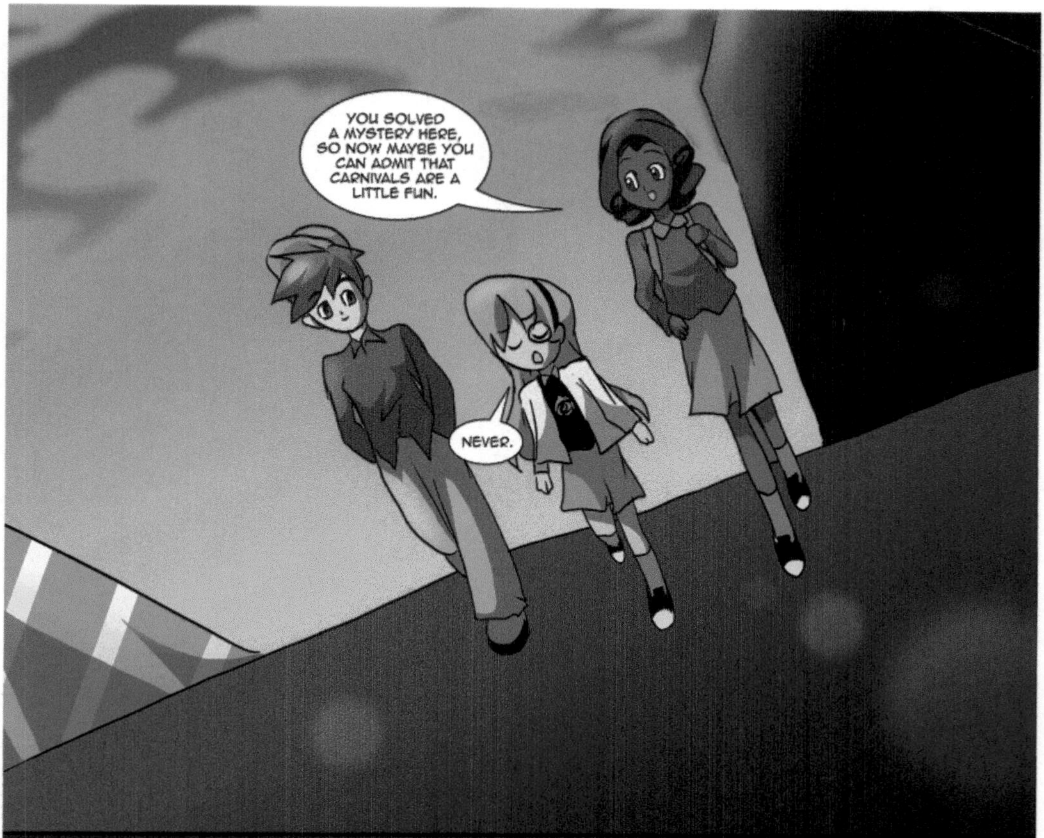
YOU SOLVED A MYSTERY HERE, SO NOW MAYBE YOU CAN ADMIT THAT CARNIVALS ARE A LITTLE FUN.
NEVER.

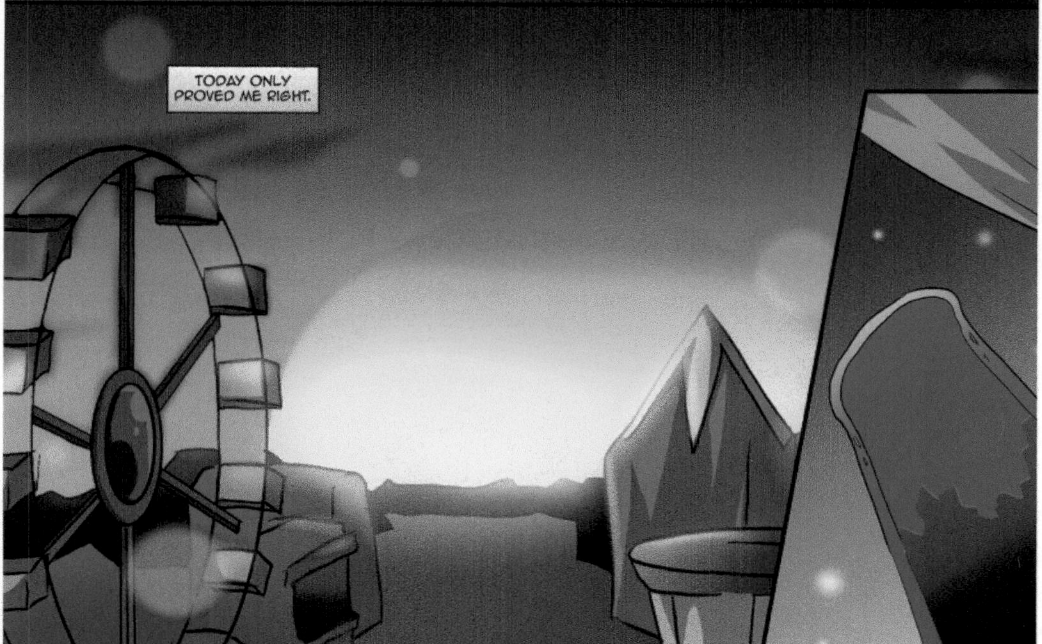
TODAY ONLY PROVED ME RIGHT.

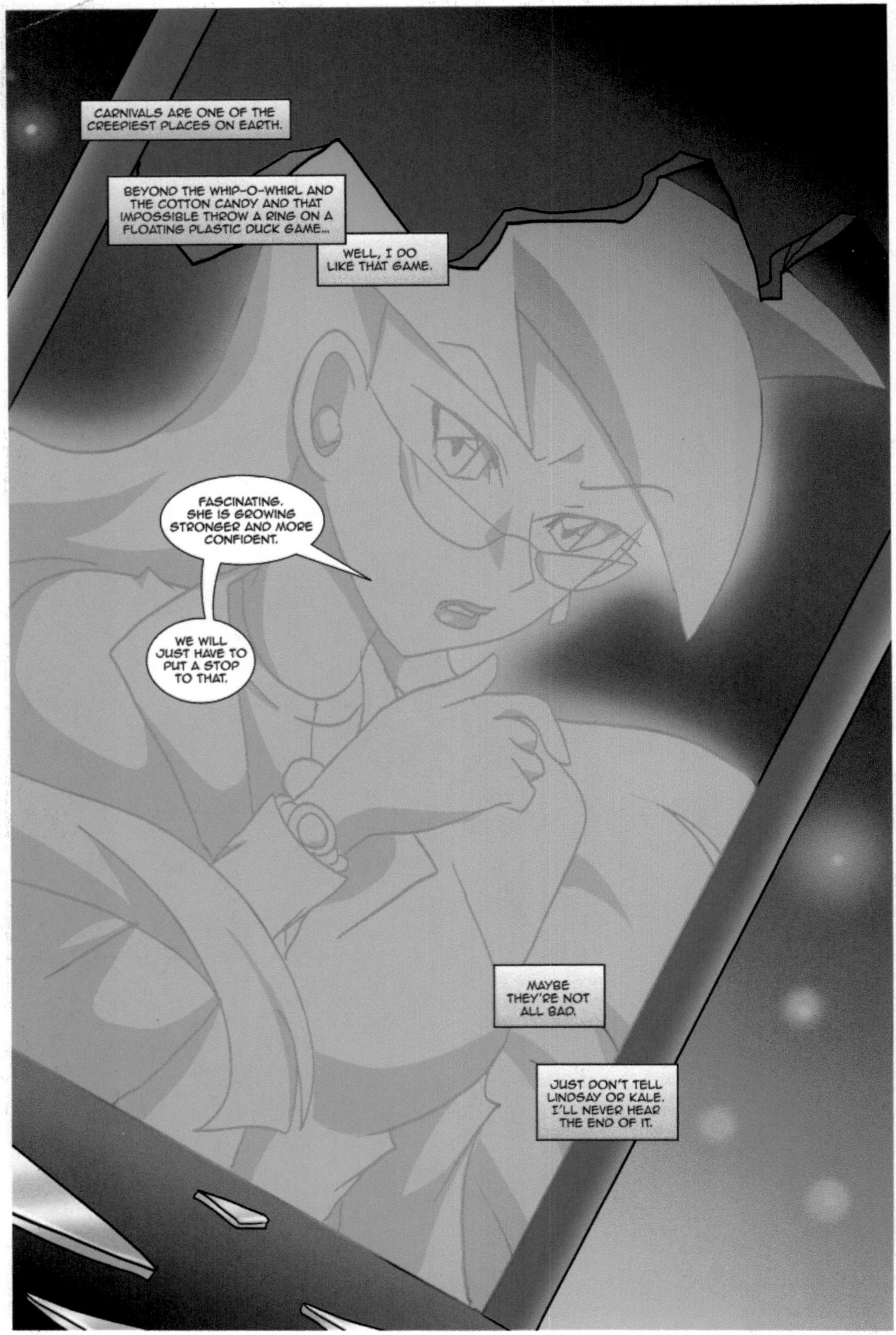
CARNIVALS ARE ONE OF THE CREEPIEST PLACES ON EARTH.
BEYOND THE WHIP-O-WHIRL AND THE COTTON CANDY AND THAT IMPOSSIBLE THROW A RING ON A FLOATING PLASTIC DUCK GAME...
WELL, I DO LIKE THAT GAME.
FASCINATING. SHE IS GROWING STRONGER AND MORE CONFIDENT.
WE WILL JUST HAVE TO PUT A STOP TO THAT.
MAYBE THEY'RE NOT ALL BAD.
JUST DON'T TELL LINDSAY OR KALE. I'LL NEVER HEAR THE END OF IT.

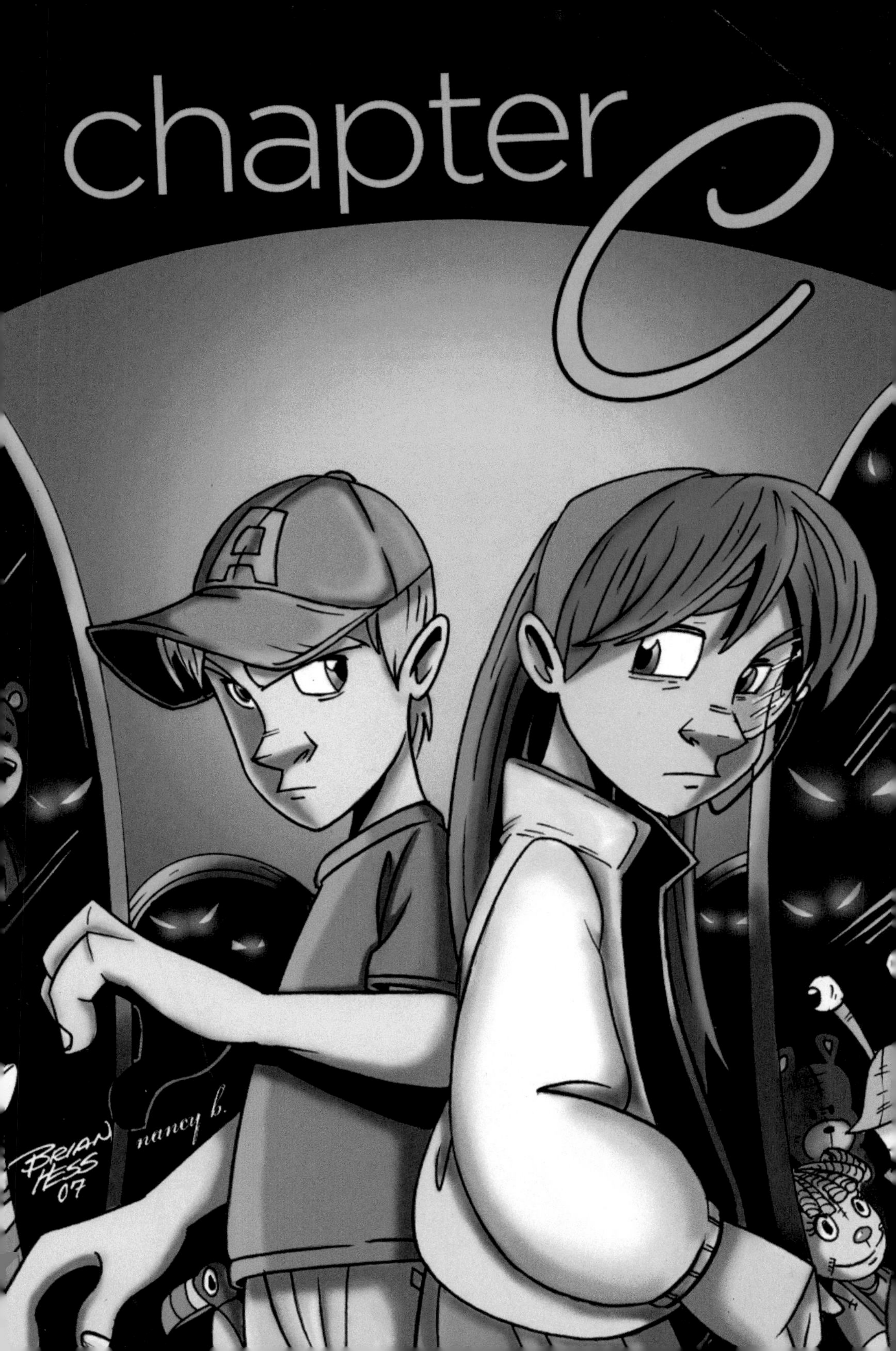
chapter C
BRIAN HESS 07
nancy b.

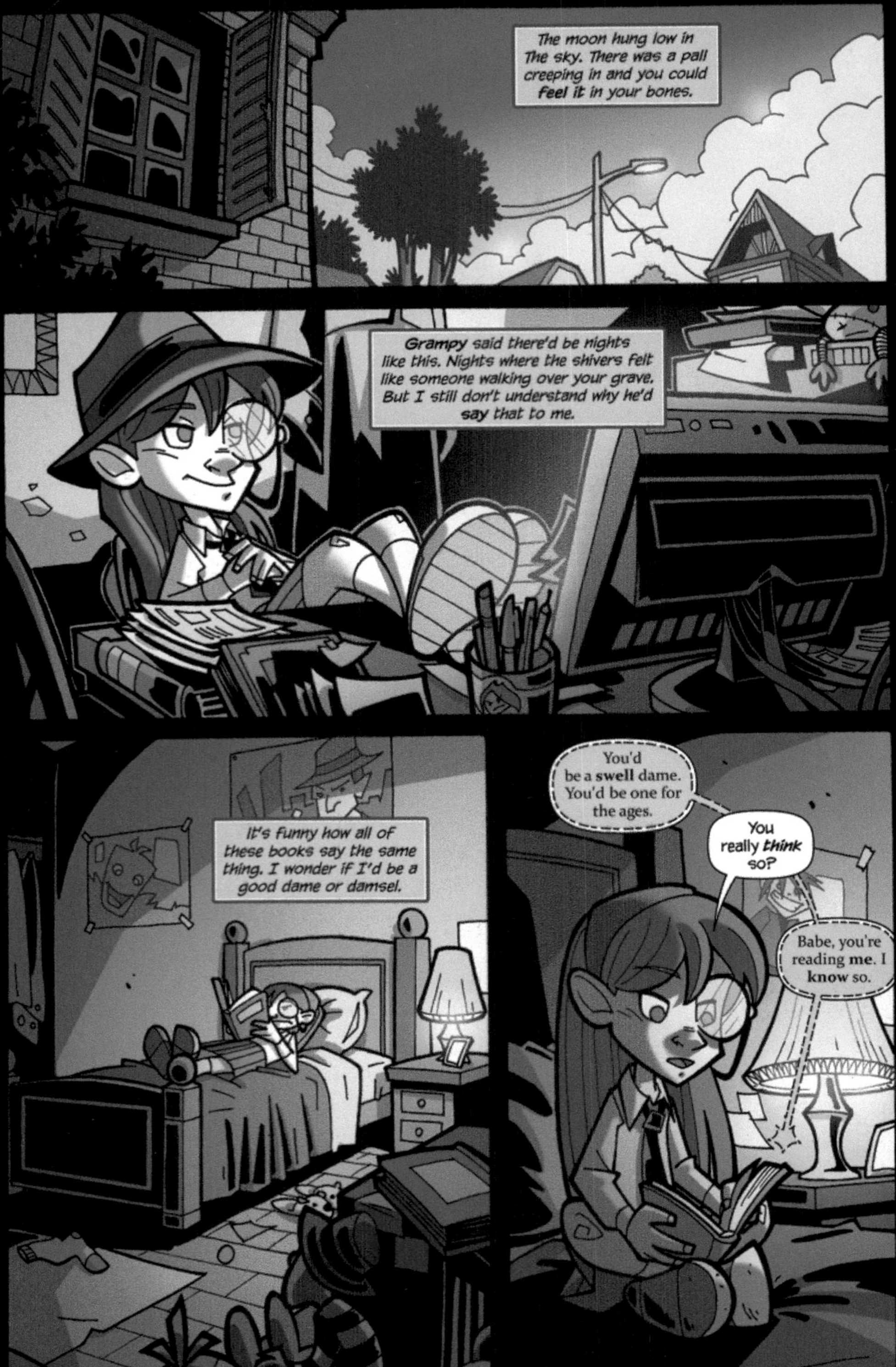
The moon hung low in the sky. There was a pall creeping in and you could feel it in your bones.
Grampy said there'd be nights like this. Nights where the shivers felt like someone walking over your grave. But I still don't understand why he'd say that to me.
It's funny how all of these books say the same thing. I wonder if I'd be a good dame or damsel.
You'd be a swell dame. You'd be one for the ages.
You really think so?
Babe, you're reading me. I know so.

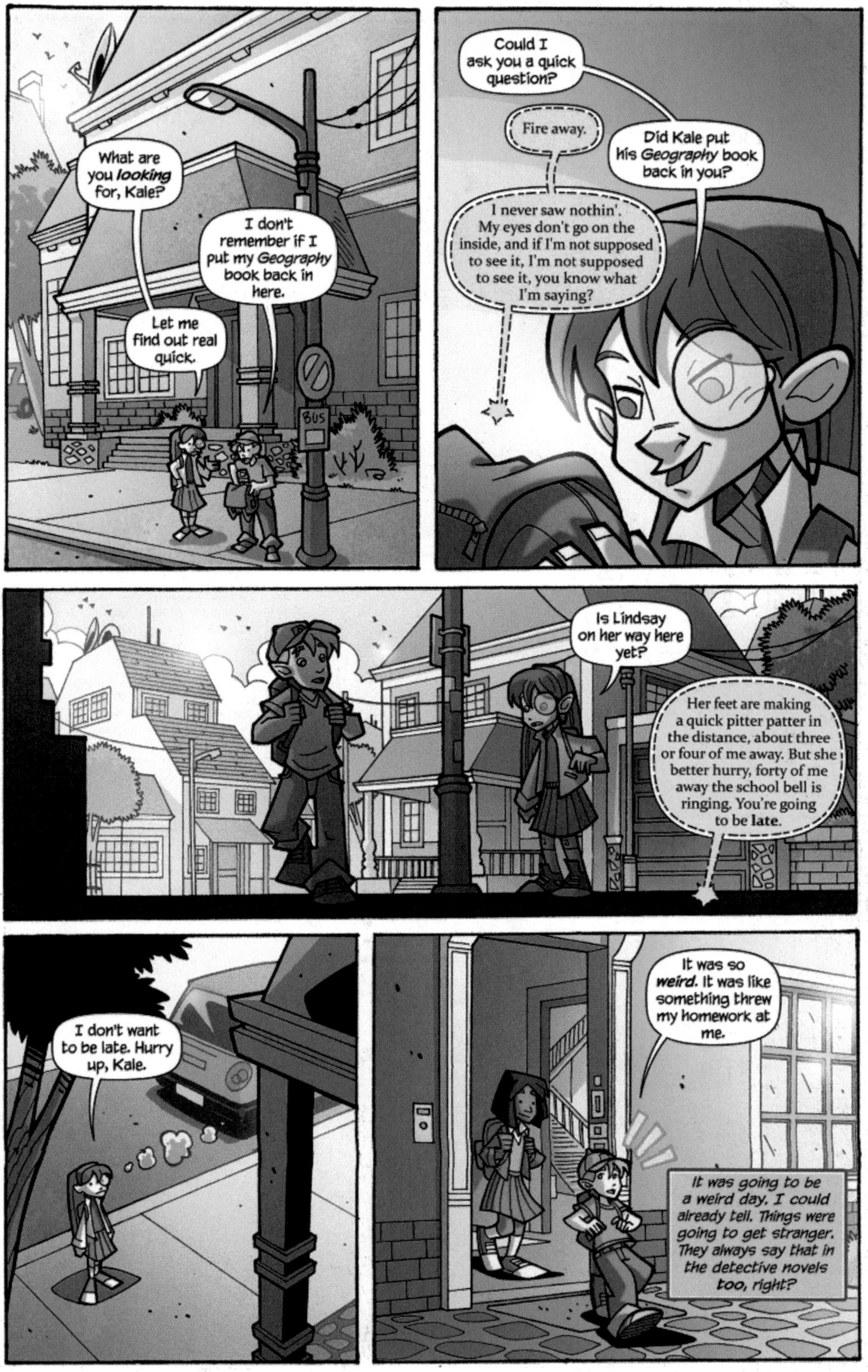
What are you *looking* for, Kale?
I don't remember if I put my *Geography* book back in here.
Let me find out real quick.
Could I ask you a quick question?
Fire away.
Did Kale put his *Geography* book back in you?
I never saw nothin'. My eyes don't go on the inside, and if I'm not supposed to see it, I'm not supposed to see it, you know what I'm saying?
Is Lindsay on her way here yet?
Her feet are making a quick pitter patter in the distance, about three or four of me away. But she better hurry, forty of me away the school bell is ringing. You're going to be **late**.
I don't want to be late. Hurry up, Kale.
It was so *weird*. It was like something threw my homework at me.
It was going to be a weird day. I could already tell. Things were going to get stranger. They always say that in the detective novels ***too****, right?*

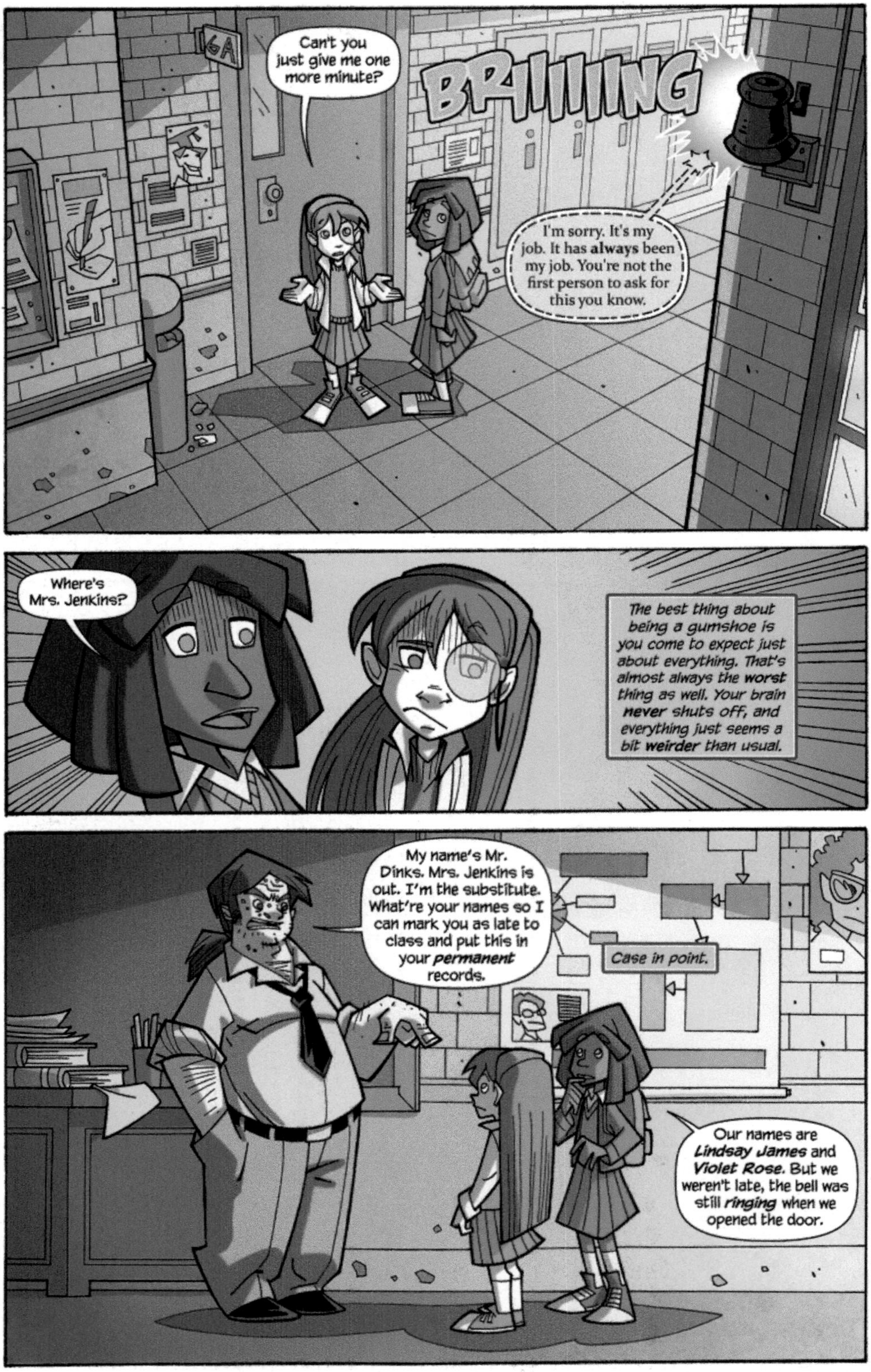
6A
Can't you just give me one more minute?
BRIIIIIING
I'm sorry. It's my job. It has **always** been my job. You're not the first person to ask for this you know.
Where's Mrs. Jenkins?
*The best thing about being a gumshoe is you come to expect just about everything. That's almost always the **worst** thing as well. Your brain **never** shuts off, and everything just seems a bit **weirder** than usual.*
My name's Mr. Dinks. Mrs. Jenkins is out. I'm the substitute. What're your names so I can mark you as late to class and put this in your ***permanent*** records.
Case in point.
Our names are ***Lindsay James*** and ***Violet Rose.*** But we weren't late, the bell was still ***ringing*** when we opened the door.

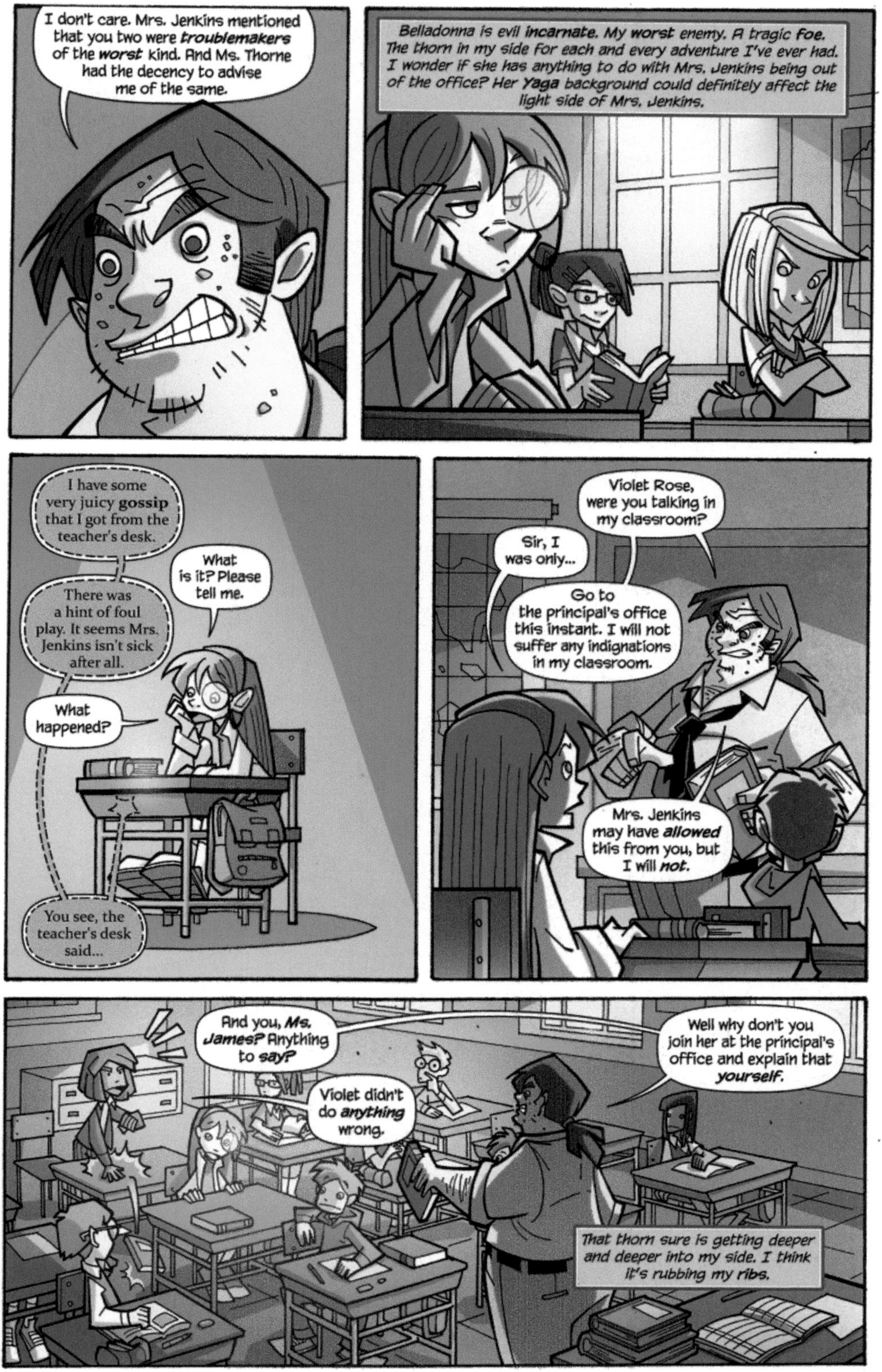

I don't care. Mrs. Jenkins mentioned that you two were ***troublemakers*** of the ***worst*** kind. And Ms. Thorne had the decency to advise me of the same.
Belladonna is evil ***incarnate.*** *My* ***worst*** *enemy. A tragic* ***foe.*** *The thorn in my side for each and every adventure I've ever had. I wonder if she has anything to do with Mrs. Jenkins being out of the office? Her* ***Yaga*** *background could definitely affect the light side of Mrs. Jenkins.*
I have some very juicy **gossip** that I got from the teacher's desk.
What is it? Please tell me.
There was a hint of foul play. It seems Mrs. Jenkins isn't sick after all.
What happened?
You see, the teacher's desk said...
Violet Rose, were you talking in my classroom?
Sir, I was only...
Go to the principal's office this instant. I will not suffer any indignations in my classroom.
Mrs. Jenkins may have ***allowed*** this from you, but I will ***not.***
And you, ***Ms. James?*** Anything to ***say?***
Violet didn't do ***anything*** wrong.
Well why don't you join her at the principal's office and explain that ***yourself.***
That thorn sure is getting deeper and deeper into my side. I think it's rubbing my ***ribs.***

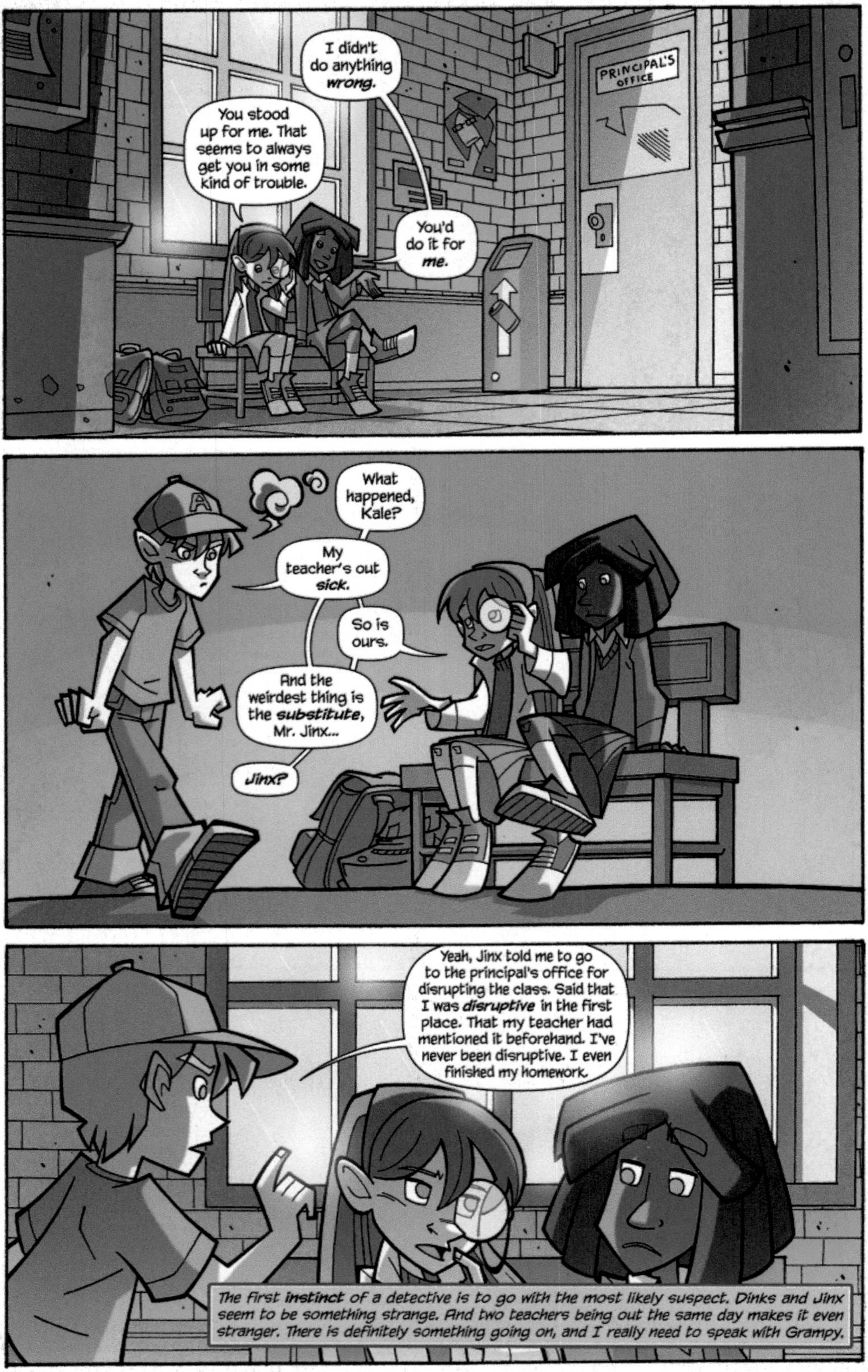
PRINCIPAL'S OFFICE
You stood up for me. That seems to always get you in some kind of trouble.
I didn't do anything wrong.
You'd do it for me.
What happened, Kale?
My teacher's out sick.
So is ours.
And the weirdest thing is the substitute, Mr. Jinx...
Jinx?
Yeah, Jinx told me to go to the principal's office for disrupting the class. Said that I was disruptive in the first place. That my teacher had mentioned it beforehand. I've never been disruptive. I even finished my homework.
The first instinct of a detective is to go with the most likely suspect. Dinks and Jinx seem to be something strange. And two teachers being out the same day makes it even stranger. There is definitely something going on, and I really need to speak with Grampy.

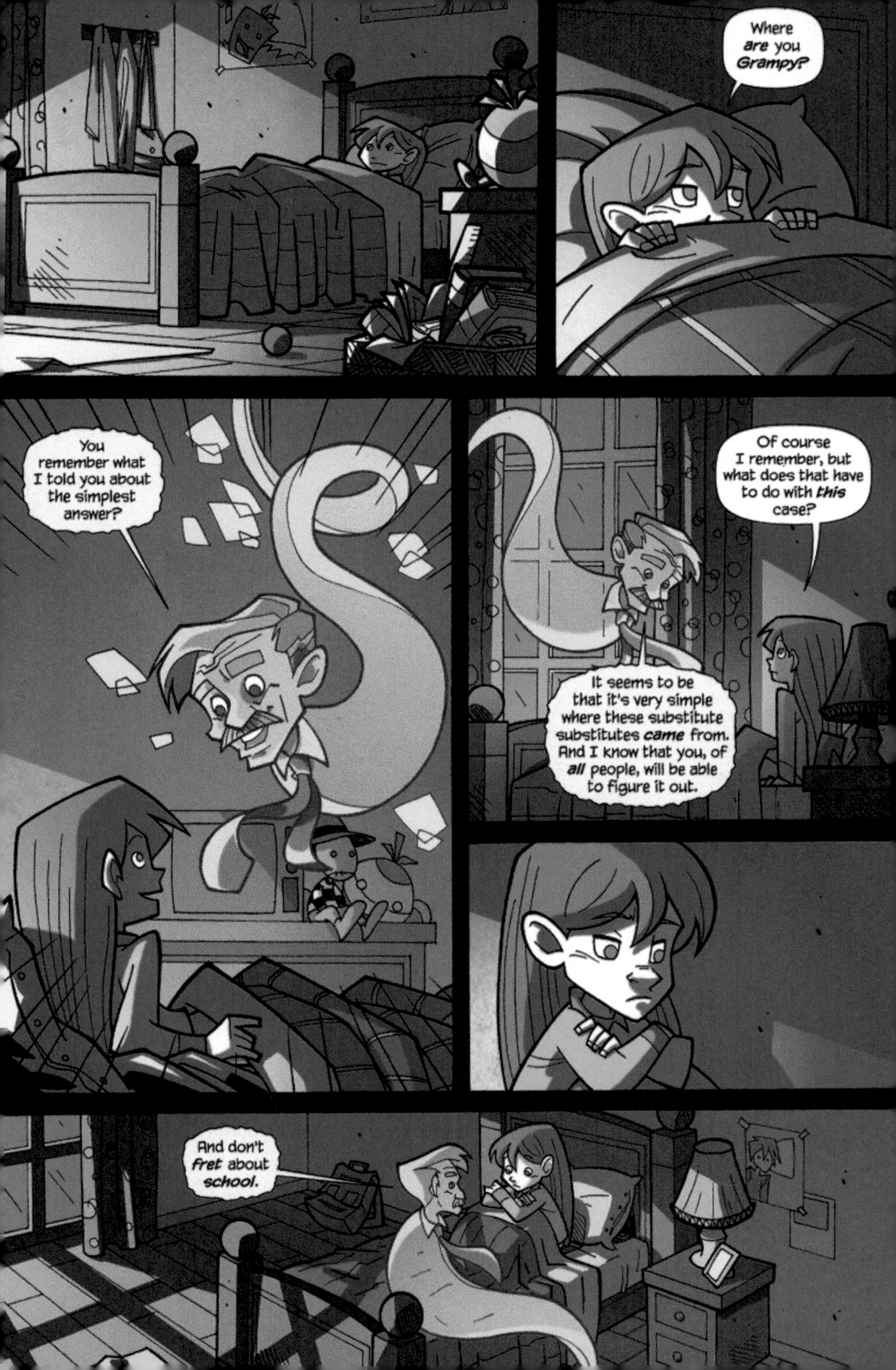
Where are you Grampy?
You remember what I told you about the simplest answer?
Of course I remember, but what does that have to do with this case?
It seems to be that it's very simple where these substitute substitutes came from. And I know that you, of all people, will be able to figure it out.
And don't fret about school.

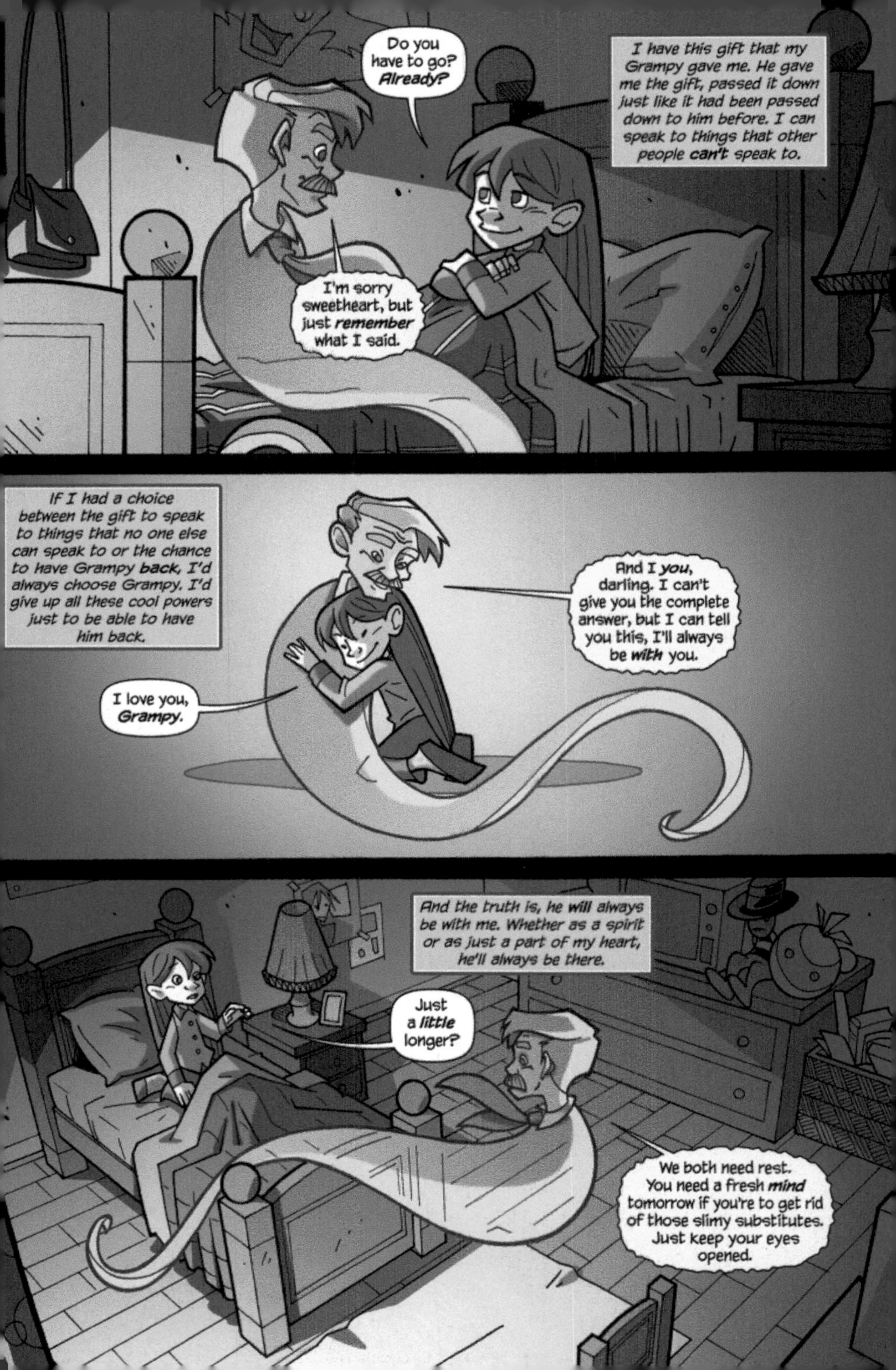
Do you have to go? *Already?*
I have this gift that my Grampy gave me. He gave me the gift, passed it down just like it had been passed down to him before. I can speak to things that other people *can't* speak to.
I'm sorry sweetheart, but just *remember* what I said.
If I had a choice between the gift to speak to things that no one else can speak to or the chance to have Grampy *back*, I'd always choose Grampy. I'd give up all these cool powers just to be able to have him back.
I love you, *Grampy*.
And I *you*, darling. I can't give you the complete answer, but I can tell you this, I'll always be *with* you.
And the truth is, he *will* always be with me. Whether as a spirit or as just a part of my heart, he'll always be there.
Just a *little* longer?
We both need rest. You need a fresh *mind* tomorrow if you're to get rid of those slimy substitutes. Just keep your eyes opened.

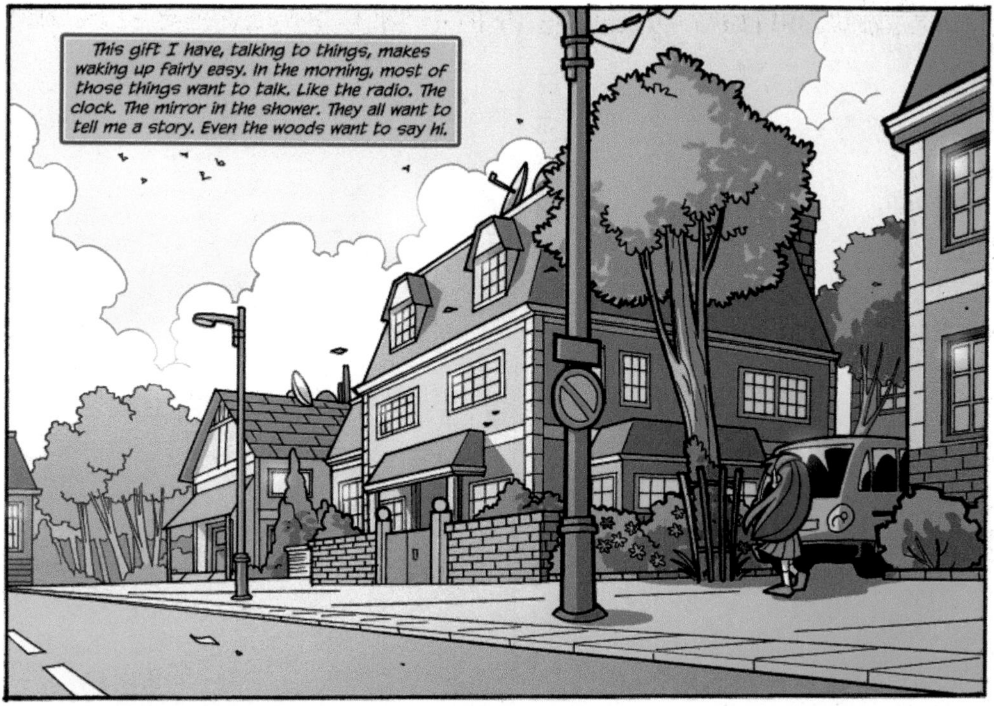
This gift I have, talking to things, makes waking up fairly easy. In the morning, most of those things want to talk. Like the radio. The clock. The mirror in the shower. They all want to tell me a story. Even the woods want to say hi.

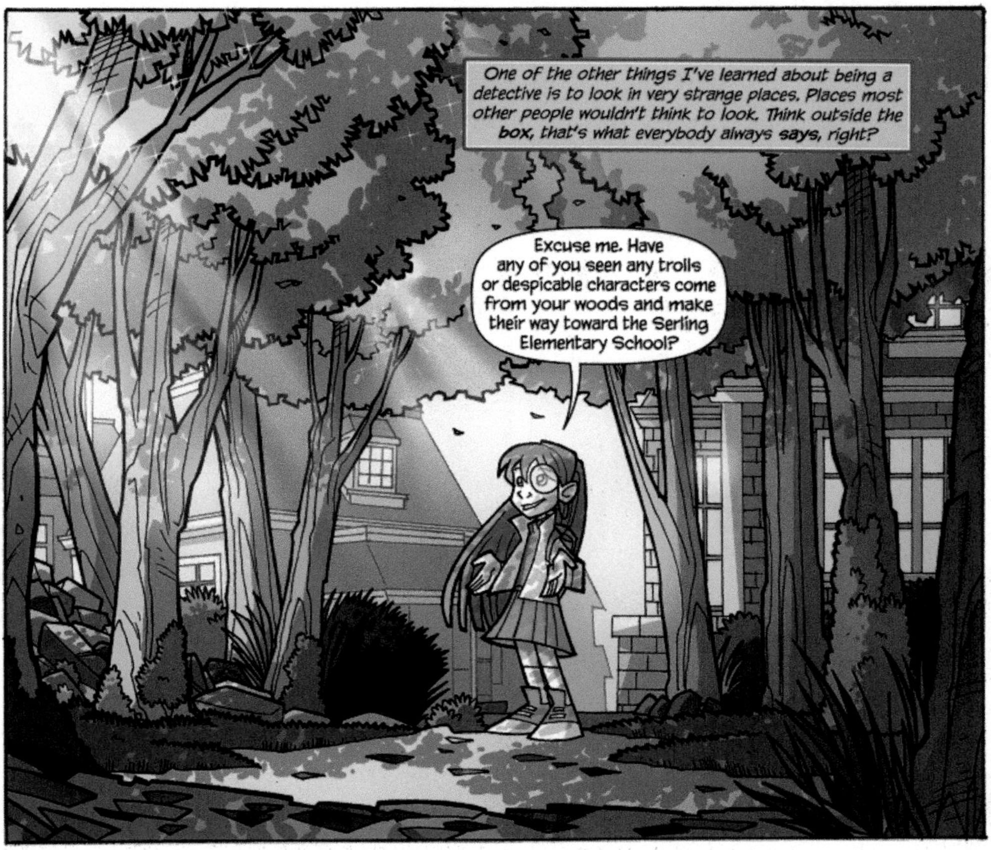
One of the other things I've learned about being a detective is to look in very strange places. Places most other people wouldn't think to look. Think outside the box, that's what everybody always says, right?
Excuse me. Have any of you seen any trolls or despicable characters come from your woods and make their way toward the Serling Elementary School?

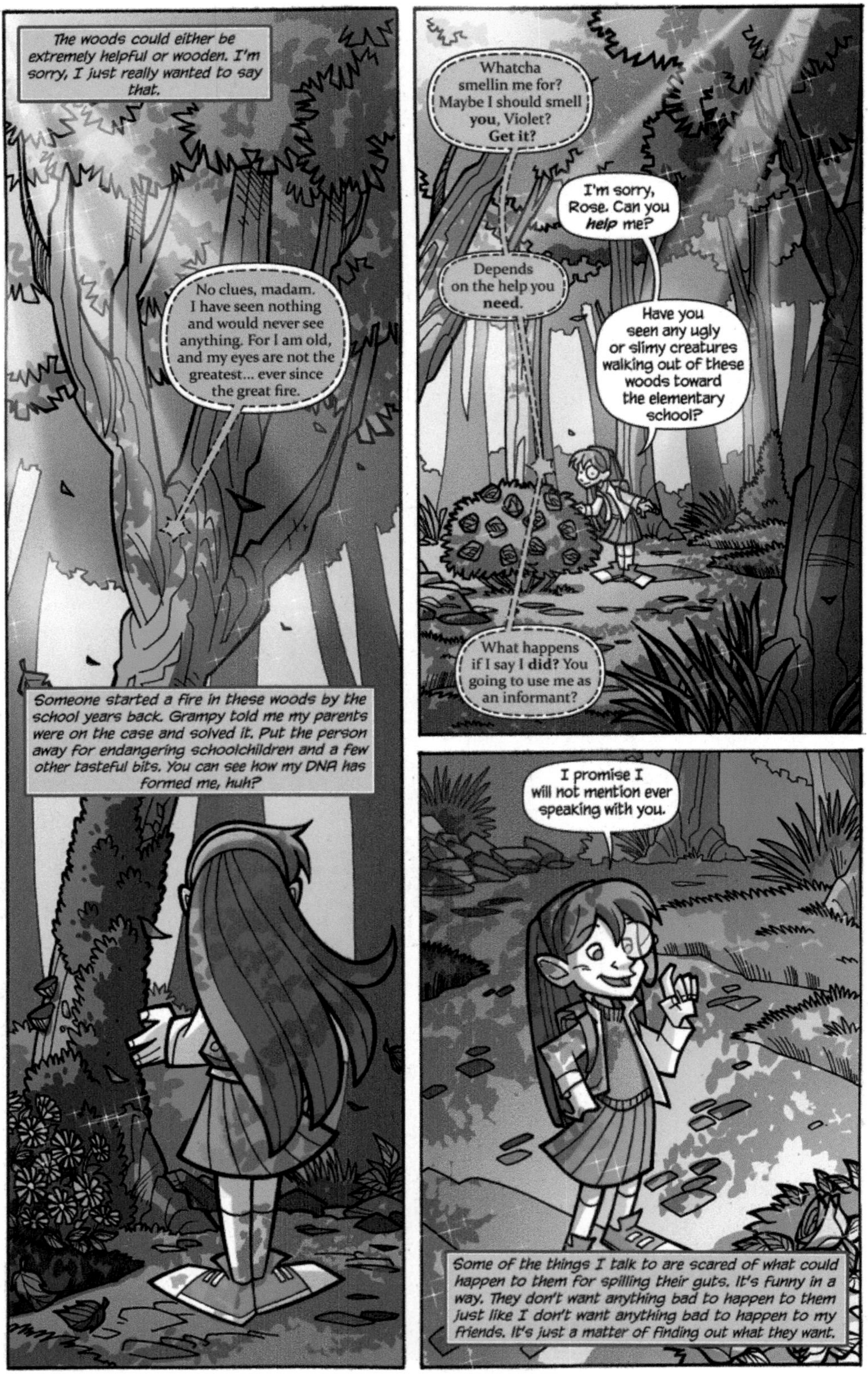

The woods could either be extremely helpful or wooden. I'm sorry, I just really wanted to say that.
No clues, madam. I have seen nothing and would never see anything. For I am old, and my eyes are not the greatest... ever since the great fire.
Someone started a fire in these woods by the school years back. Grampy told me my parents were on the case and solved it. Put the person away for endangering schoolchildren and a few other tasteful bits. You can see how my DNA has formed me, huh?
Whatcha smellin me for? Maybe I should smell **you**, Violet? **Get it?**
I'm sorry, Rose. Can you ***help*** me?
Depends on the help you **need**.
Have you seen any ugly or slimy creatures walking out of these woods toward the elementary school?
What happens if I say I **did?** You going to use me as an informant?
I promise I will not mention ever speaking with you.
Some of the things I talk to are scared of what could happen to them for spilling their guts. It's funny in a way. They don't want anything bad to happen to them just like I don't want anything bad to happen to my friends. It's just a matter of finding out what they want.

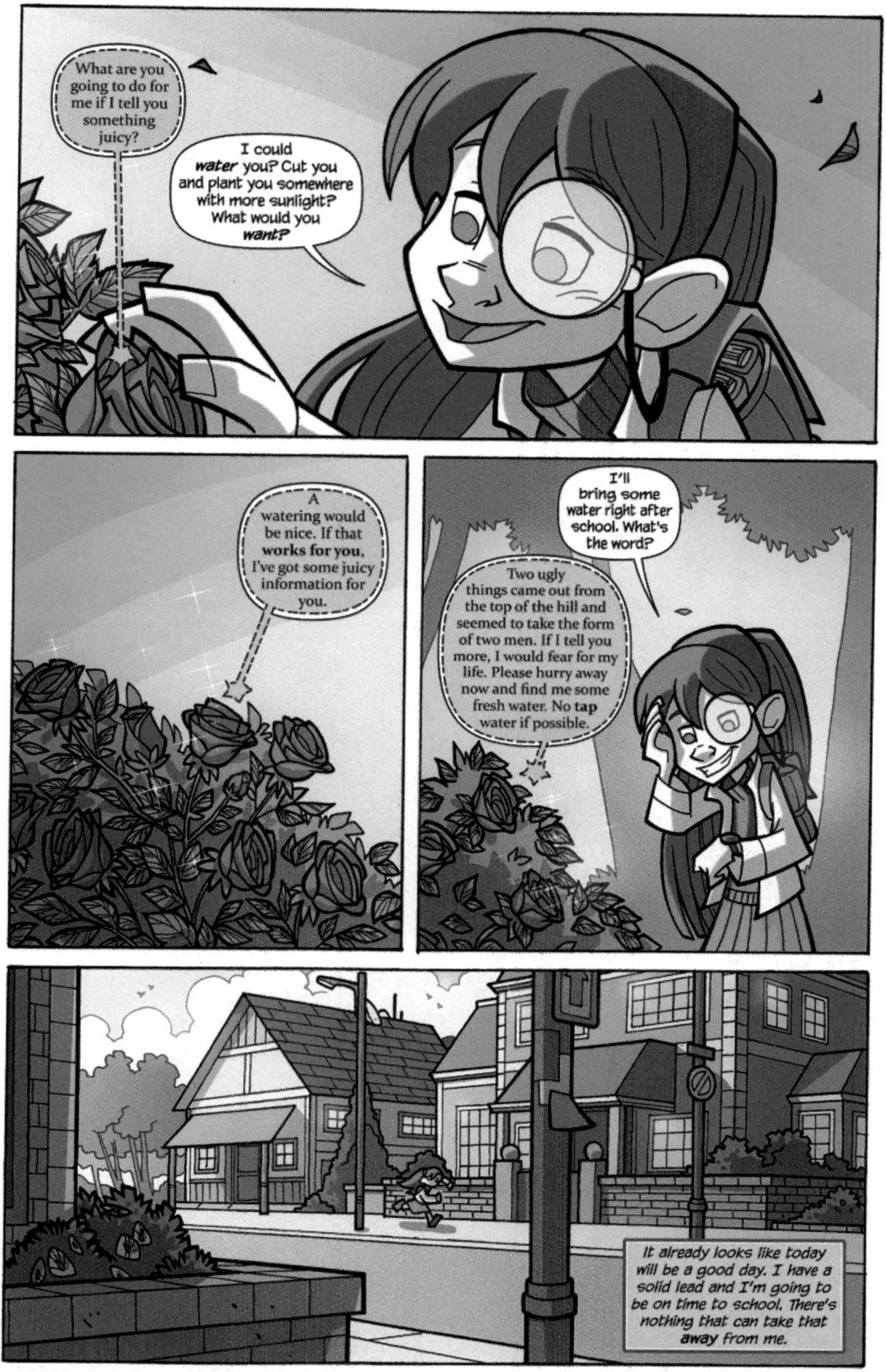
What are you going to do for me if I tell you something juicy?
I could water you? Cut you and plant you somewhere with more sunlight? What would you want?
A watering would be nice. If that works for you, I've got some juicy information for you.
I'll bring some water right after school. What's the word?
Two ugly things came out from the top of the hill and seemed to take the form of two men. If I tell you more, I would fear for my life. Please hurry away now and find me some fresh water. No tap water if possible.
It already looks like today will be a good day. I have a solid lead and I'm going to be on time to school. There's nothing that can take that away from me.

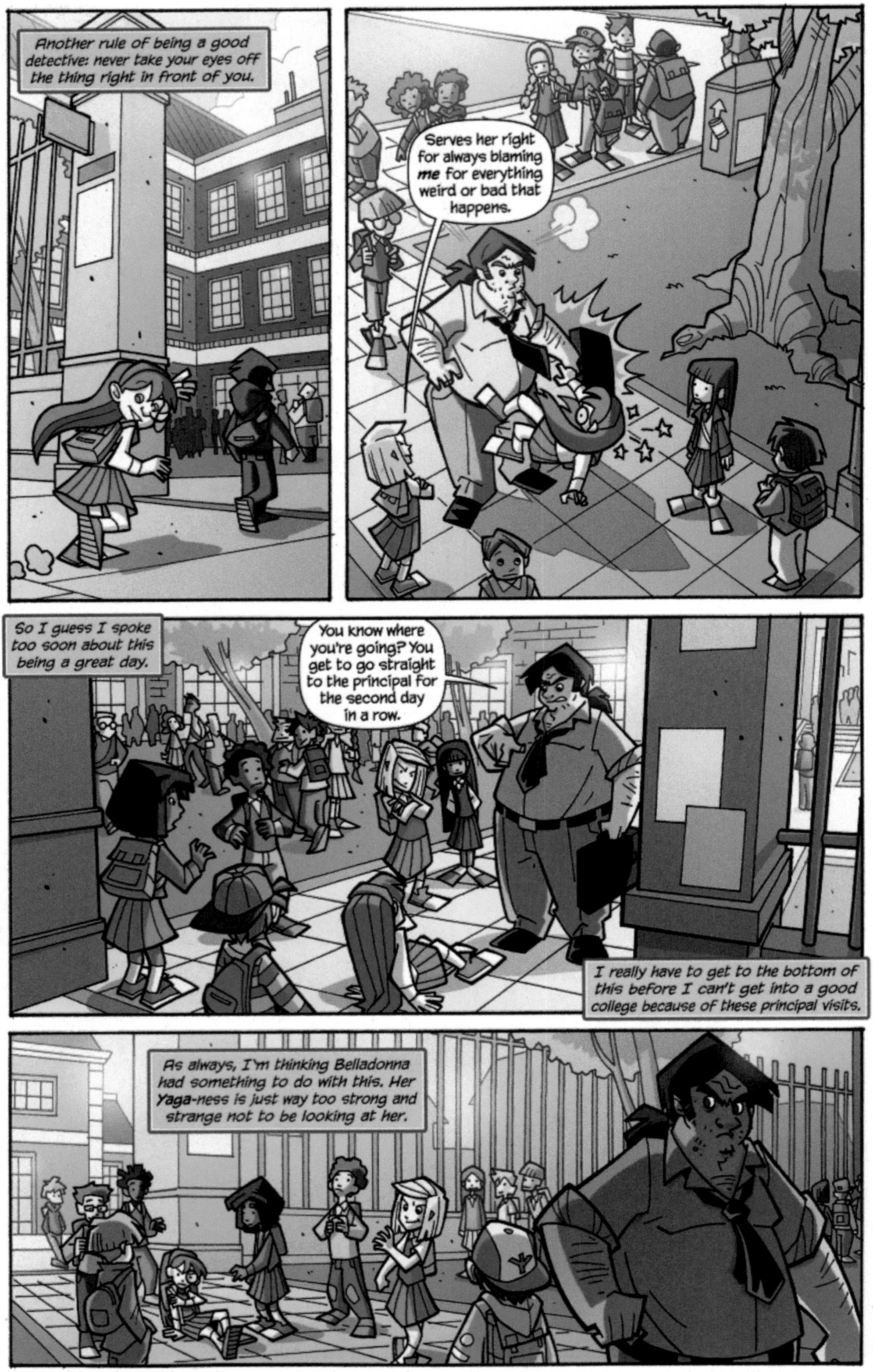
Another rule of being a good detective: never take your eyes off the thing right in front of you.
Serves her right for always blaming *me* for everything weird or bad that happens.
So I guess I spoke too soon about this being a great day.
You know where you're going? You get to go straight to the principal for the second day in a row.
I really have to get to the bottom of this before I can't get into a good college because of these principal visits.
As always, I'm thinking Belladonna had something to do with this. Her *Yaga*-ness is just way too strong and strange not to be looking at her.

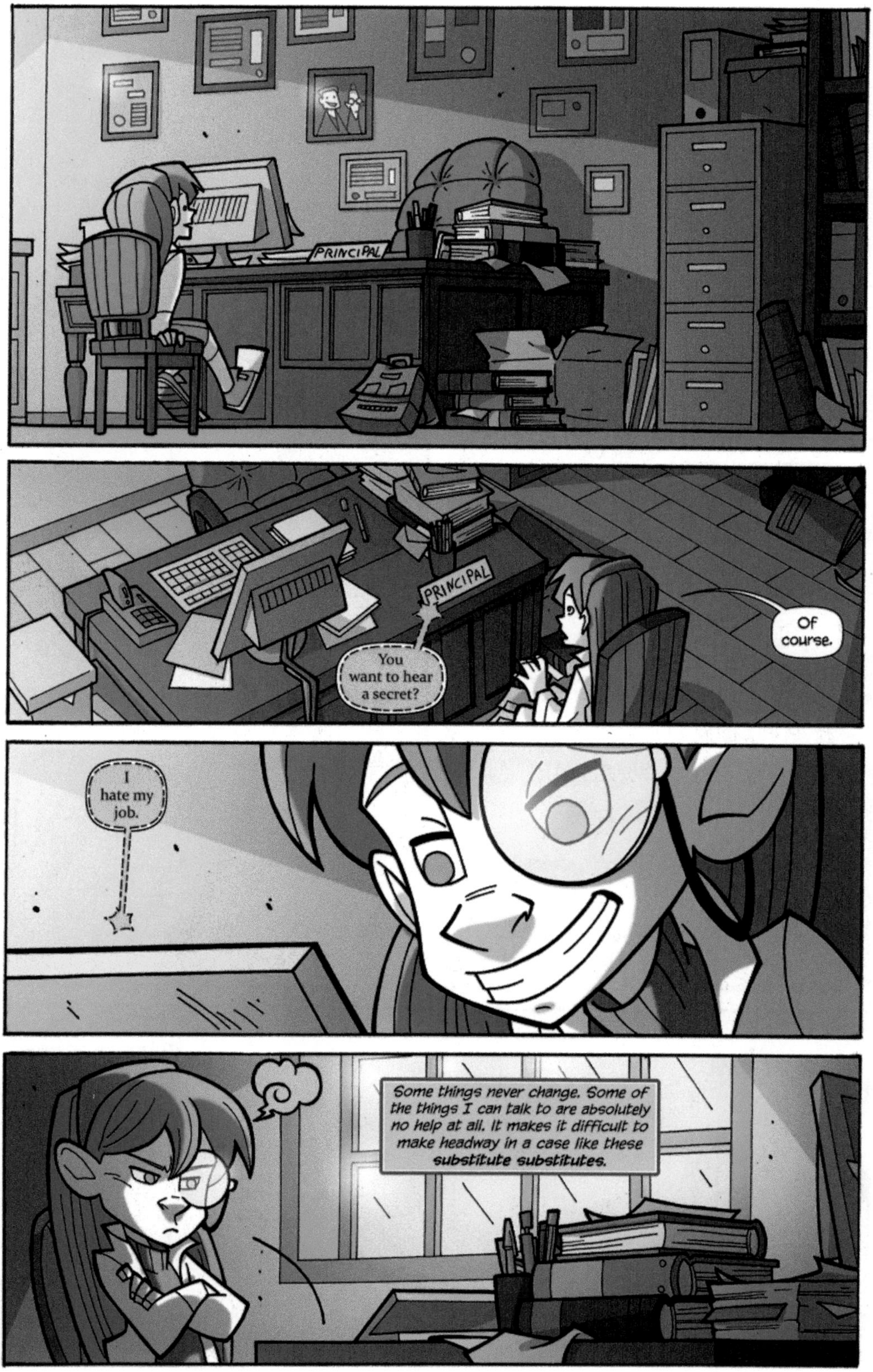
PRINCIPAL
PRINCIPAL
You want to hear a secret?
Of course.
I hate my job.
Some things never change. Some of the things I can talk to are absolutely no help at all. It makes it difficult to make headway in a case like these **substitute substitutes**.

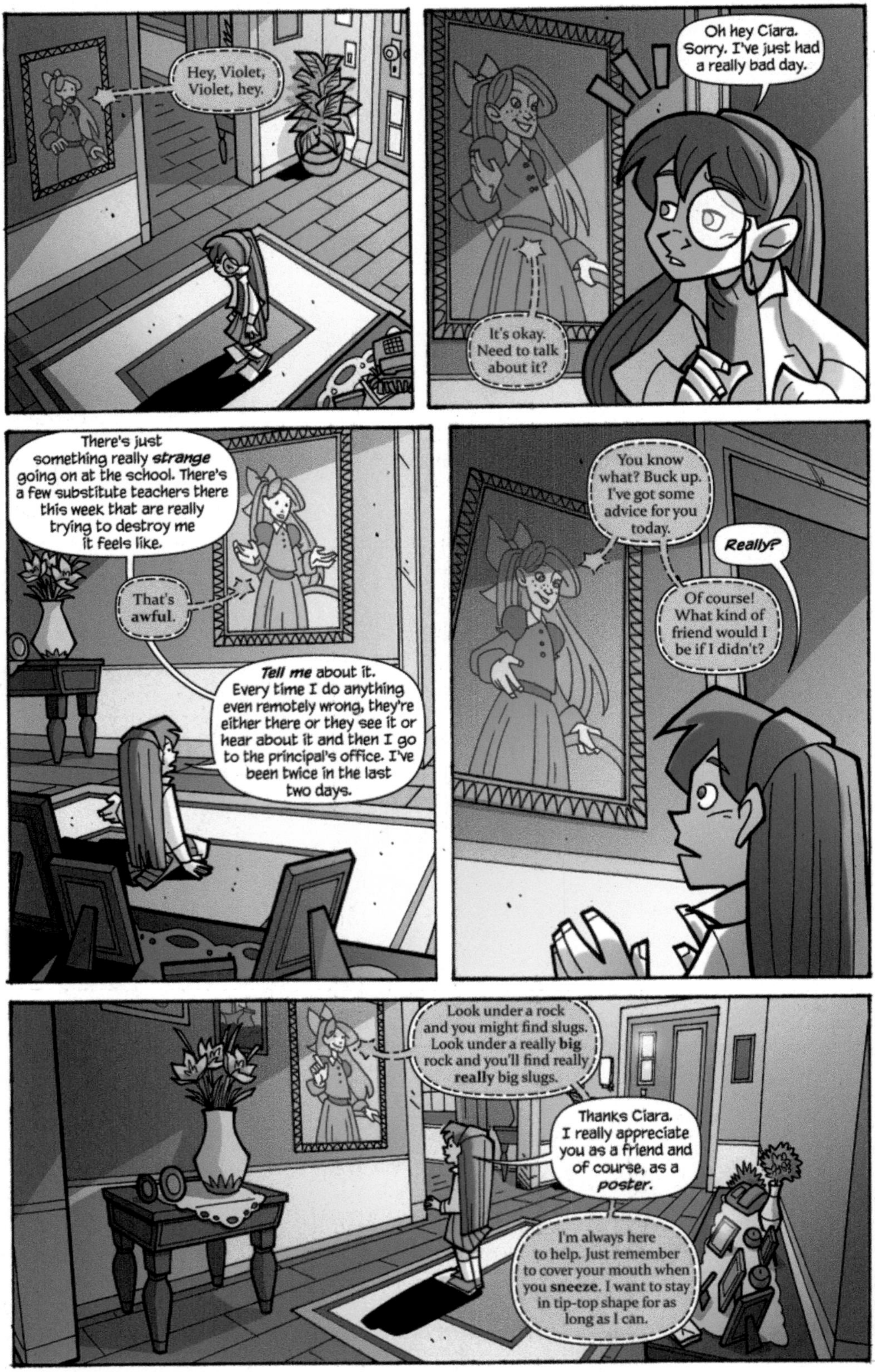
Hey, Violet, Violet, hey.
Oh hey Ciara. Sorry. I've just had a really bad day.
It's okay. Need to talk about it?
There's just something really *strange* going on at the school. There's a few substitute teachers there this week that are really trying to destroy me it feels like.
That's **awful**.
Tell me about it. Every time I do anything even remotely wrong, they're either there or they see it or hear about it and then I go to the principal's office. I've been twice in the last two days.
You know what? Buck up. I've got some advice for you today.
Really?
Of course! What kind of friend would I be if I didn't?
Look under a rock and you might find slugs. Look under a really **big** rock and you'll find really **really** big slugs.
Thanks Ciara. I really appreciate you as a friend and of course, as a ***poster***.
I'm always here to help. Just remember to cover your mouth when you **sneeze**. I want to stay in tip-top shape for as long as I can.

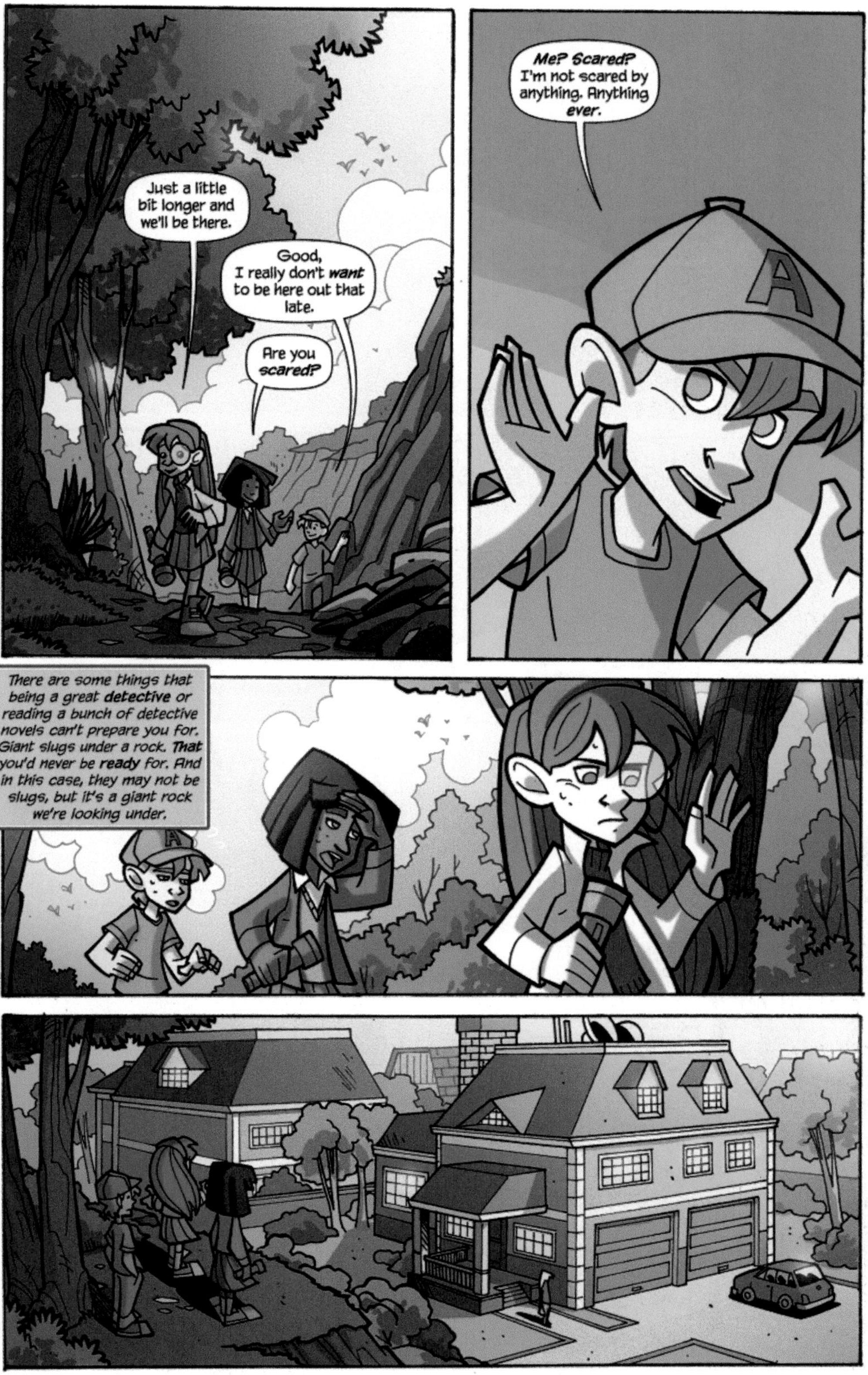
Just a little bit longer and we'll be there.
Good, I really don't *want* to be here out that late.
Are you *scared?*
Me? Scared? I'm not scared by anything. Anything *ever.*
*There are some things that being a great **detective** or reading a bunch of detective novels can't prepare you for. Giant slugs under a rock. **That** you'd never be **ready** for. And in this case, they may not be slugs, but it's a giant rock we're looking under.*

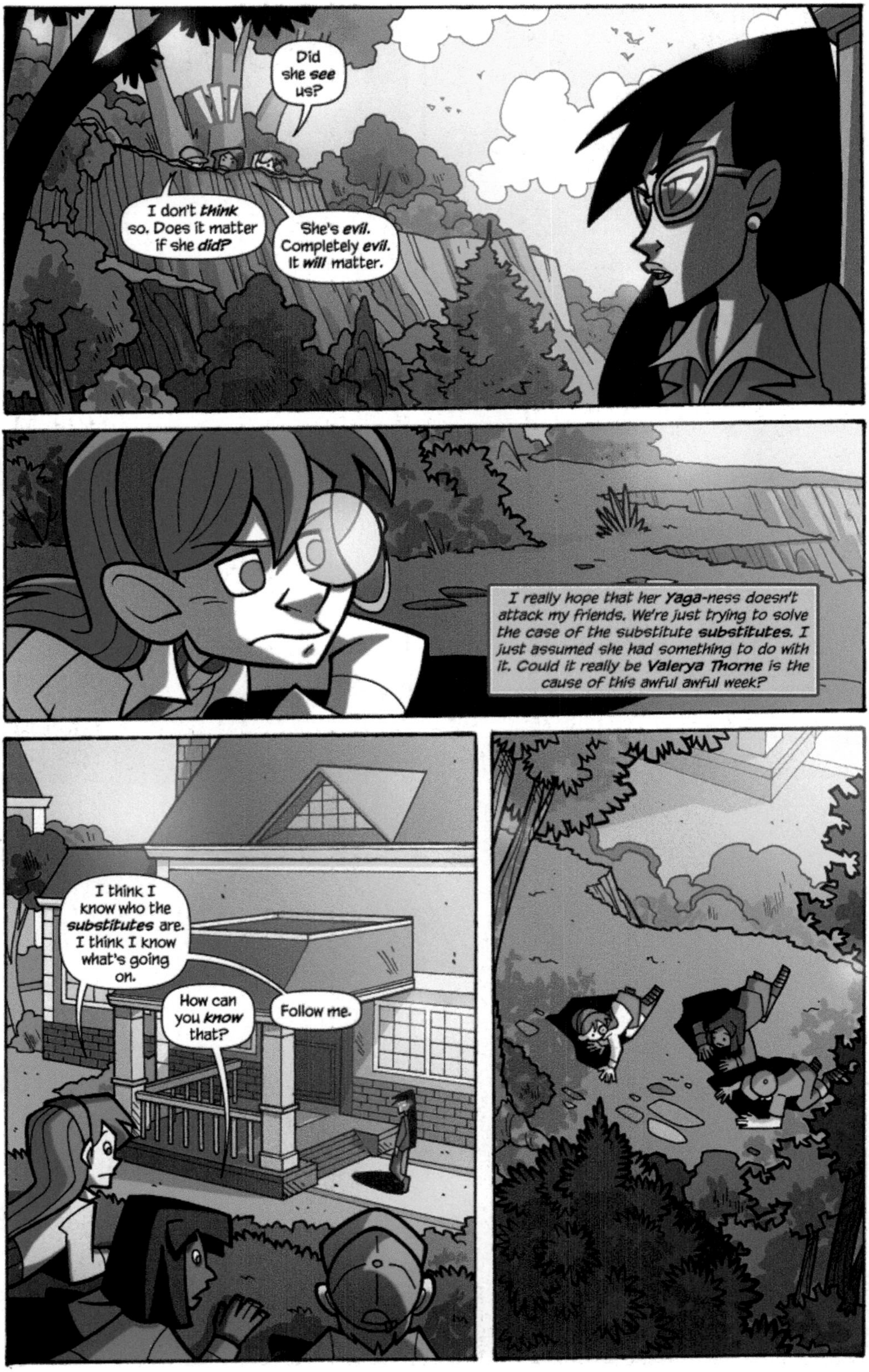
Did she *see* us?
I don't *think* so. Does it matter if she *did?*
She's *evil.* Completely *evil.* It *will* matter.
I really hope that her *Yaga*-ness doesn't attack my friends. We're just trying to solve the case of the substitute **substitutes**. I just assumed she had something to do with it. Could it really be **Valerya Thorne** is the cause of this awful awful week?
I think I know who the *substitutes* are. I think I know what's going on.
How can you *know* that?
Follow me.

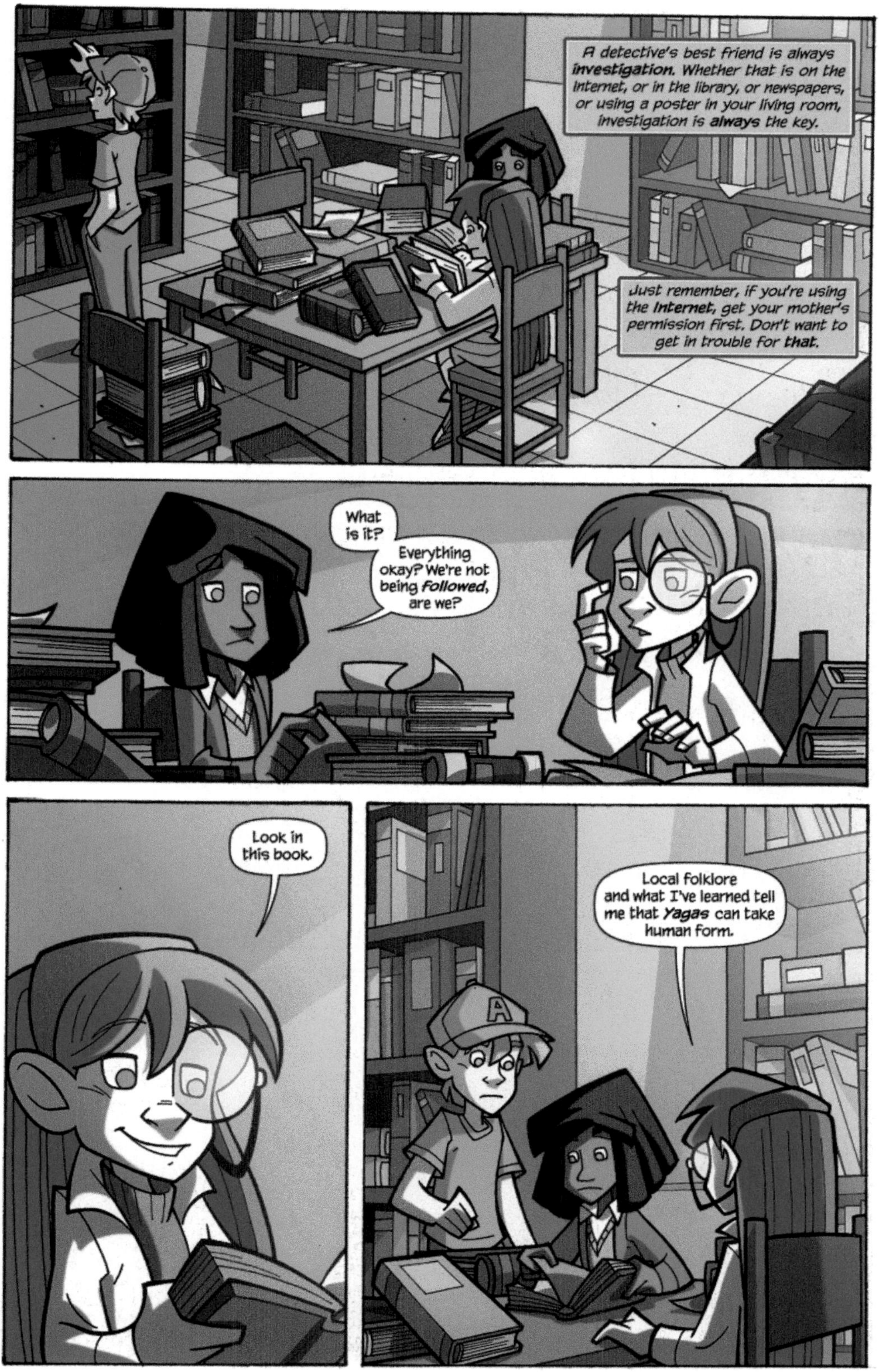
A detective's best friend is always **investigation**. Whether that is on the Internet, or in the library, or newspapers, or using a poster in your living room, investigation is **always** the key.
Just remember, if you're using the **Internet**, get your mother's permission first. Don't want to get in trouble for **that**.
What is it?
Everything okay? We're not being ***followed***, are we?
Look in this book.
Local folklore and what I've learned tell me that ***Yagas*** can take human form.

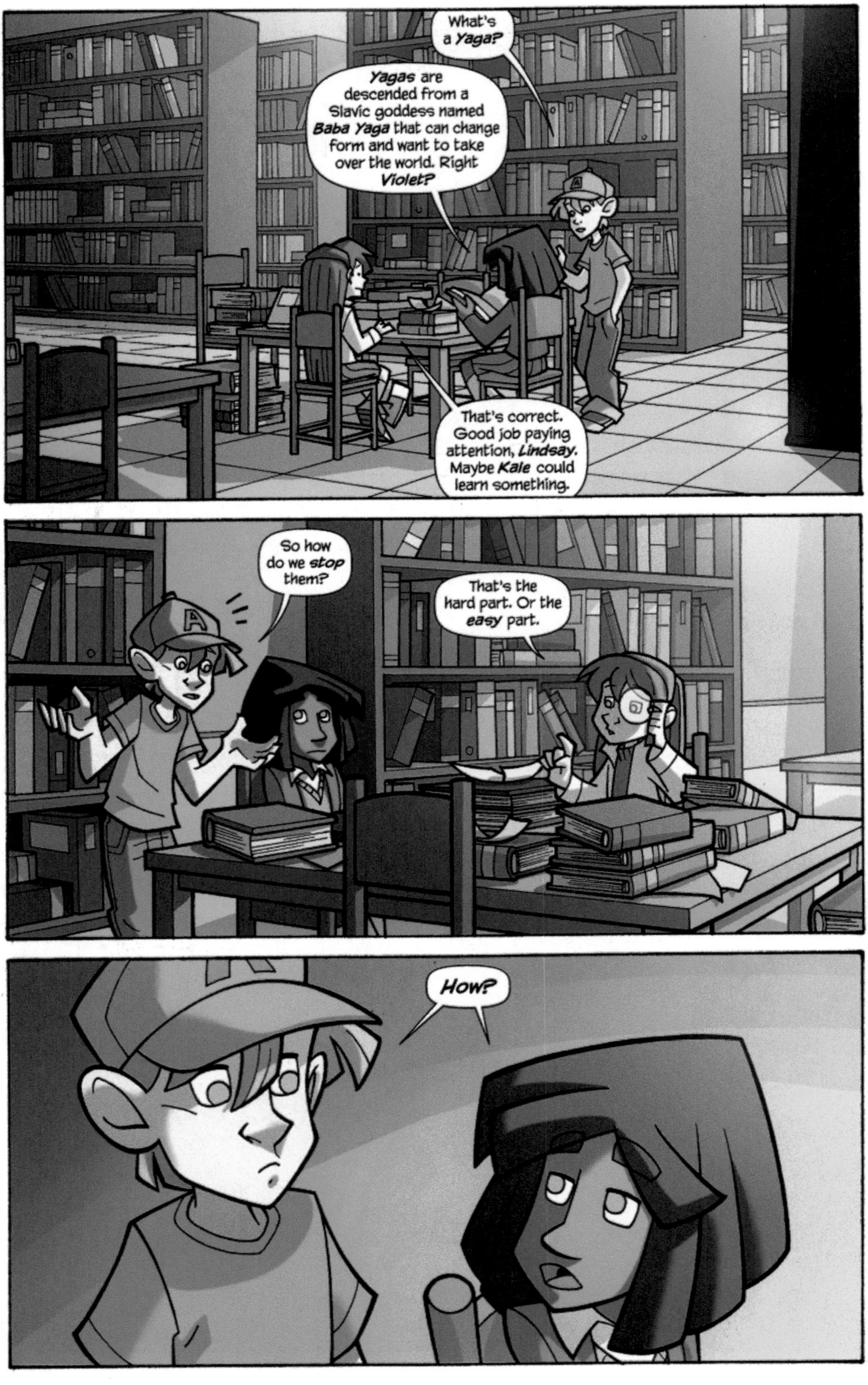
What's a Yaga?
Yagas are descended from a Slavic goddess named Baba Yaga that can change form and want to take over the world. Right Violet?
That's correct. Good job paying attention, Lindsay. Maybe Kale could learn something.
So how do we stop them?
That's the hard part. Or the easy part.
How?

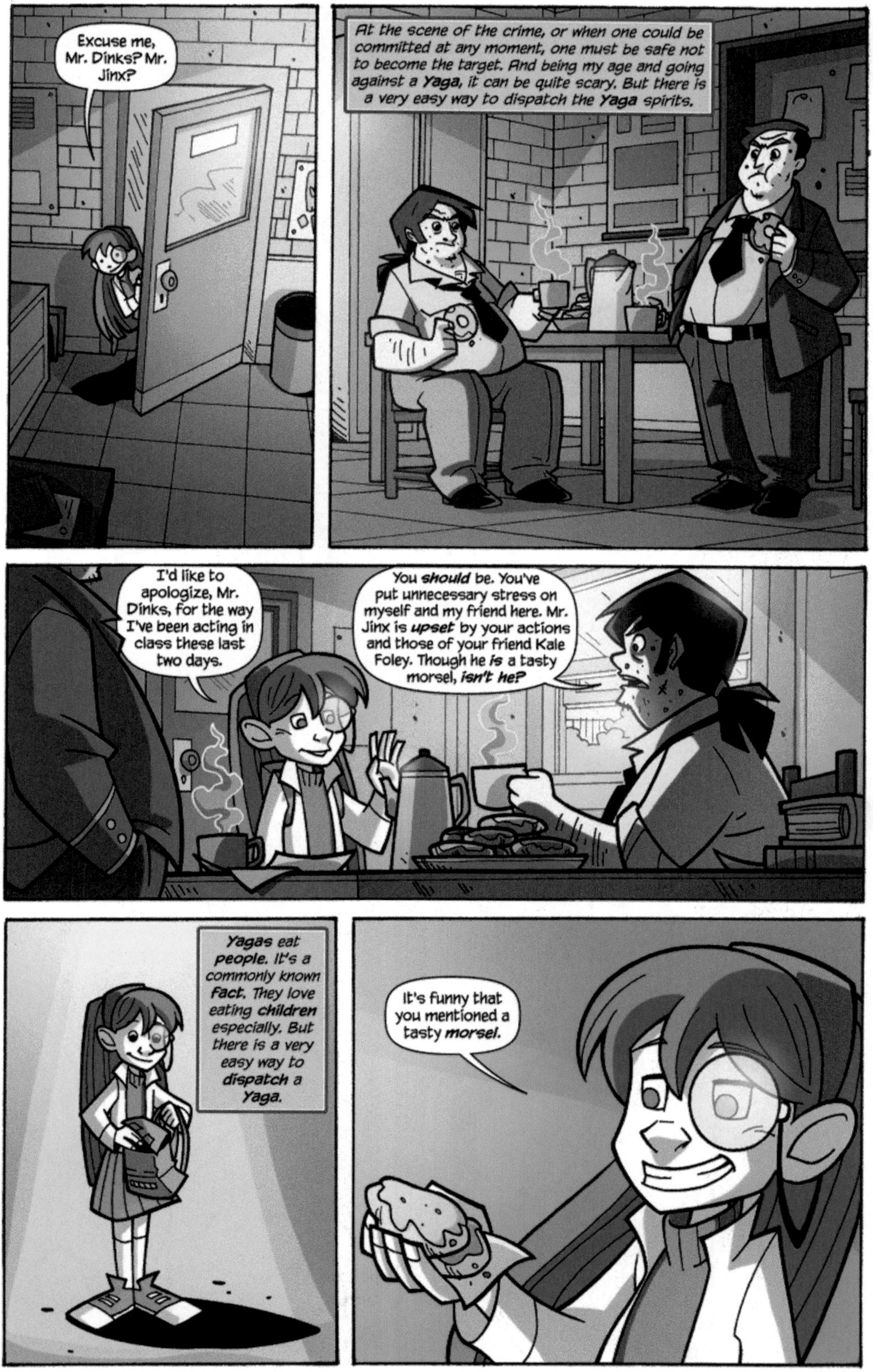

Excuse me, Mr. Dinks? Mr. Jinx?
At the scene of the crime, or when one could be committed at any moment, one must be safe not to become the target. And being my age and going against a Yaga, it can be quite scary. But there is a very easy way to dispatch the Yaga spirits.
I'd like to apologize, Mr. Dinks, for the way I've been acting in class these last two days.
You should be. You've put unnecessary stress on myself and my friend here. Mr. Jinx is upset by your actions and those of your friend Kale Foley. Though he is a tasty morsel, isn't he?
Yagas eat people. It's a commonly known fact. They love eating children especially. But there is a very easy way to dispatch a Yaga.
It's funny that you mentioned a tasty morsel.

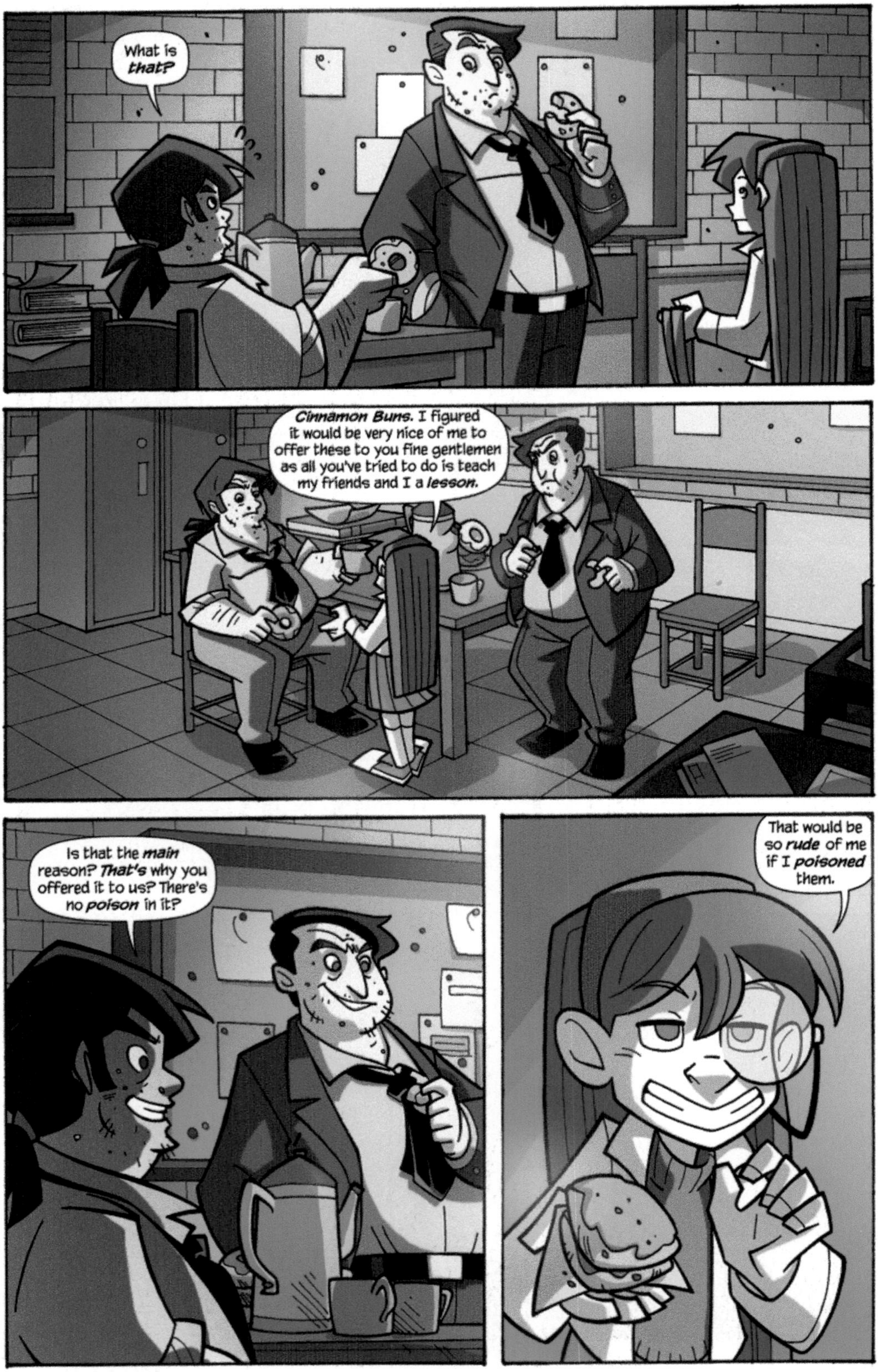
What is *that?*
Cinnamon Buns. I figured it would be very nice of me to offer these to you fine gentlemen as all you've tried to do is teach my friends and I a *lesson.*
Is that the *main* reason? *That's* why you offered it to us? There's no *poison* in it?
That would be so *rude* of me if I *poisoned* them.

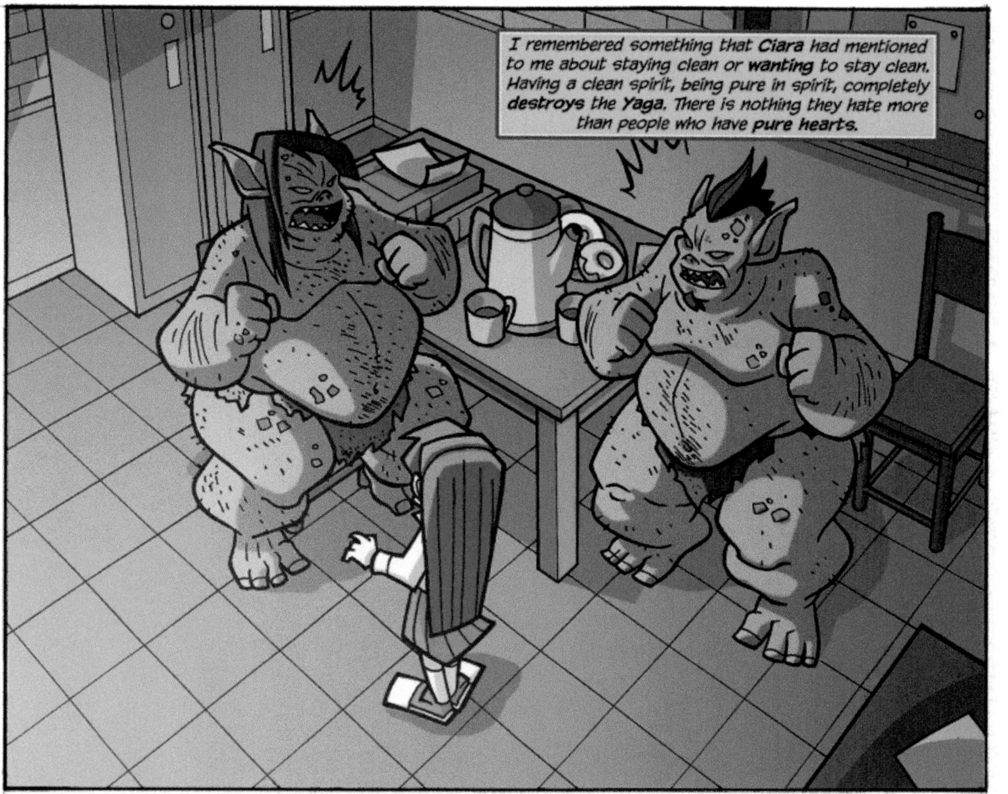
I remembered something that Ciara had mentioned to me about staying clean or wanting to stay clean. Having a clean spirit, being pure in spirit, completely destroys the Yaga. There is nothing they hate more than people who have pure hearts.

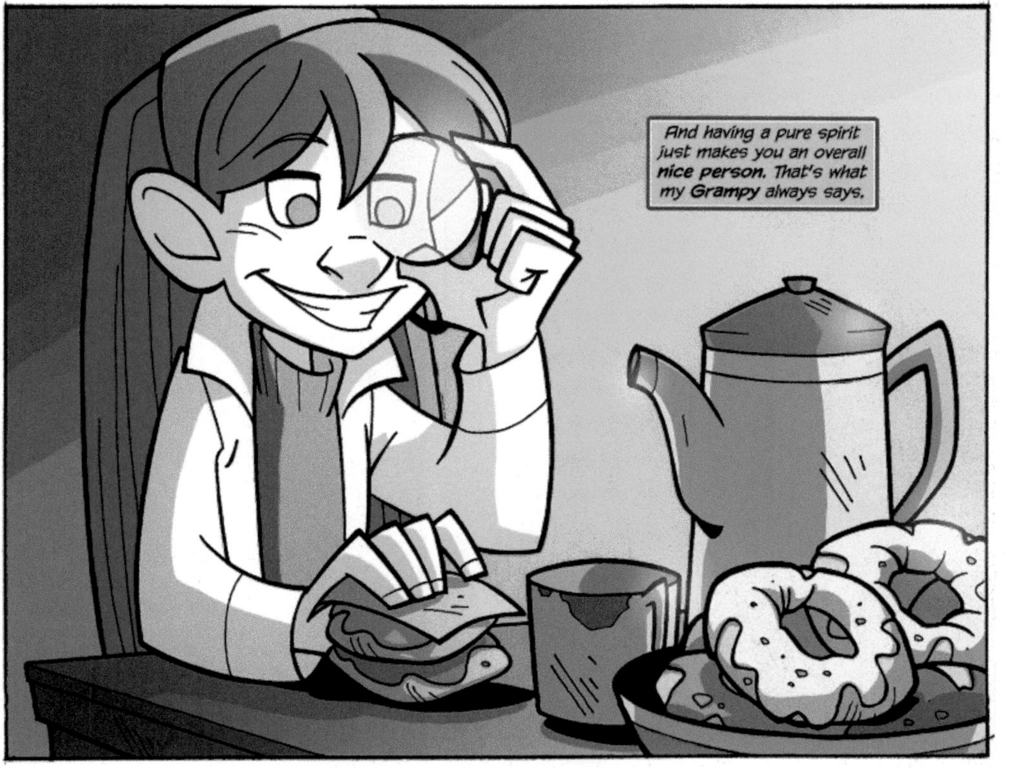
And having a pure spirit just makes you an overall nice person. That's what my Grampy always says.

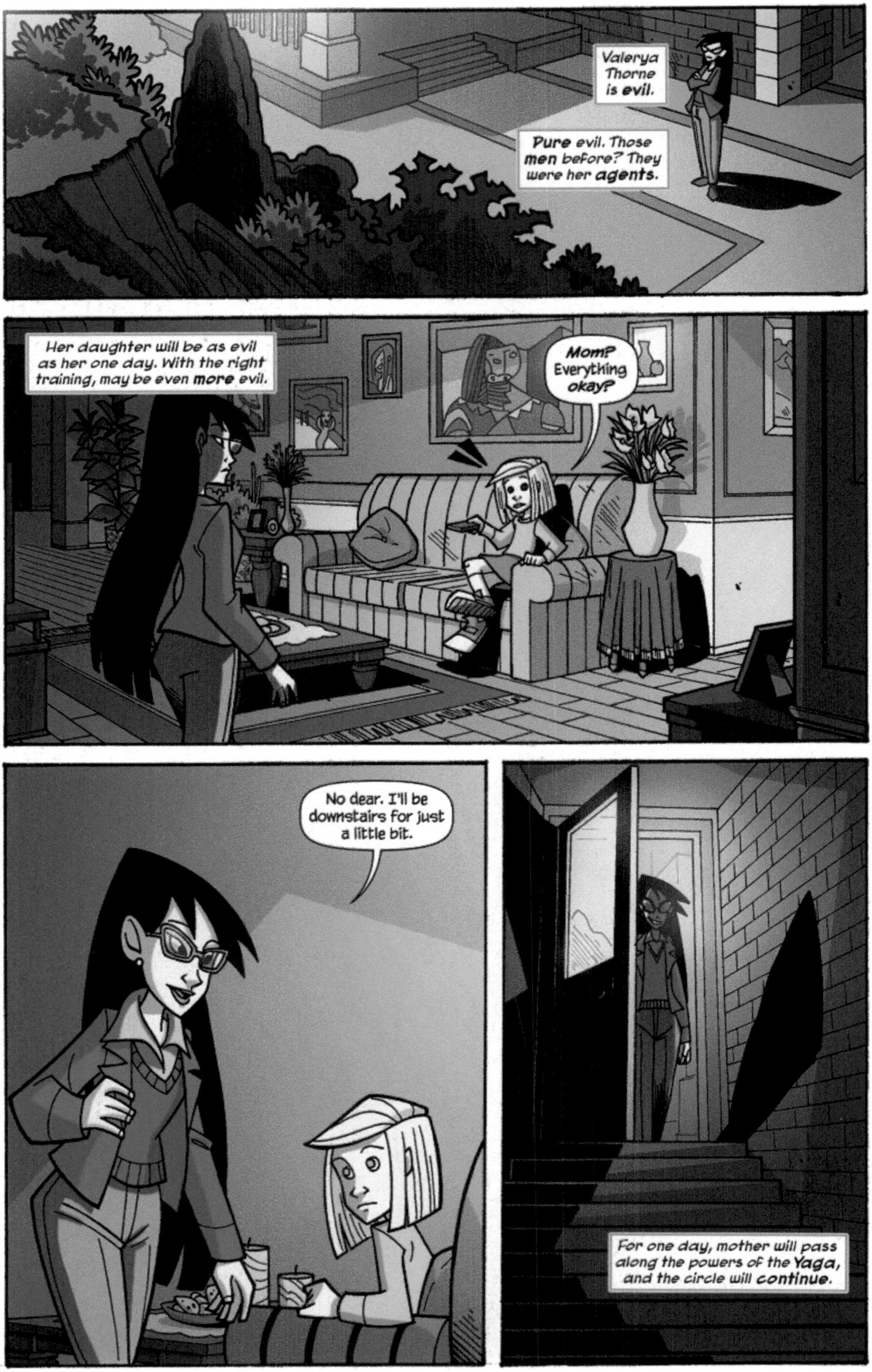
Valerya Thorne is evil.
Pure evil. Those men before? They were her agents.
Her daughter will be as evil as her one day. With the right training, may be even more evil.
Mom? Everything okay?
No dear. I'll be downstairs for just a little bit.
For one day, mother will pass along the powers of the Yaga, and the circle will continue.

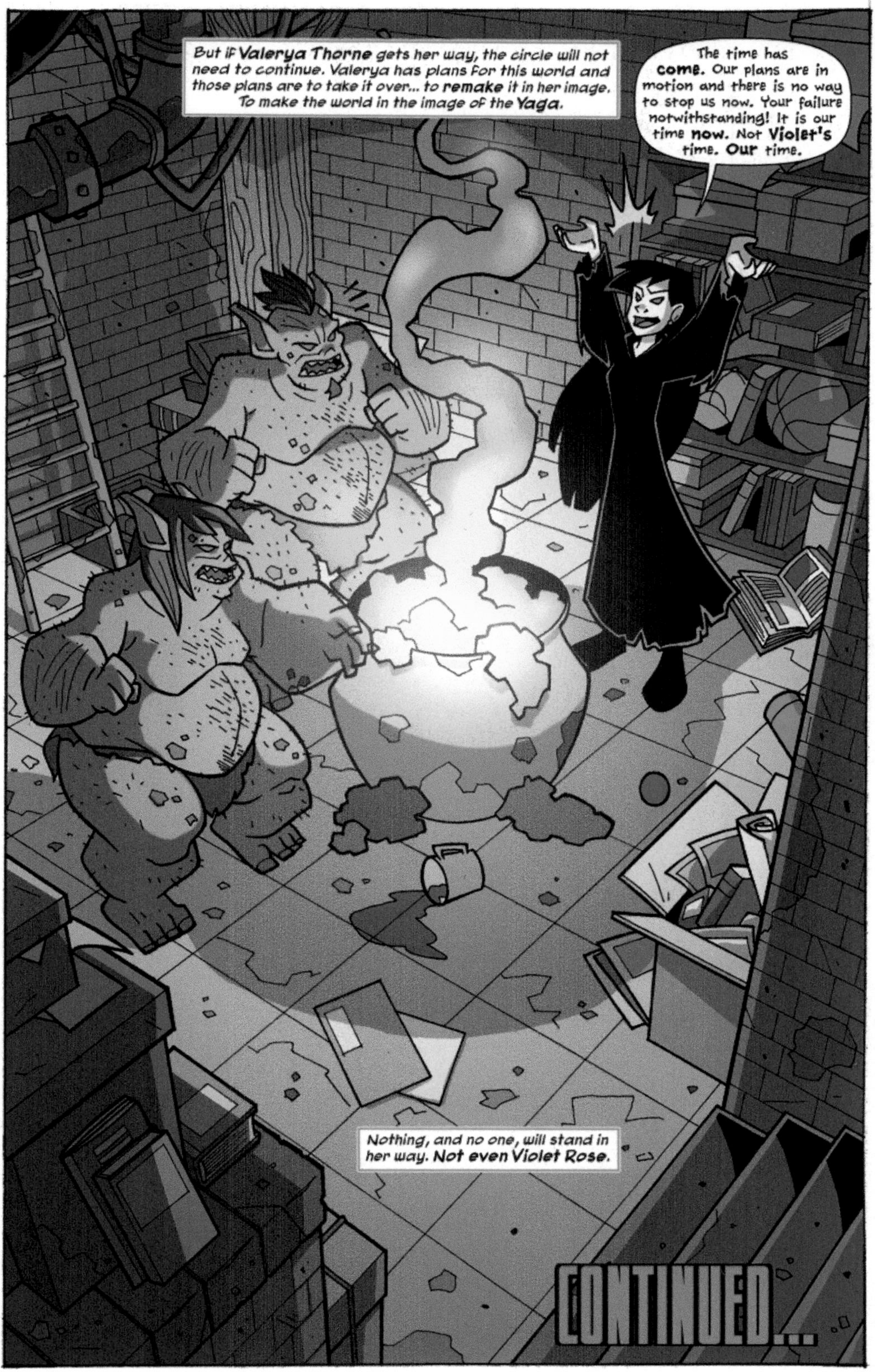
But if Valerya Thorne gets her way, the circle will not need to continue. Valerya has plans for this world and those plans are to take it over... to remake it in her image. To make the world in the image of the Yaga.
The time has come. Our plans are in motion and there is no way to stop us now. Your failure notwithstanding! It is our time now. Not Violet's time. Our time.
Nothing, and no one, will stand in her way. Not even Violet Rose.
CONTINUED...

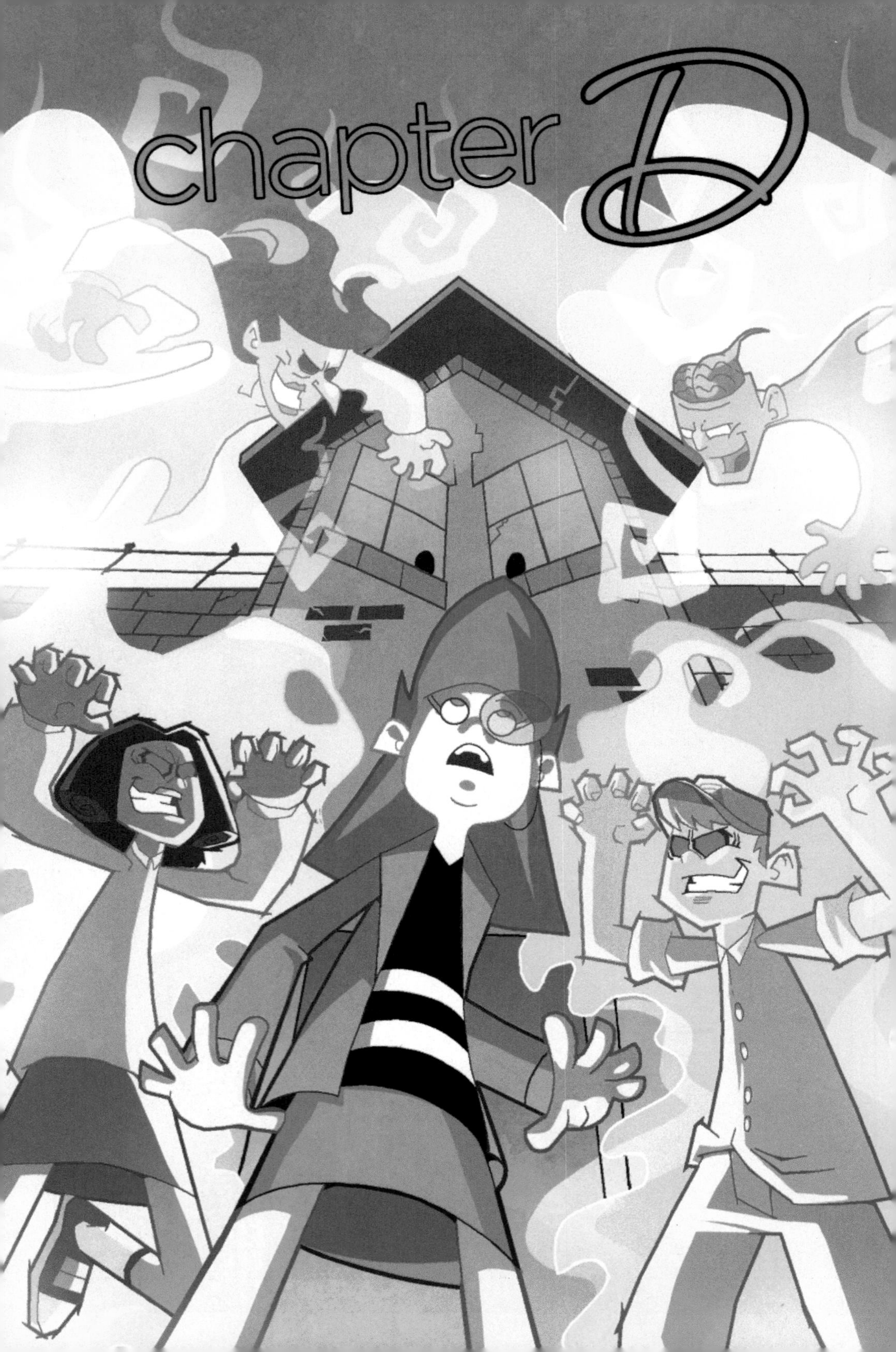
chapter D

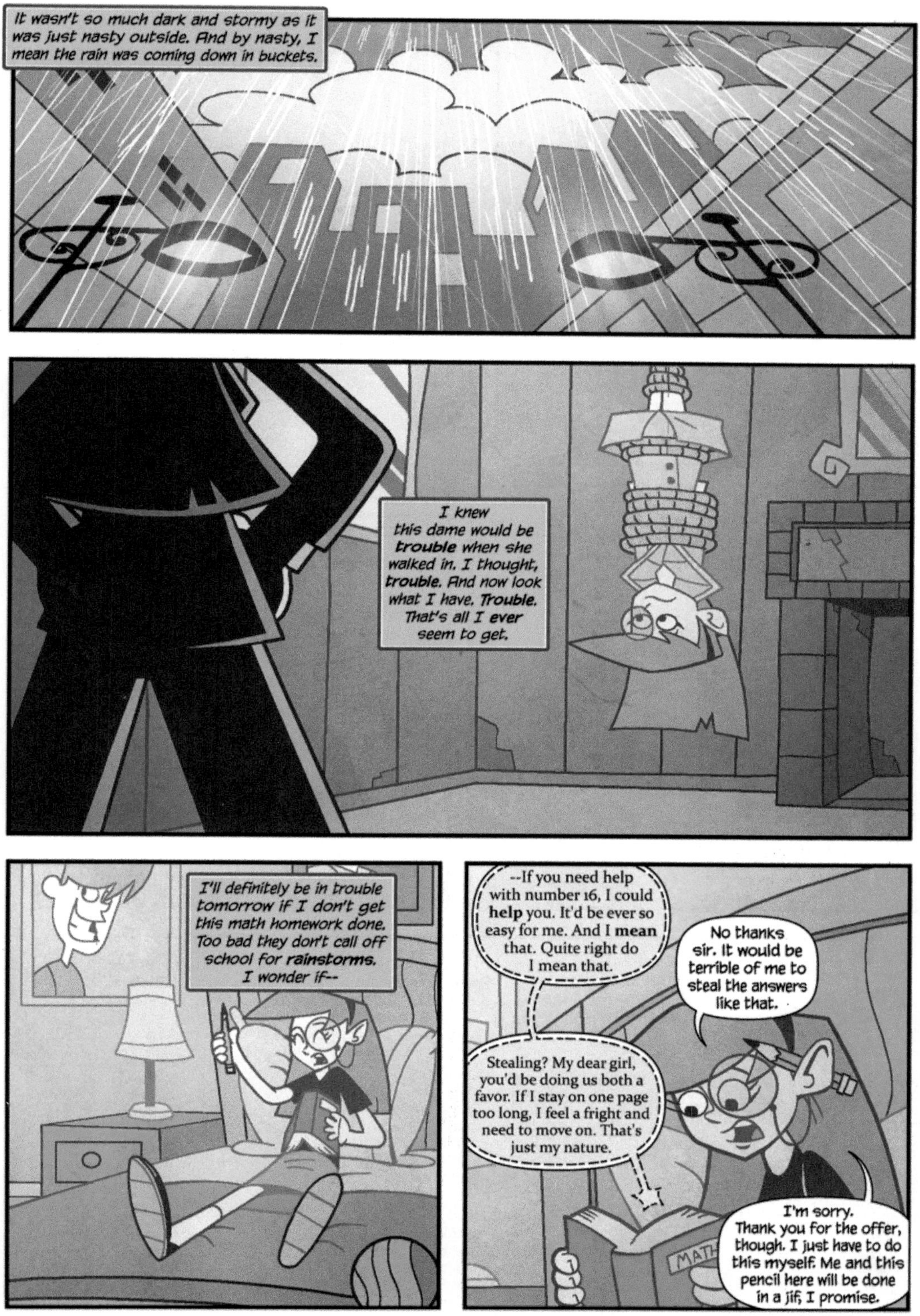
It wasn't so much dark and stormy as it was just nasty outside. And by nasty, I mean the rain was coming down in buckets.
I knew this dame would be trouble when she walked in. I thought, trouble. And now look what I have. Trouble. That's all I ever seem to get.
I'll definitely be in trouble tomorrow if I don't get this math homework done. Too bad they don't call off school for rainstorms. I wonder if--
--If you need help with number 16, I could help you. It'd be ever so easy for me. And I mean that. Quite right do I mean that.
No thanks sir. It would be terrible of me to steal the answers like that.
Stealing? My dear girl, you'd be doing us both a favor. If I stay on one page too long, I feel a fright and need to move on. That's just my nature.
I'm sorry. Thank you for the offer, though. I just have to do this myself. Me and this pencil here will be done in a jif, I promise.
MATH

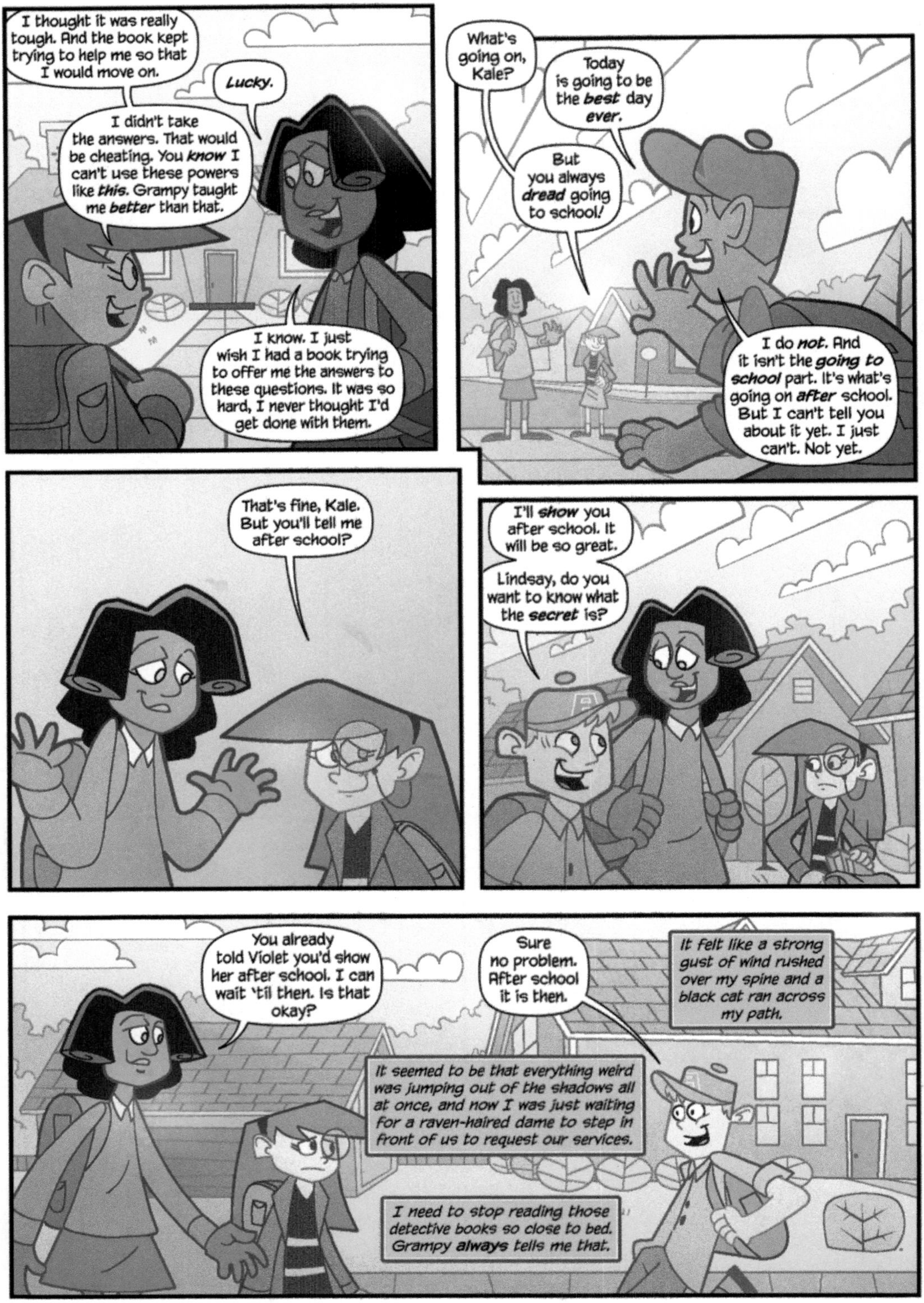
I thought it was really tough. And the book kept trying to help me so that I would move on.
Lucky.
I didn't take the answers. That would be cheating. You **know** I can't use these powers like **this**. Grampy taught me **better** than that.
I know. I just wish I had a book trying to offer me the answers to these questions. It was so hard, I never thought I'd get done with them.
What's going on, Kale?
Today is going to be the **best** day **ever**.
But you always **dread** going to school!
I do **not**. And it isn't the **going to school** part. It's what's going on **after** school. But I can't tell you about it yet. I just can't. Not yet.
That's fine, Kale. But you'll tell me after school?
I'll **show** you after school. It will be so great.
Lindsay, do you want to know what the **secret** is?
You already told Violet you'd show her after school. I can wait 'til then. Is that okay?
Sure no problem. After school it is then.
It felt like a strong gust of wind rushed over my spine and a black cat ran across my path.
It seemed to be that everything weird was jumping out of the shadows all at once, and now I was just waiting for a raven-haired dame to step in front of us to request our services.
*I need to stop reading those detective books so close to bed. Grampy **always** tells me that.*

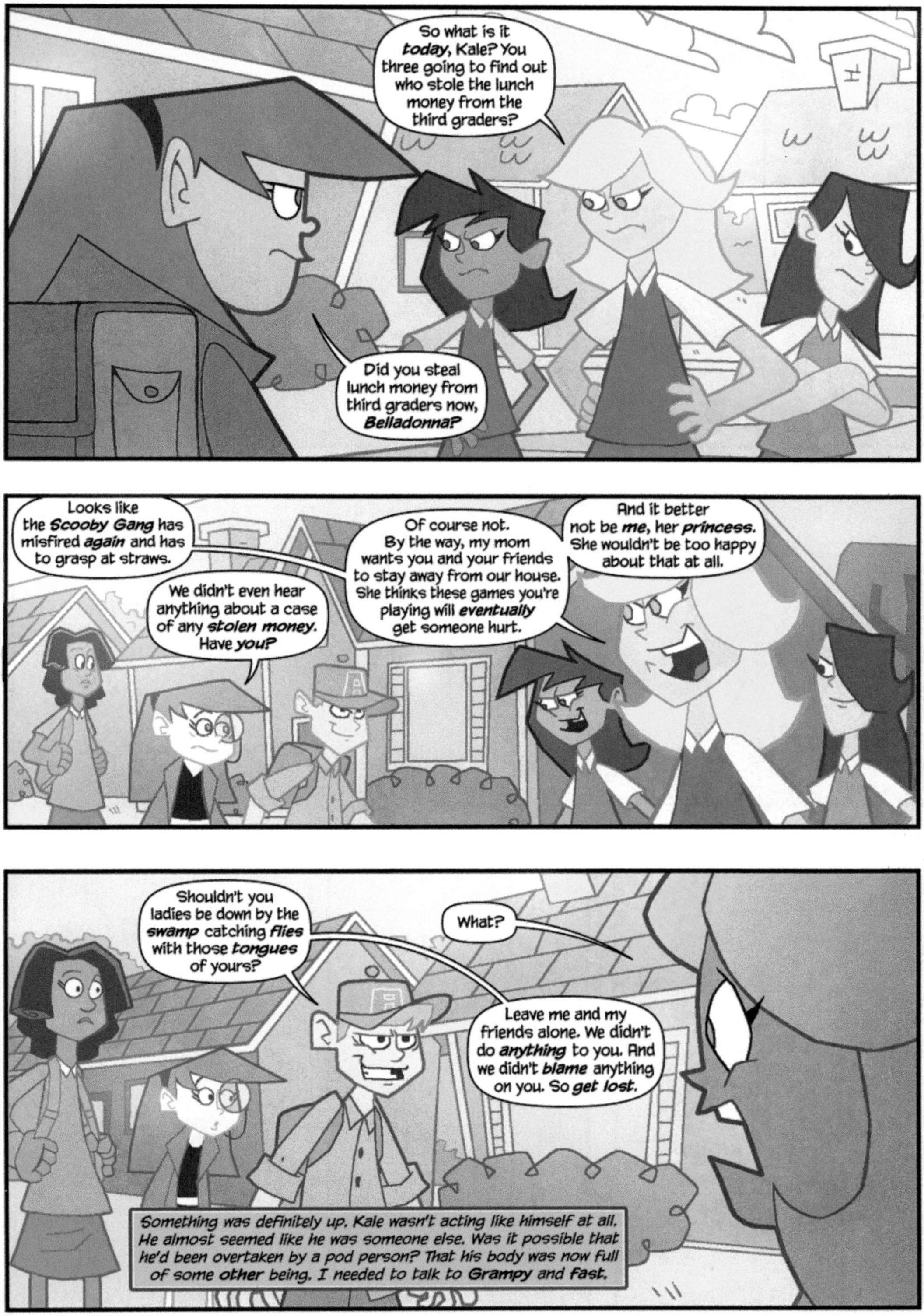
So what is it today, Kale? You three going to find out who stole the lunch money from the third graders?
Did you steal lunch money from third graders now, Belladonna?
Looks like the Scooby Gang has misfired again and has to grasp at straws.
We didn't even hear anything about a case of any stolen money. Have you?
Of course not. By the way, my mom wants you and your friends to stay away from our house. She thinks these games you're playing will eventually get someone hurt.
And it better not be me, her princess. She wouldn't be too happy about that at all.
Shouldn't you ladies be down by the swamp catching flies with those tongues of yours?
What?
Leave me and my friends alone. We didn't do anything to you. And we didn't blame anything on you. So get lost.
Something was definitely up. Kale wasn't acting like himself at all. He almost seemed like he was someone else. Was it possible that he'd been overtaken by a pod person? That his body was now full of some other being. I needed to talk to Grampy and fast.

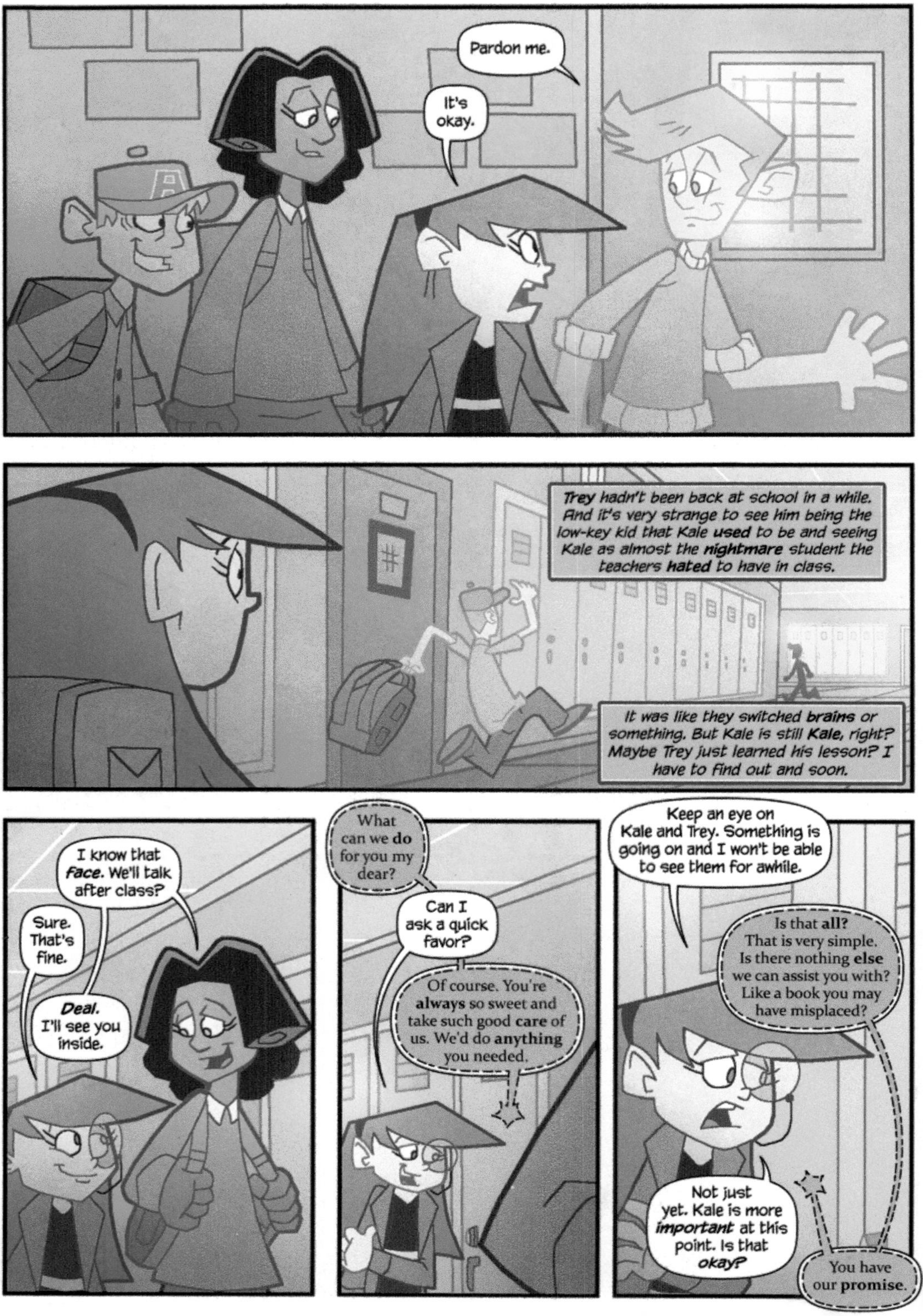
Pardon me.
It's okay.
Trey hadn't been back at school in a while. And it's very strange to see him being the low-key kid that Kale used to be and seeing Kale as almost the nightmare student the teachers hated to have in class.
It was like they switched brains or something. But Kale is still Kale, right? Maybe Trey just learned his lesson? I have to find out and soon.
I know that face. We'll talk after class?
Sure. That's fine.
Deal. I'll see you inside.
What can we do for you my dear?
Can I ask a quick favor?
Of course. You're always so sweet and take such good care of us. We'd do anything you needed.
Keep an eye on Kale and Trey. Something is going on and I won't be able to see them for awhile.
Is that all? That is very simple. Is there nothing else we can assist you with? Like a book you may have misplaced?
Not just yet. Kale is more important at this point. Is that okay?
You have our promise.

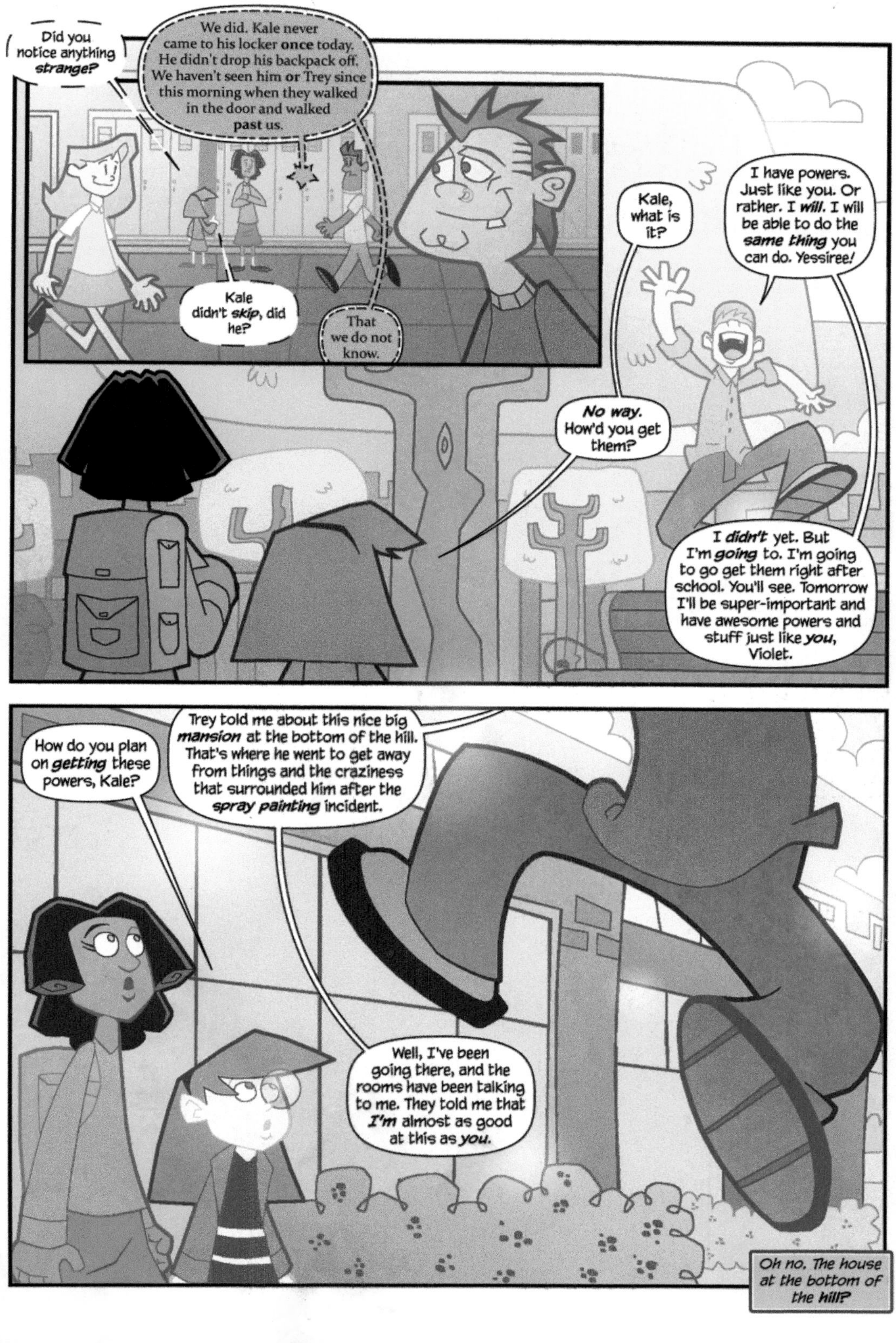
Did you notice anything *strange?*
We did. Kale never came to his locker **once** today. He didn't drop his backpack off. We haven't seen him **or** Trey since this morning when they walked in the door and walked **past us**.
Kale didn't *skip*, did he?
That we do not know.
Kale, what is it?
I have powers. Just like you. Or rather. I *will*. I will be able to do the *same thing* you can do. Yessiree!
No way. How'd you get them?
I *didn't* yet. But I'm *going* to. I'm going to go get them right after school. You'll see. Tomorrow I'll be super-important and have awesome powers and stuff just like *you*, Violet.
How do you plan on *getting* these powers, Kale?
Trey told me about this nice big *mansion* at the bottom of the hill. That's where he went to get away from things and the craziness that surrounded him after the *spray painting* incident.
Well, I've been going there, and the rooms have been talking to me. They told me that *I'm* almost as good at this as *you*.
Oh no. The house at the bottom of the hill?

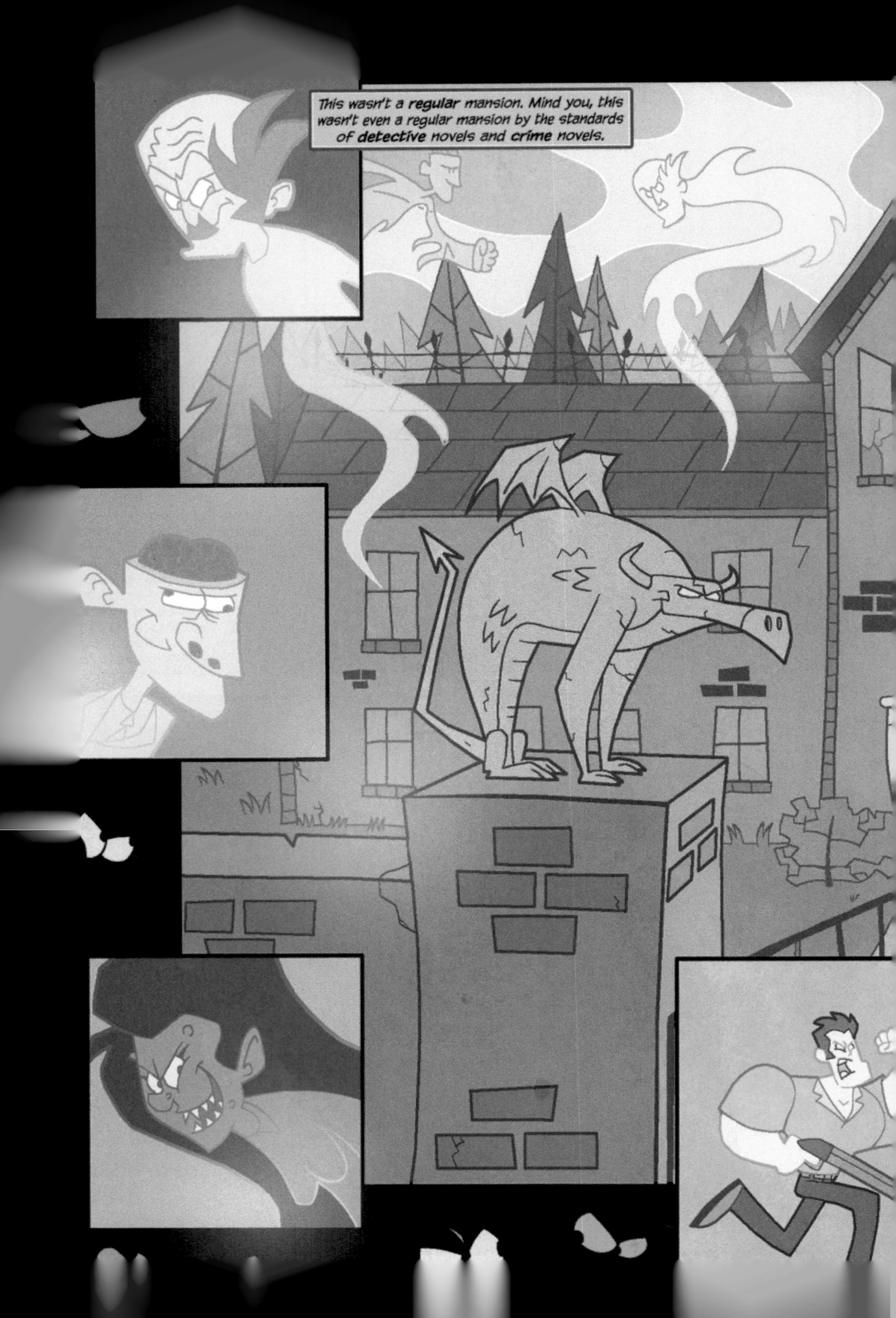
This wasn't a **regular** mansion. Mind you, this wasn't even a regular mansion by the standards of ***detective*** novels and ***crime*** novels.

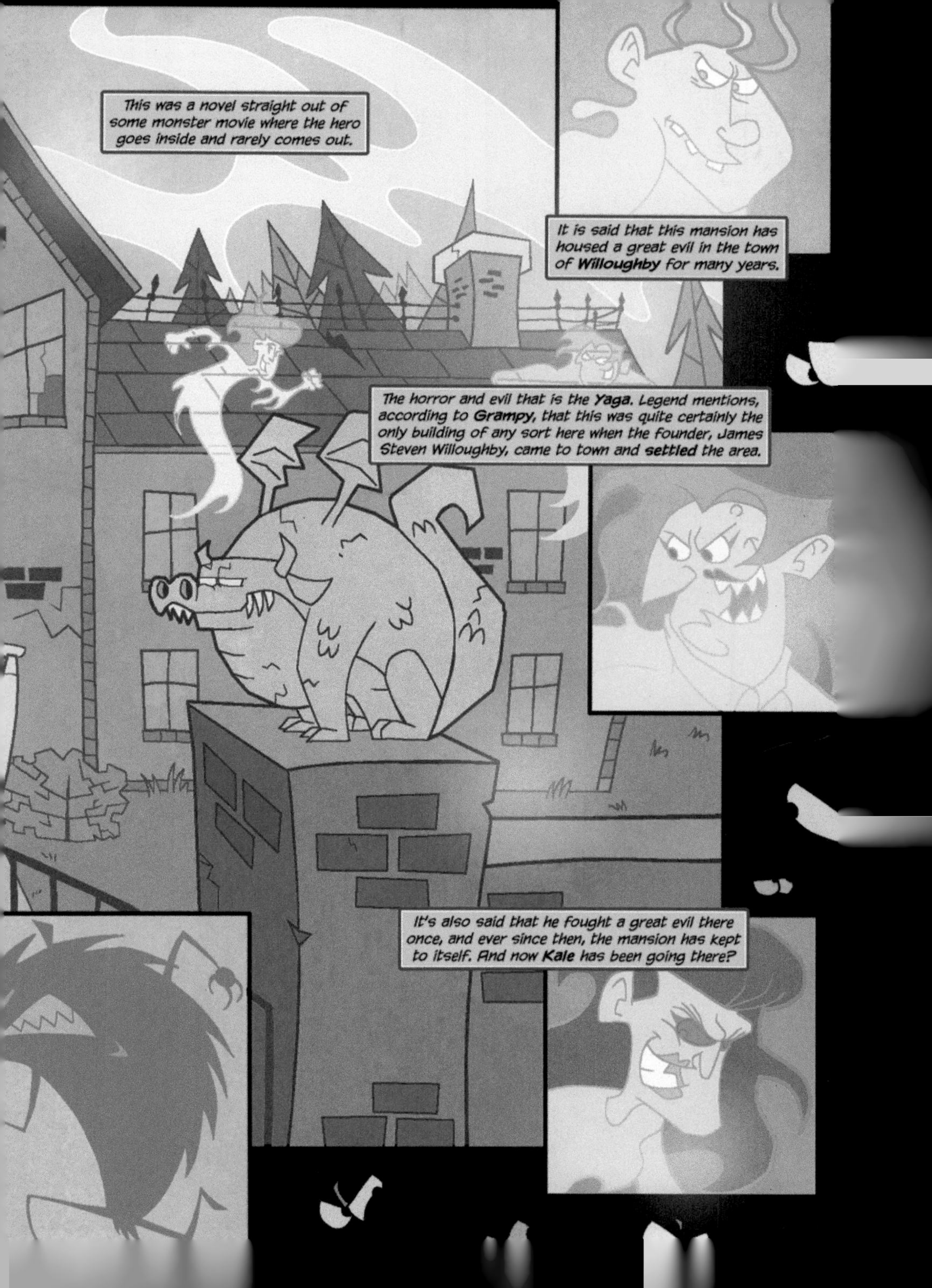
This was a novel straight out of some monster movie where the hero goes inside and rarely comes out.
It is said that this mansion has housed a great evil in the town of Willoughby for many years.
The horror and evil that is the Yaga. Legend mentions, according to Grampy, that this was quite certainly the only building of any sort here when the founder, James Steven Willoughby, came to town and settled the area.
It's also said that he fought a great evil there once, and ever since then, the mansion has kept to itself. And now Kale has been going there?

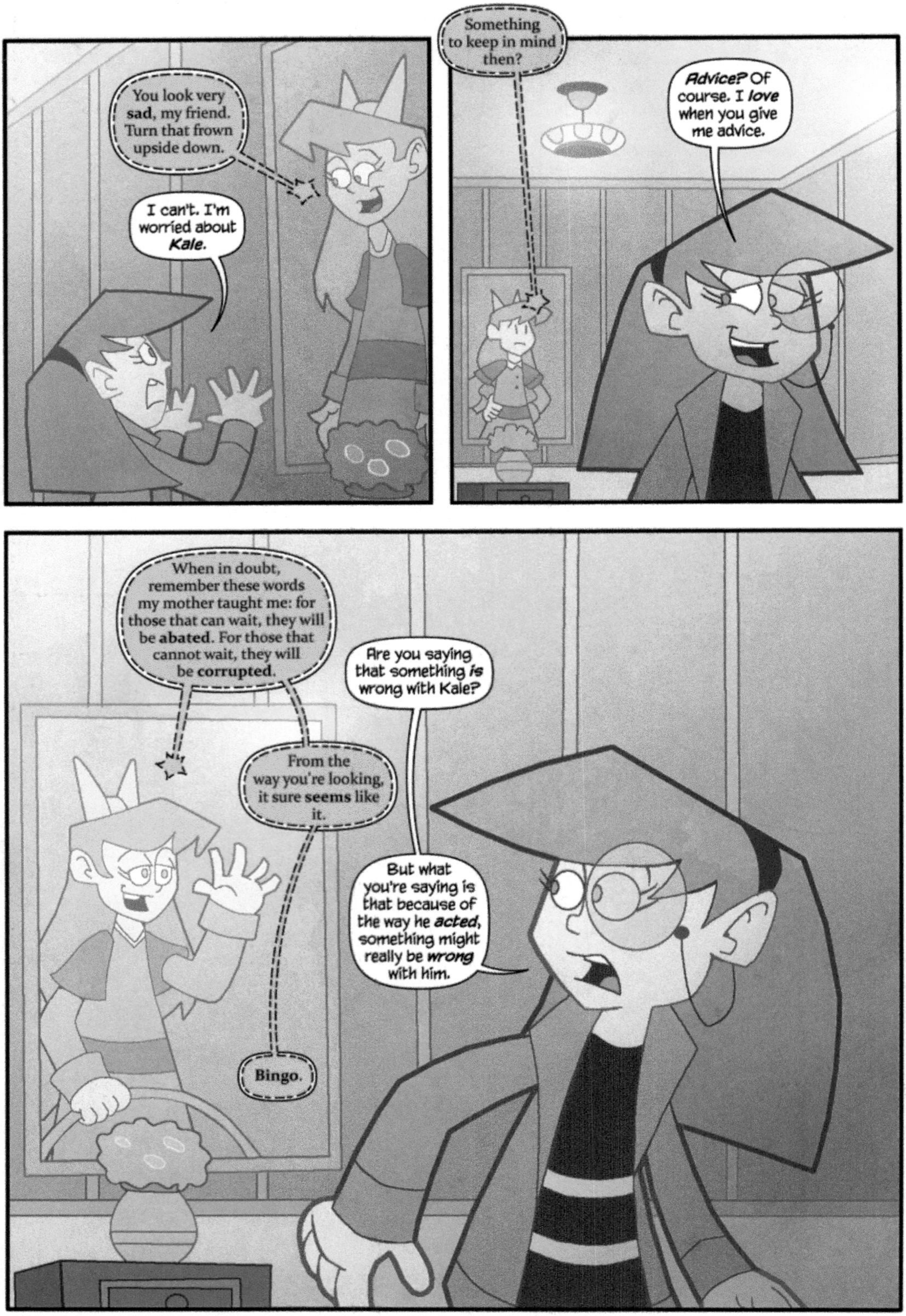
You look very **sad**, my friend. Turn that frown upside down.
I can't. I'm worried about ***Kale***.
Something to keep in mind then?
Advice? Of course. I ***love*** when you give me advice.
When in doubt, remember these words my mother taught me: for those that can wait, they will be **abated**. For those that cannot wait, they will be **corrupted**.
From the way you're looking, it sure **seems** like it.
Are you saying that something ***is*** wrong with Kale?
But what you're saying is that because of the way he ***acted***, something might really be ***wrong*** with him.
Bingo.

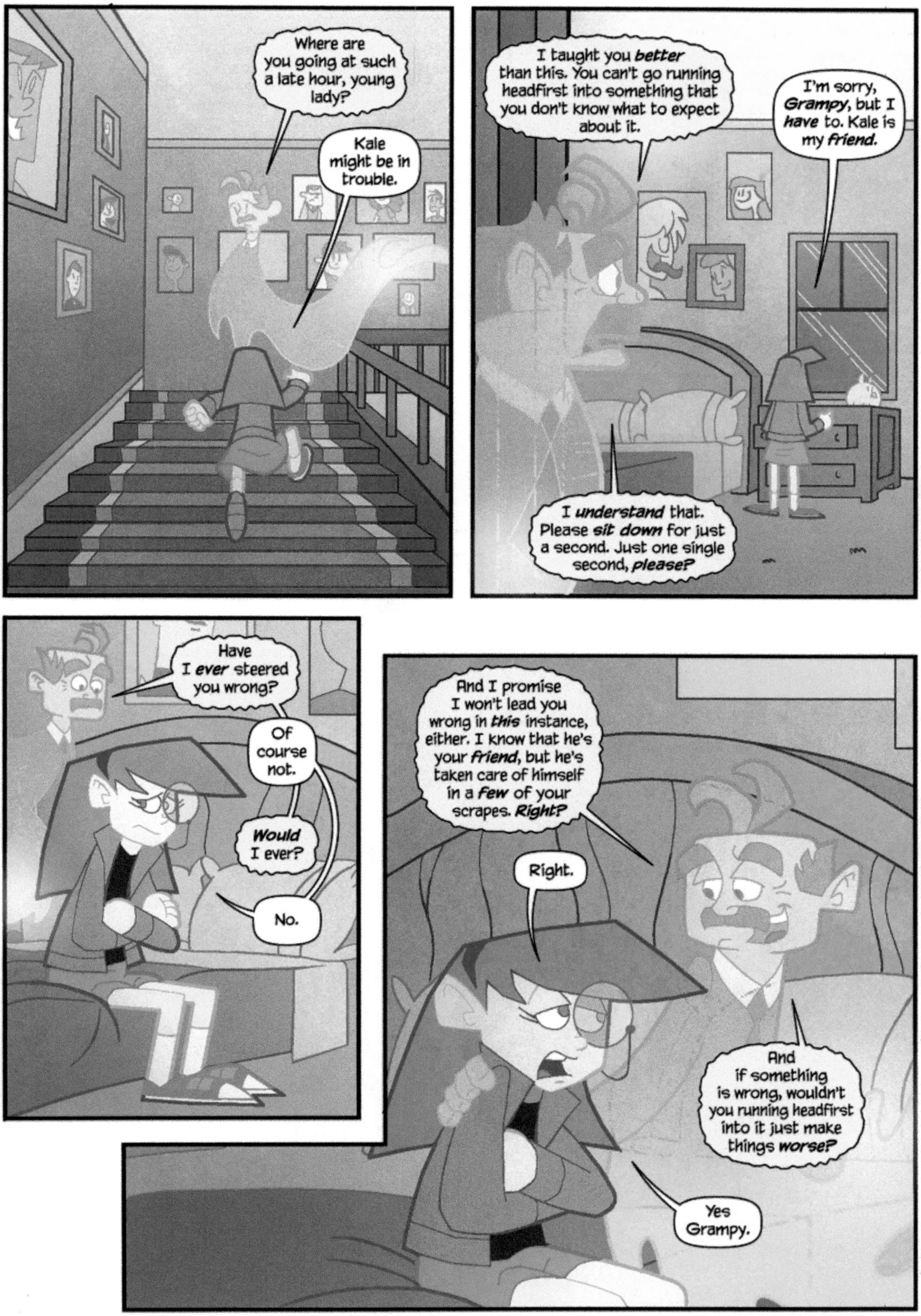
Where are you going at such a late hour, young lady?
Kale might be in trouble.
I taught you better than this. You can't go running headfirst into something that you don't know what to expect about it.
I'm sorry, Grampy, but I have to. Kale is my friend.
I understand that. Please sit down for just a second. Just one single second, please?
Have I ever steered you wrong?
Of course not.
Would I ever?
No.
And I promise I won't lead you wrong in this instance, either. I know that he's your friend, but he's taken care of himself in a few of your scrapes. Right?
Right.
And if something is wrong, wouldn't you running headfirst into it just make things worse?
Yes Grampy.

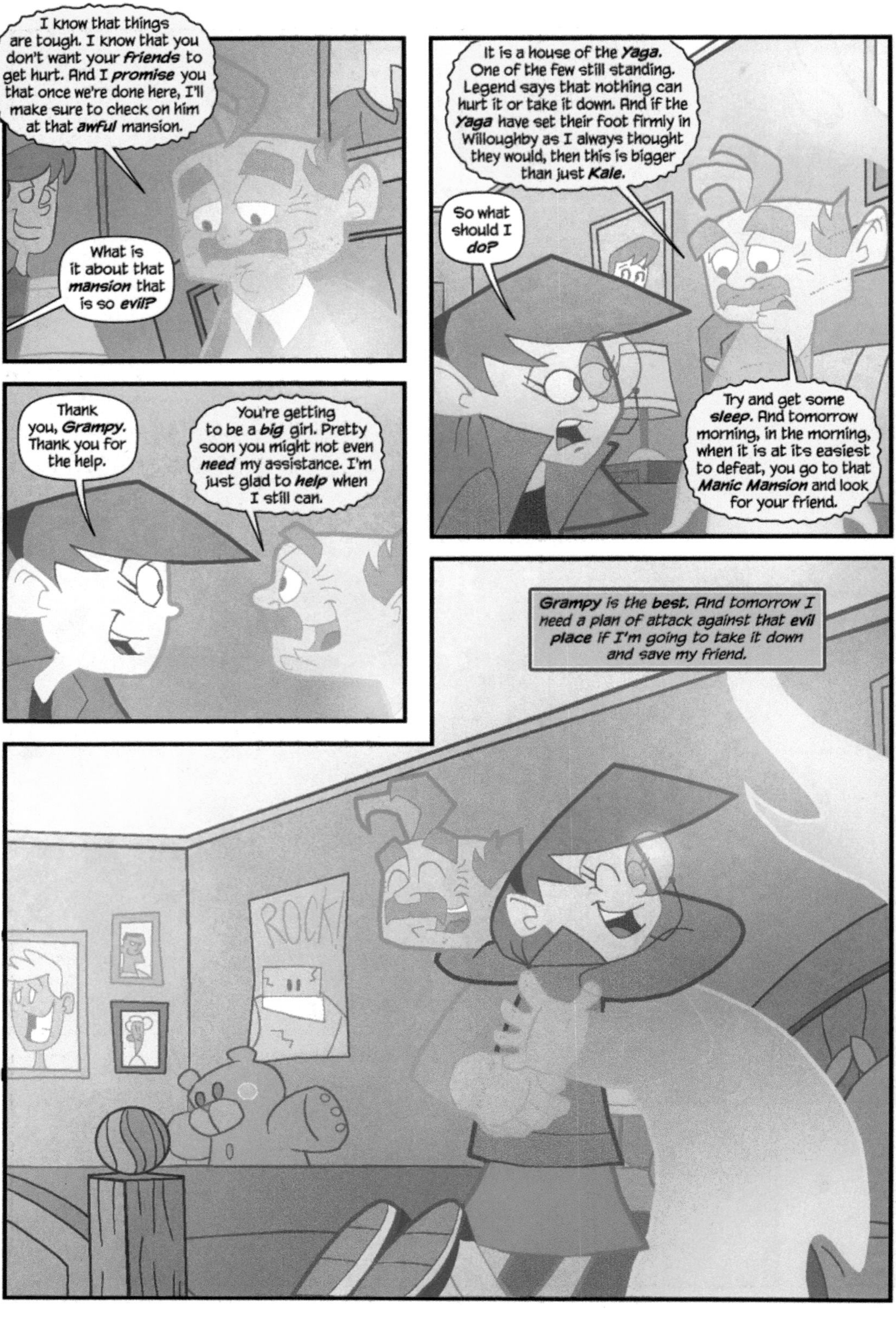
I know that things are tough. I know that you don't want your *friends* to get hurt. And I *promise* you that once we're done here, I'll make sure to check on him at that *awful* mansion.
What is it about that *mansion* that is so *evil?*
It is a house of the *Yaga*. One of the few still standing. Legend says that nothing can hurt it or take it down. And if the *Yaga* have set their foot firmly in Willoughby as I always thought they would, then this is bigger than just *Kale*.
So what should I *do?*
Try and get some *sleep*. And tomorrow morning, in the morning, when it is at its easiest to defeat, you go to that *Manic Mansion* and look for your friend.
Thank you, *Grampy*. Thank you for the help.
You're getting to be a *big* girl. Pretty soon you might not even *need* my assistance. I'm just glad to *help* when I still can.
*Grampy is the **best**. And tomorrow I need a plan of attack against that **evil place** if I'm going to take it down and save my friend.*
ROCK!

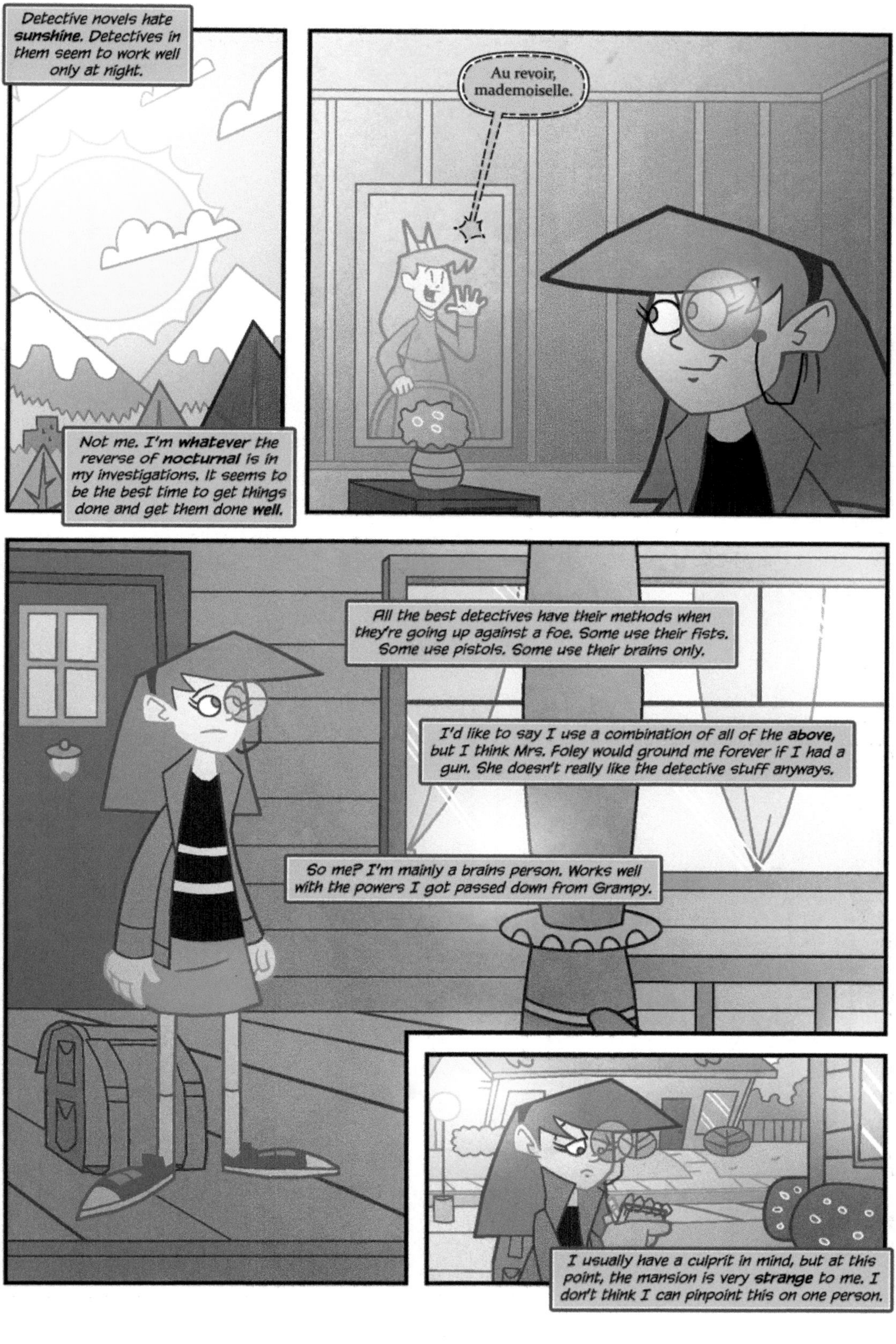
Detective novels hate sunshine. Detectives in them seem to work well only at night.
Not me. I'm whatever the reverse of nocturnal is in my investigations. It seems to be the best time to get things done and get them done well.
Au revoir, mademoiselle.
All the best detectives have their methods when they're going up against a foe. Some use their fists. Some use pistols. Some use their brains only.
I'd like to say I use a combination of all of the above, but I think Mrs. Foley would ground me forever if I had a gun. She doesn't really like the detective stuff anyways.
So me? I'm mainly a brains person. Works well with the powers I got passed down from Grampy.
I usually have a culprit in mind, but at this point, the mansion is very strange to me. I don't think I can pinpoint this on one person.

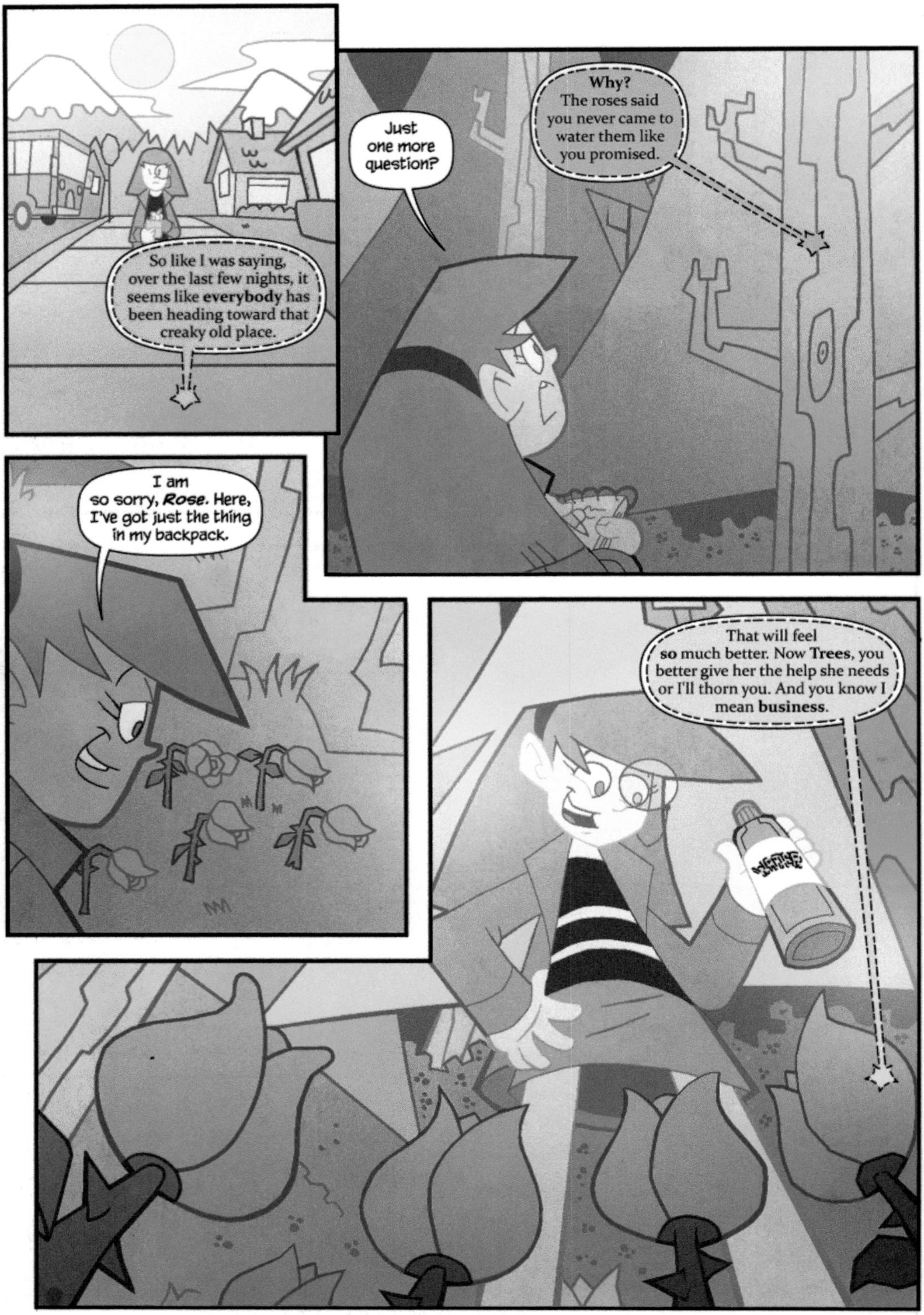
So like I was saying, over the last few nights, it seems like **everybody** has been heading toward that creaky old place.
Just one more question?
Why? The roses said you never came to water them like you promised.
I am so sorry, ***Rose.*** Here, I've got just the thing in my backpack.
That will feel **so** much better. Now **Trees**, you better give her the help she needs or I'll thorn you. And you know I mean **business**.

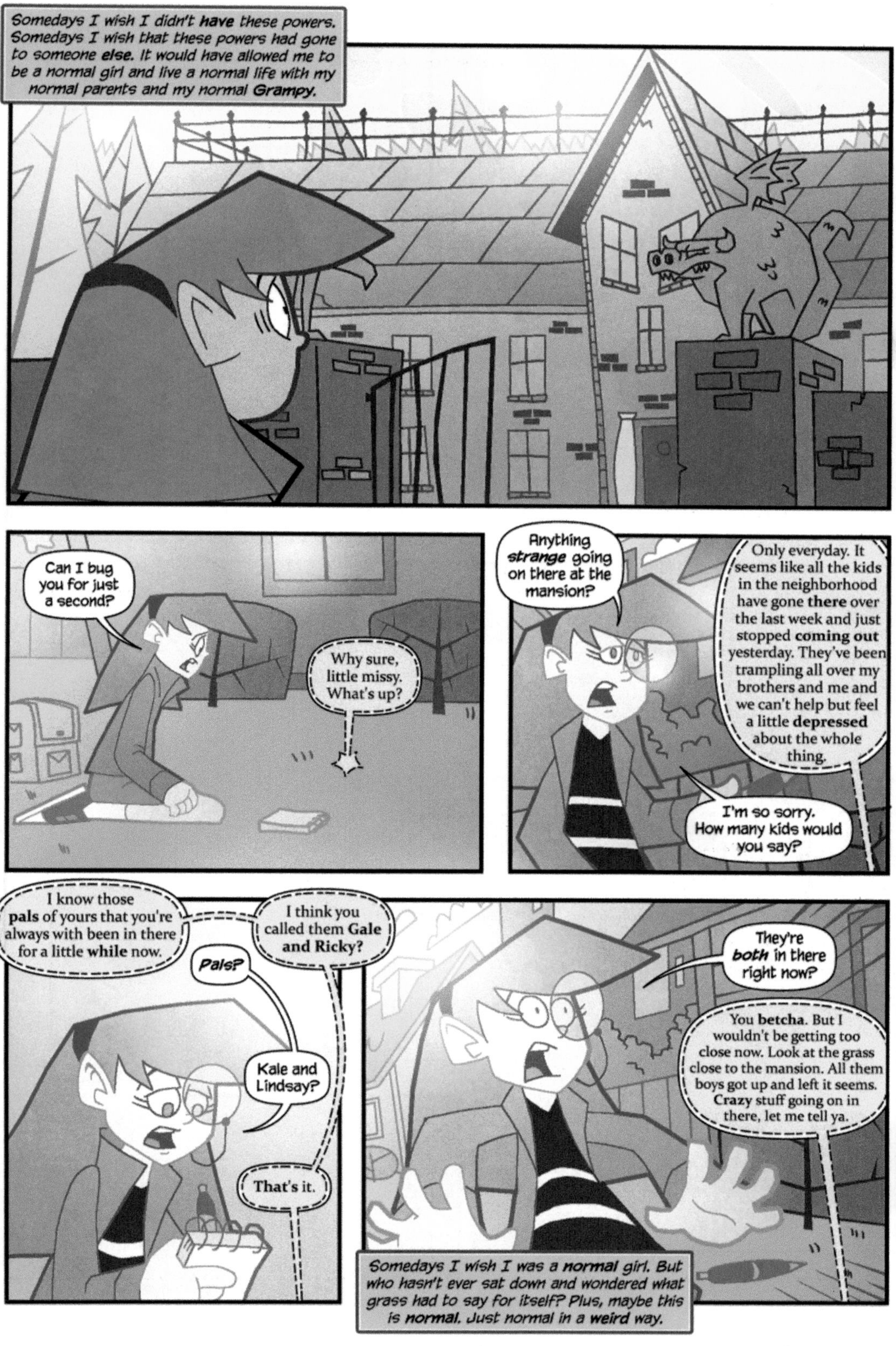

Somedays I wish I didn't **have** these powers. Somedays I wish that these powers had gone to someone **else**. It would have allowed me to be a normal girl and live a normal life with my normal parents and my normal **Grampy**.
Can I bug you for just a second?
Why sure, little missy. What's up?
Anything **strange** going on there at the mansion?
Only everyday. It seems like all the kids in the neighborhood have gone **there** over the last week and just stopped **coming out** yesterday. They've been trampling all over my brothers and me and we can't help but feel a little **depressed** about the whole thing.
I'm so sorry. How many kids would you say?
I know those **pals** of yours that you're always with been in there for a little **while** now.
I think you called them **Gale and Ricky?**
Pals?
Kale and Lindsay?
That's it.
They're **both** in there right now?
You **betcha**. But I wouldn't be getting too close now. Look at the grass close to the mansion. All them boys got up and left it seems. **Crazy** stuff going on in there, let me tell ya.
Somedays I wish I was a **normal** girl. But who hasn't ever sat down and wondered what grass had to say for itself? Plus, maybe this is **normal**. Just normal in a **weird** way.

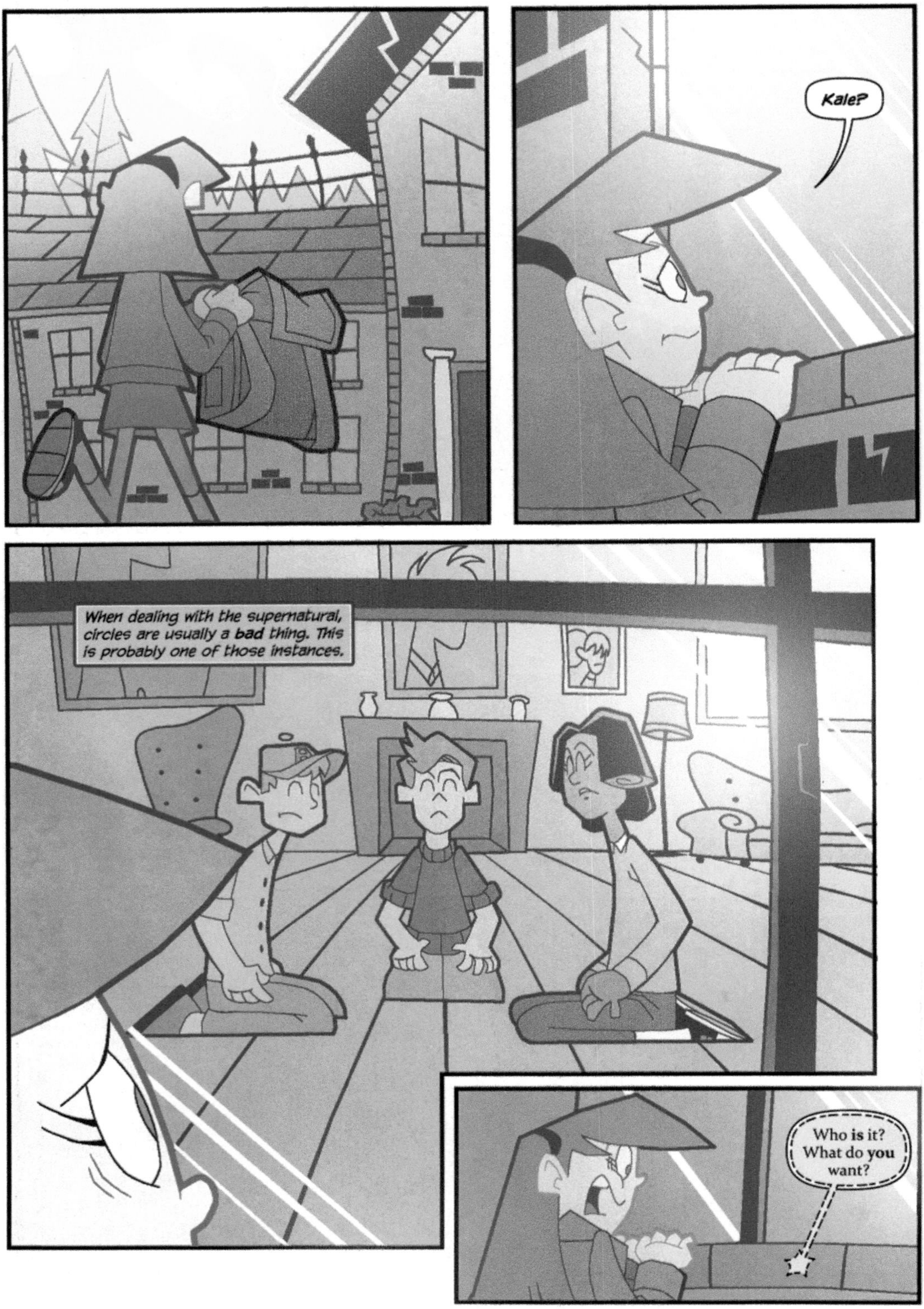
Kale?
When dealing with the supernatural, circles are usually a **bad** thing. This is probably one of those instances.
Who **is** it? What do **you** want?

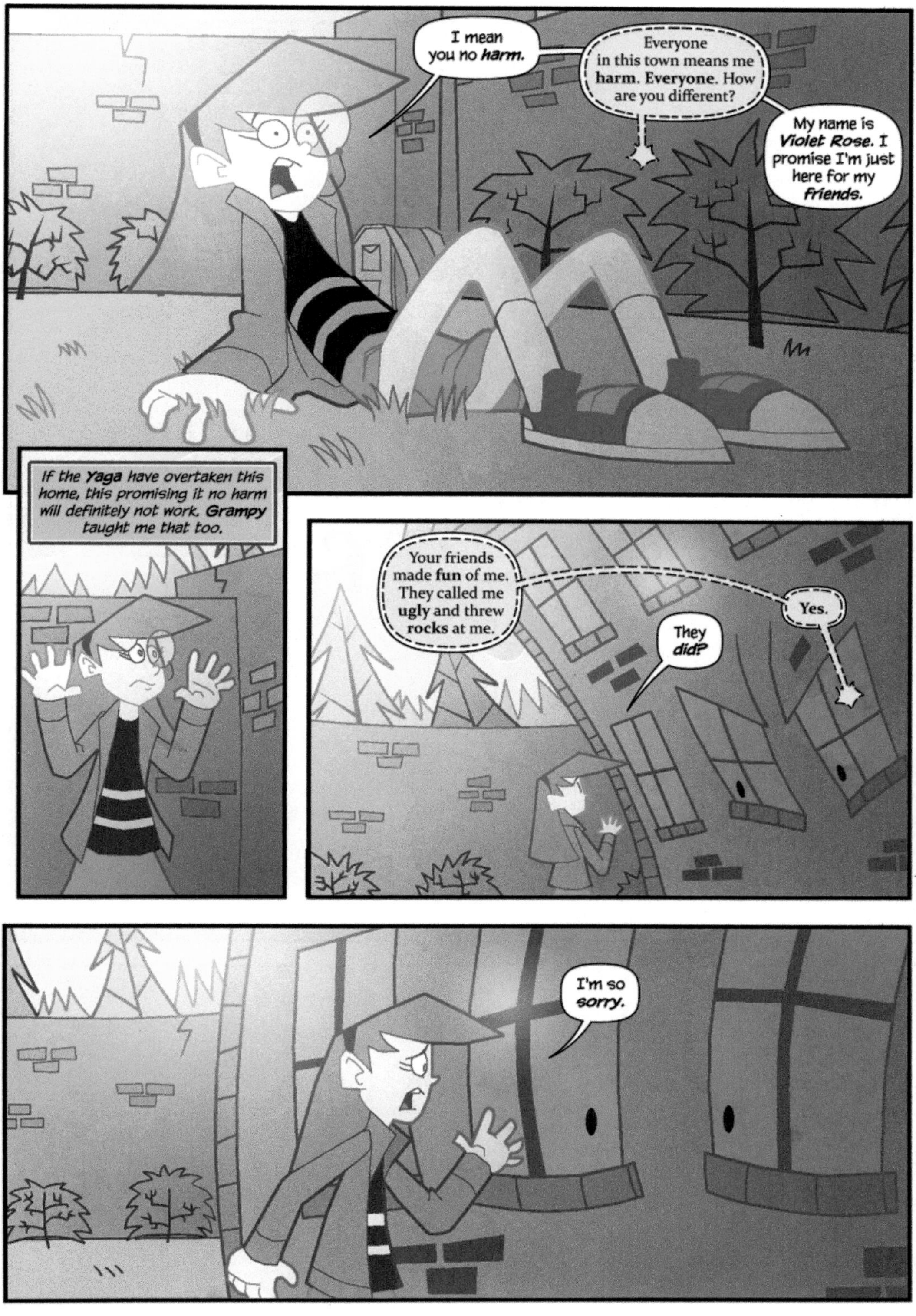
I mean you no harm.
Everyone in this town means me harm. Everyone. How are you different?
My name is Violet Rose. I promise I'm just here for my friends.
If the Yaga have overtaken this home, this promising it no harm will definitely not work. Grampy taught me that too.
Your friends made fun of me. They called me ugly and threw rocks at me.
They did?
Yes.
I'm so sorry.

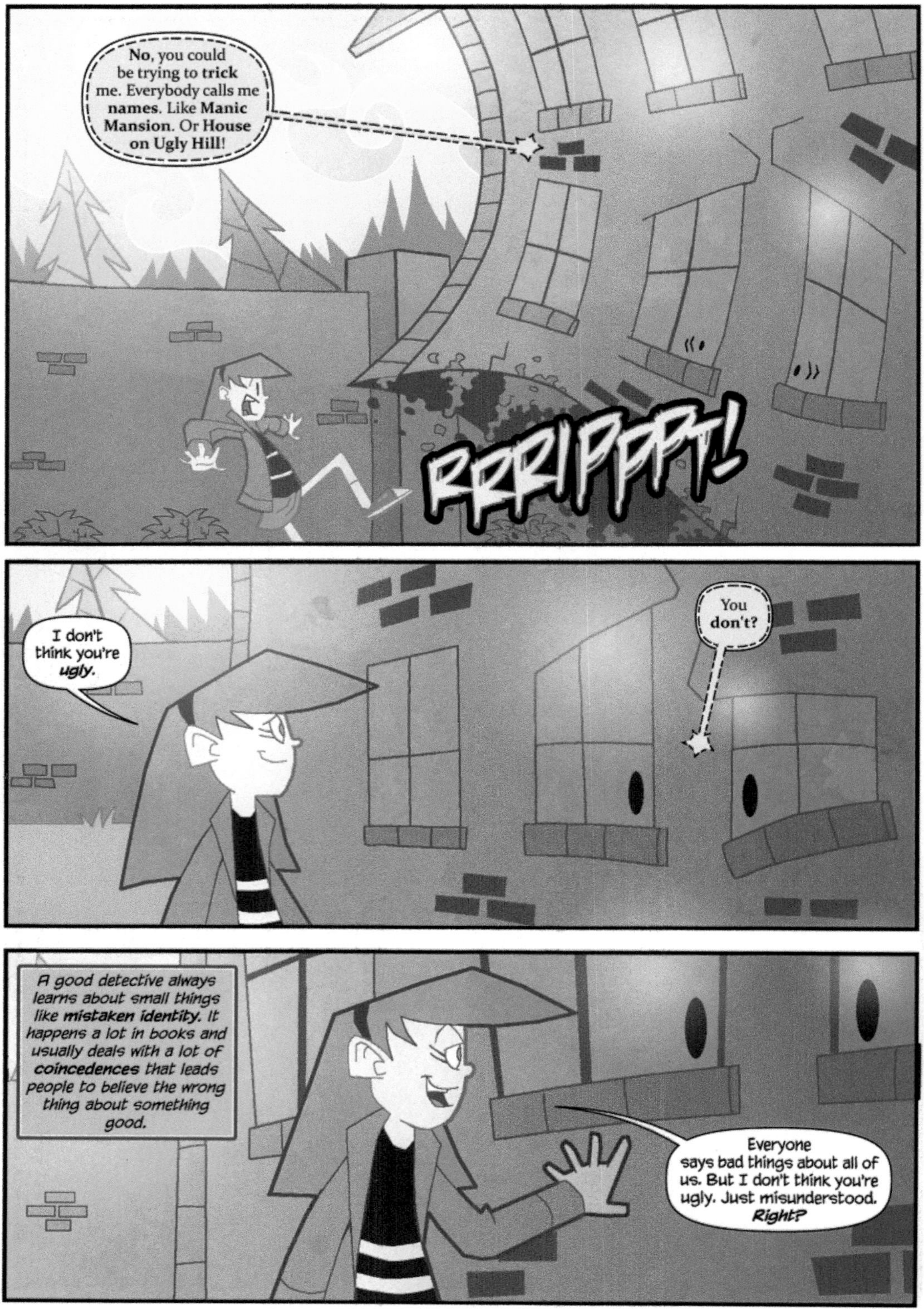
No, you could be trying to trick me. Everybody calls me names. Like Manic Mansion. Or House on Ugly Hill!
RRRIPPPT!
I don't think you're ugly.
You don't?
A good detective always learns about small things like mistaken identity. It happens a lot in books and usually deals with a lot of coincedences that leads people to believe the wrong thing about something good.
Everyone says bad things about all of us. But I don't think you're ugly. Just misunderstood. Right?

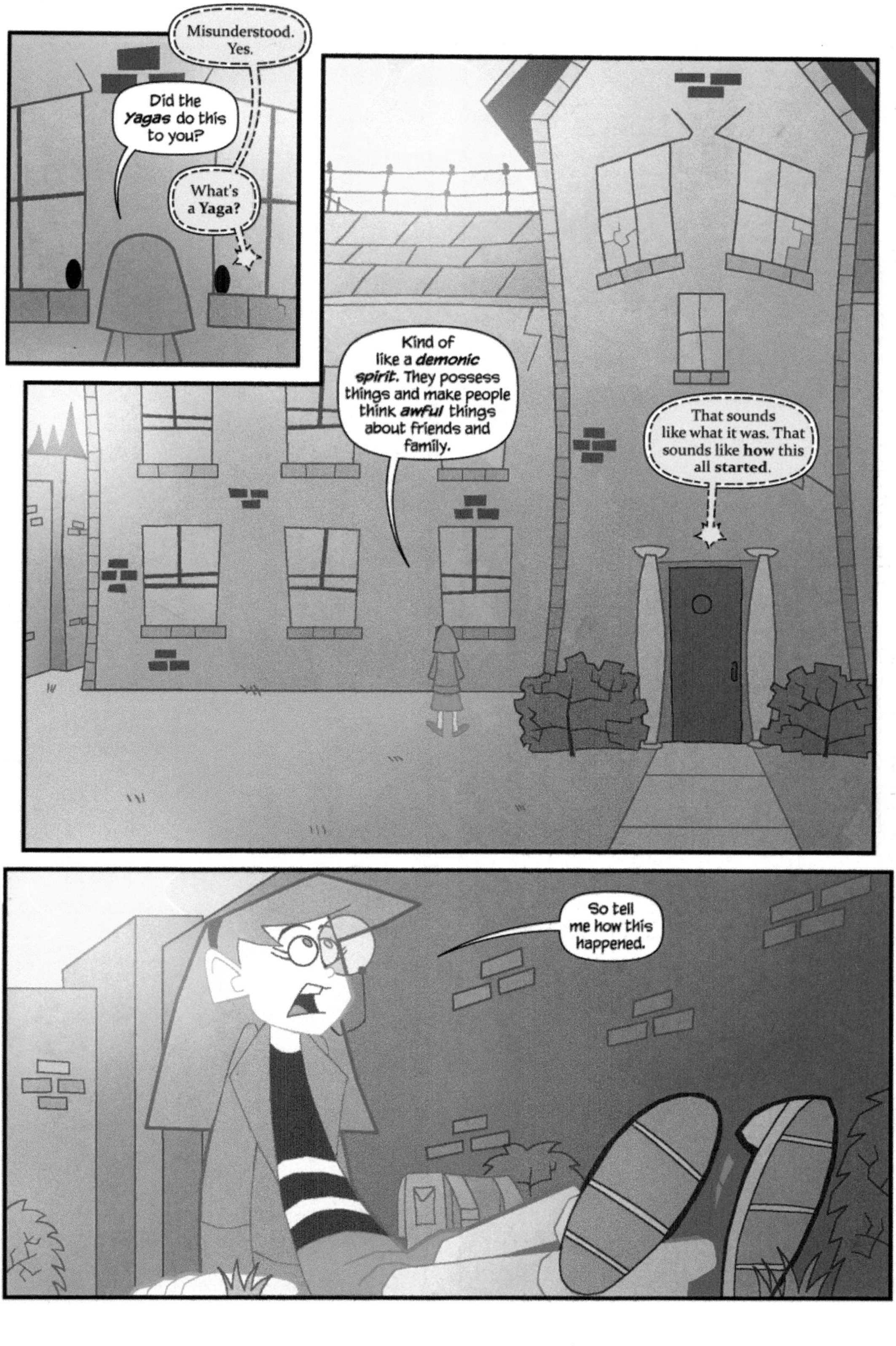
Did the *Yagas* do this to you?
Misunderstood. Yes.
What's a **Yaga?**
Kind of like a ***demonic spirit***. They possess things and make people think ***awful*** things about friends and family.
That sounds like what it was. That sounds like **how** this all **started**.
So tell me how this happened.

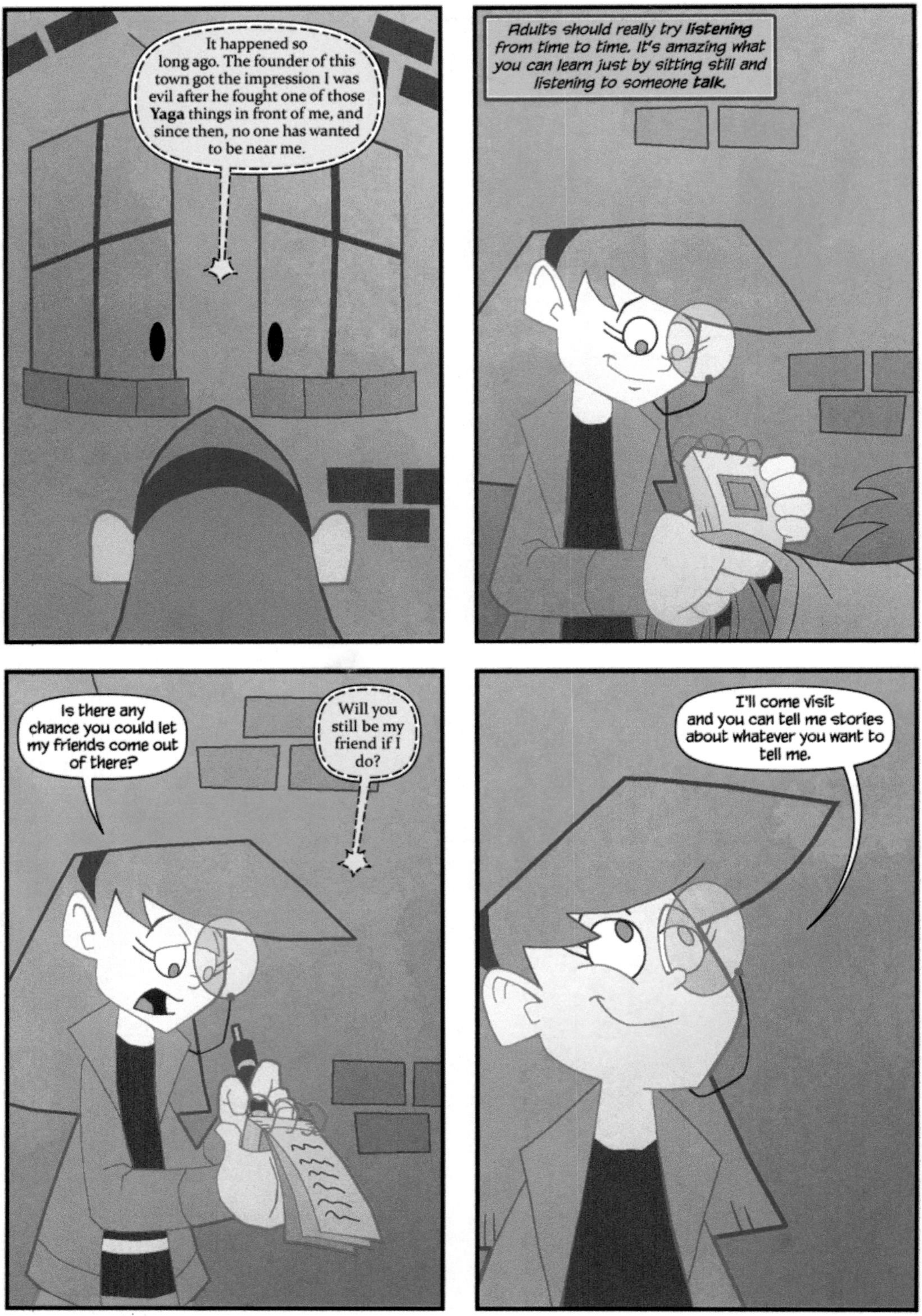
It happened so long ago. The founder of this town got the impression I was evil after he fought one of those **Yaga** things in front of me, and since then, no one has wanted to be near me.
Adults should really try **listening** from time to time. It's amazing what you can learn just by sitting still and listening to someone **talk**.
Is there any chance you could let my friends come out of there?
Will you still be my friend if I do?
I'll come visit and you can tell me stories about whatever you want to tell me.

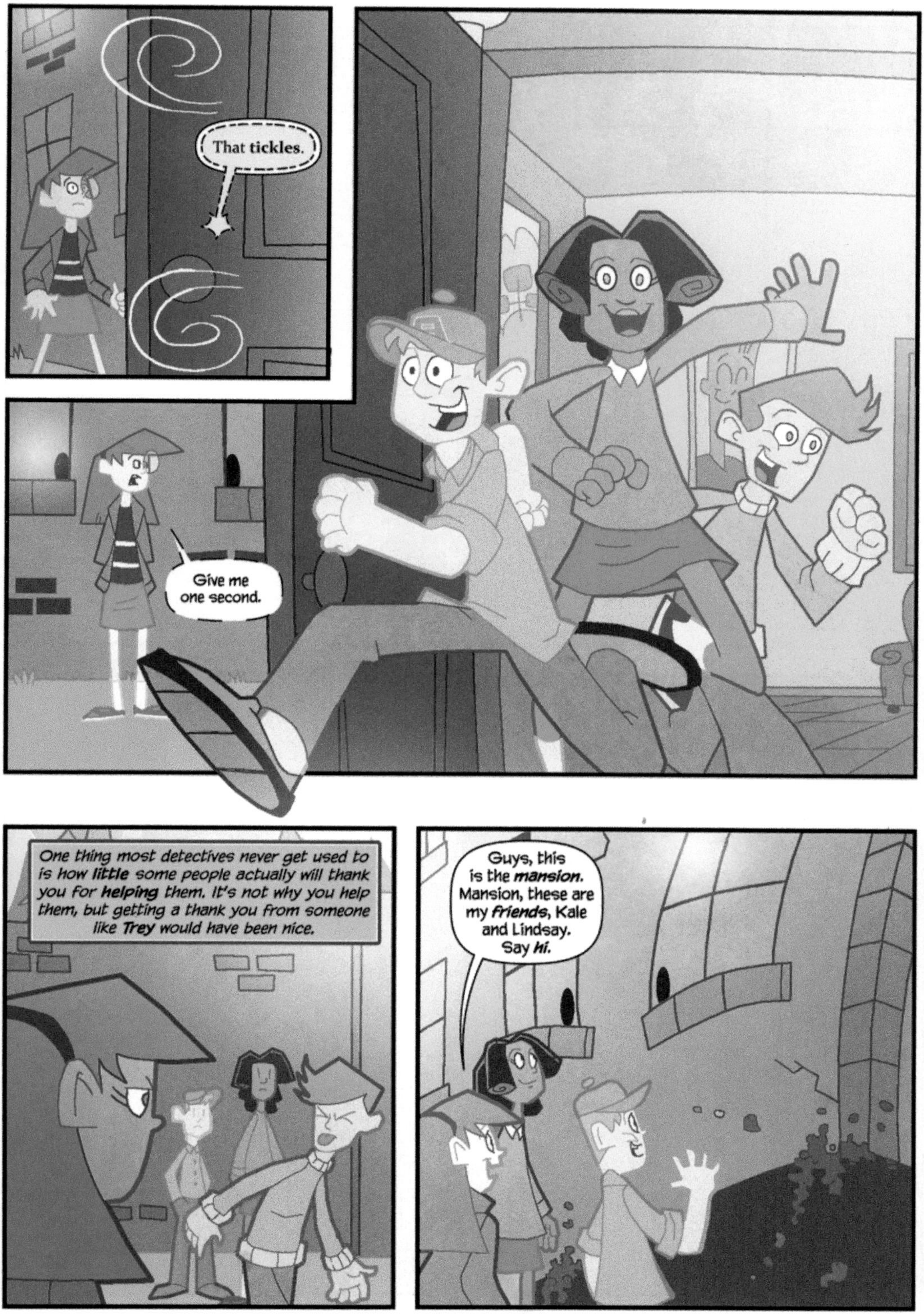
That tickles.
Give me one second.
One thing most detectives never get used to is how little some people actually will thank you for helping them. It's not why you help them, but getting a thank you from someone like Trey would have been nice.
Guys, this is the mansion. Mansion, these are my friends, Kale and Lindsay. Say hi.

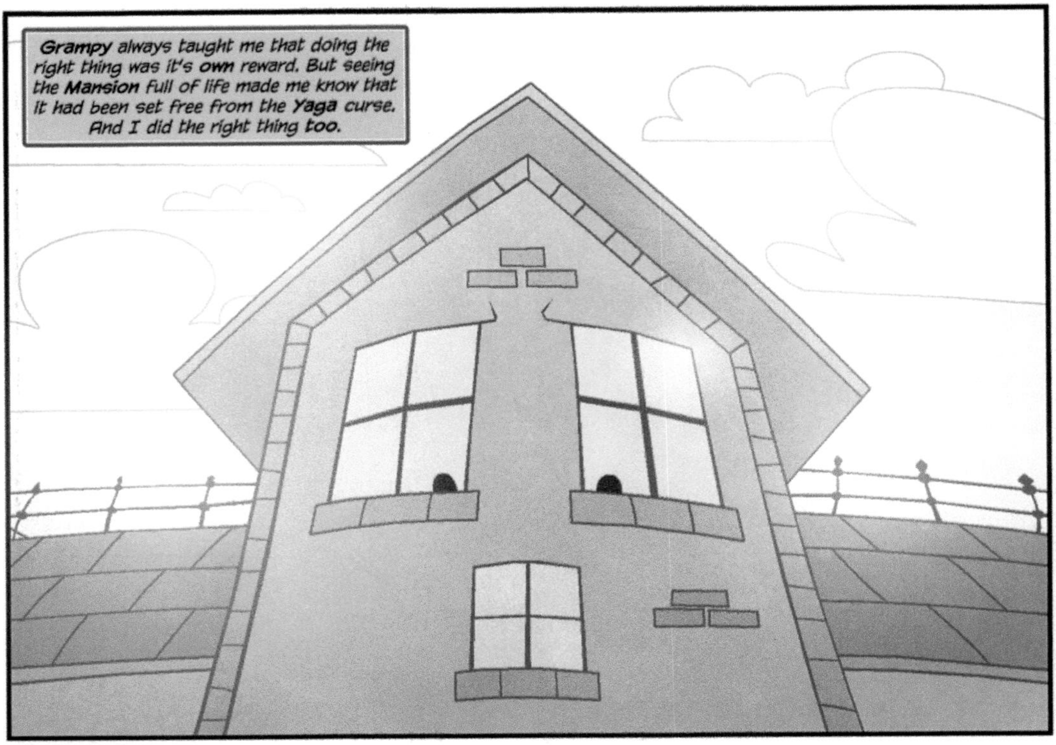
Grampy always taught me that doing the right thing was it's own reward. But seeing the Mansion full of life made me know that it had been set free from the Yaga curse. And I did the right thing too.

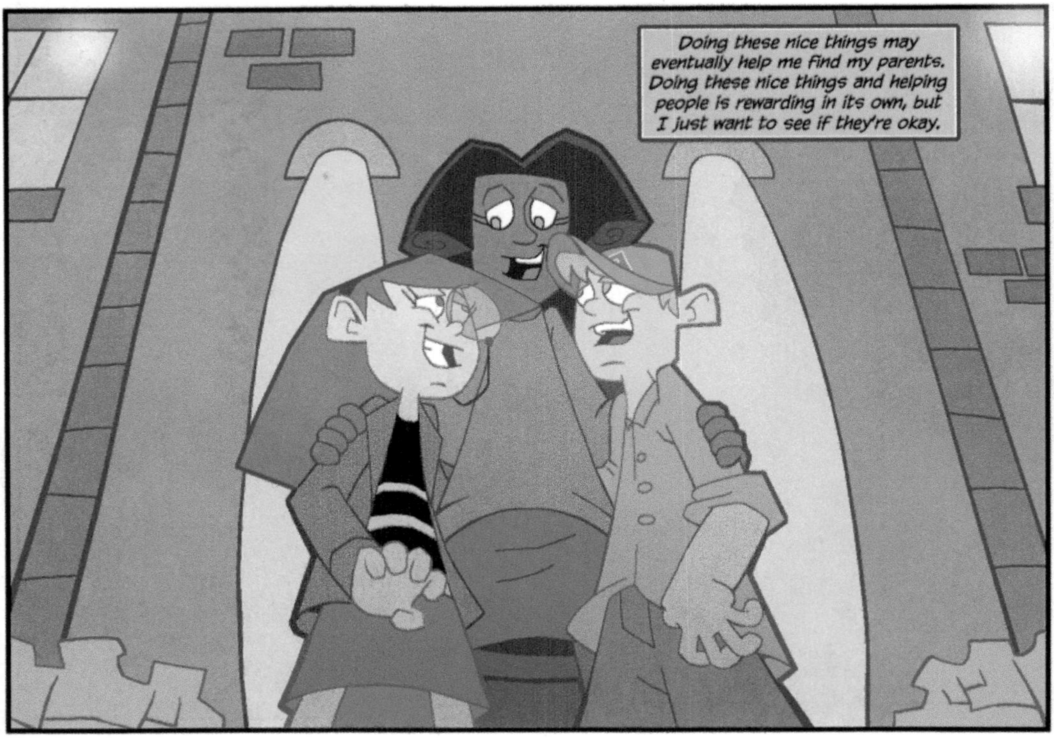
Doing these nice things may eventually help me find my parents. Doing these nice things and helping people is rewarding in its own, but I just want to see if they're okay.

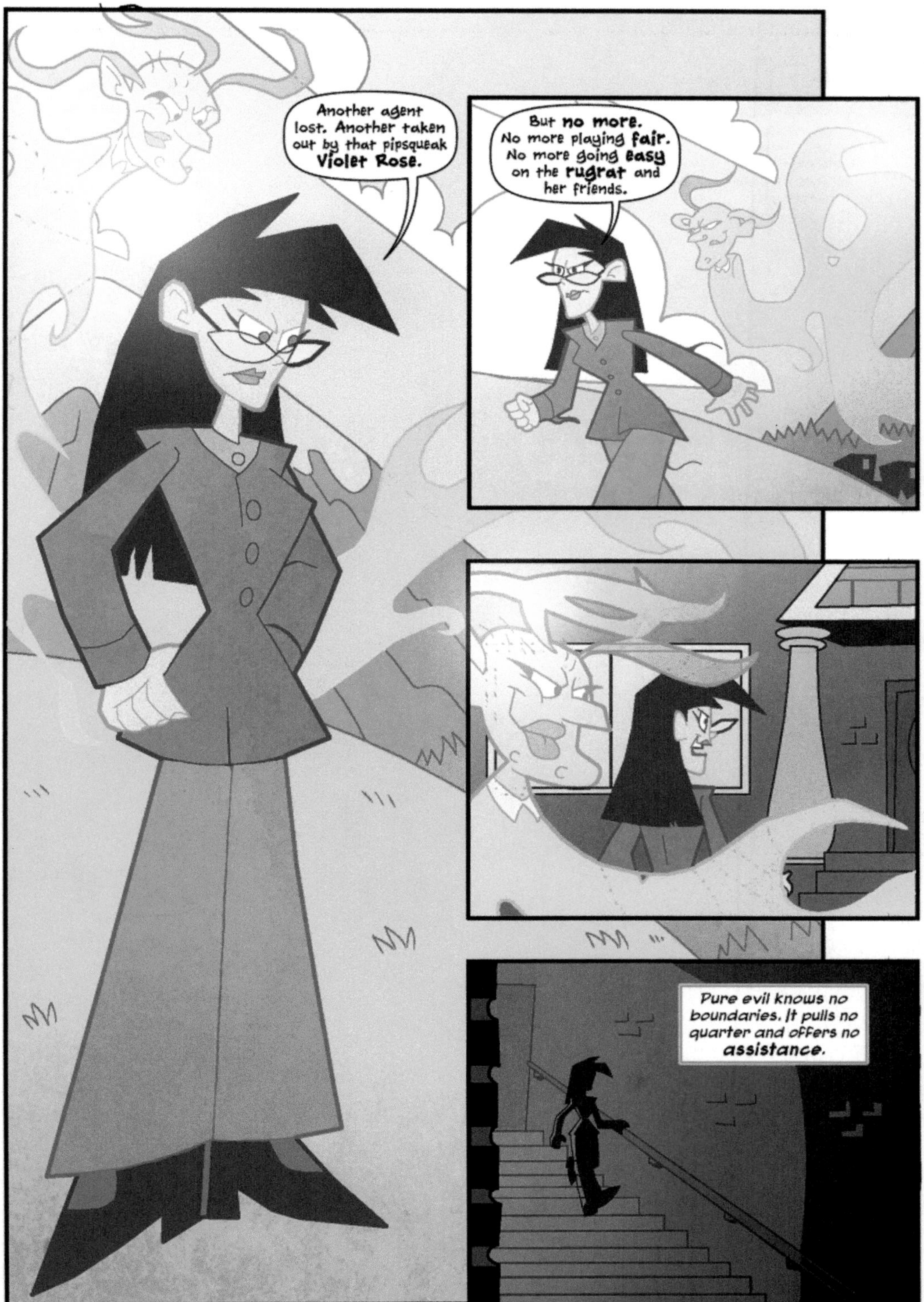
Another agent lost. Another taken out by that pipsqueak Violet Rose.
But no more. No more playing fair. No more going easy on the rugrat and her friends.
Pure evil knows no boundaries. It pulls no quarter and offers no assistance.

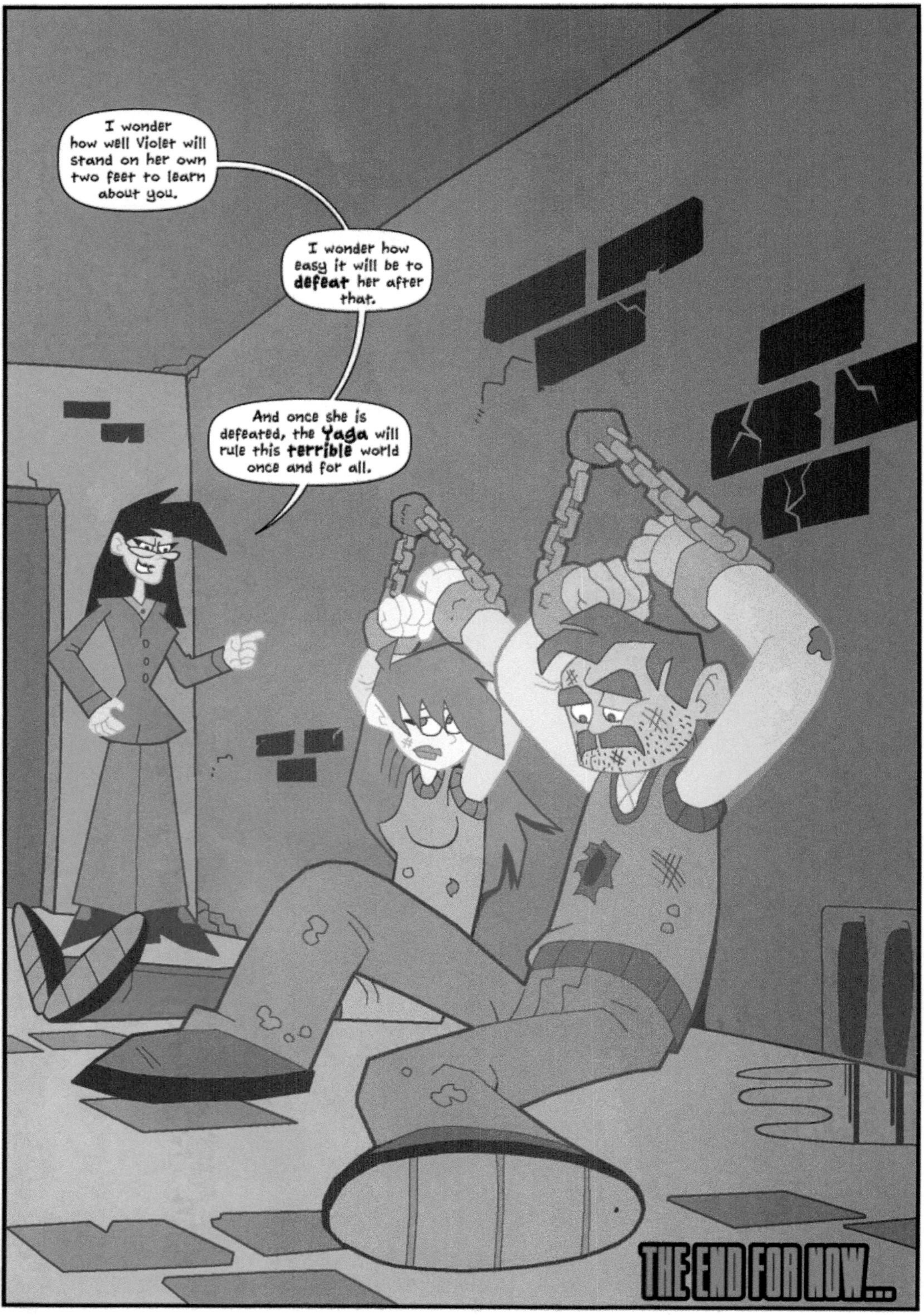
I wonder how well Violet will stand on her own two feet to learn about you.
I wonder how easy it will be to **defeat** her after that.
And once she is defeated, the **Yaga** will rule this **terrible** world once and for all.
THE END FOR NOW...

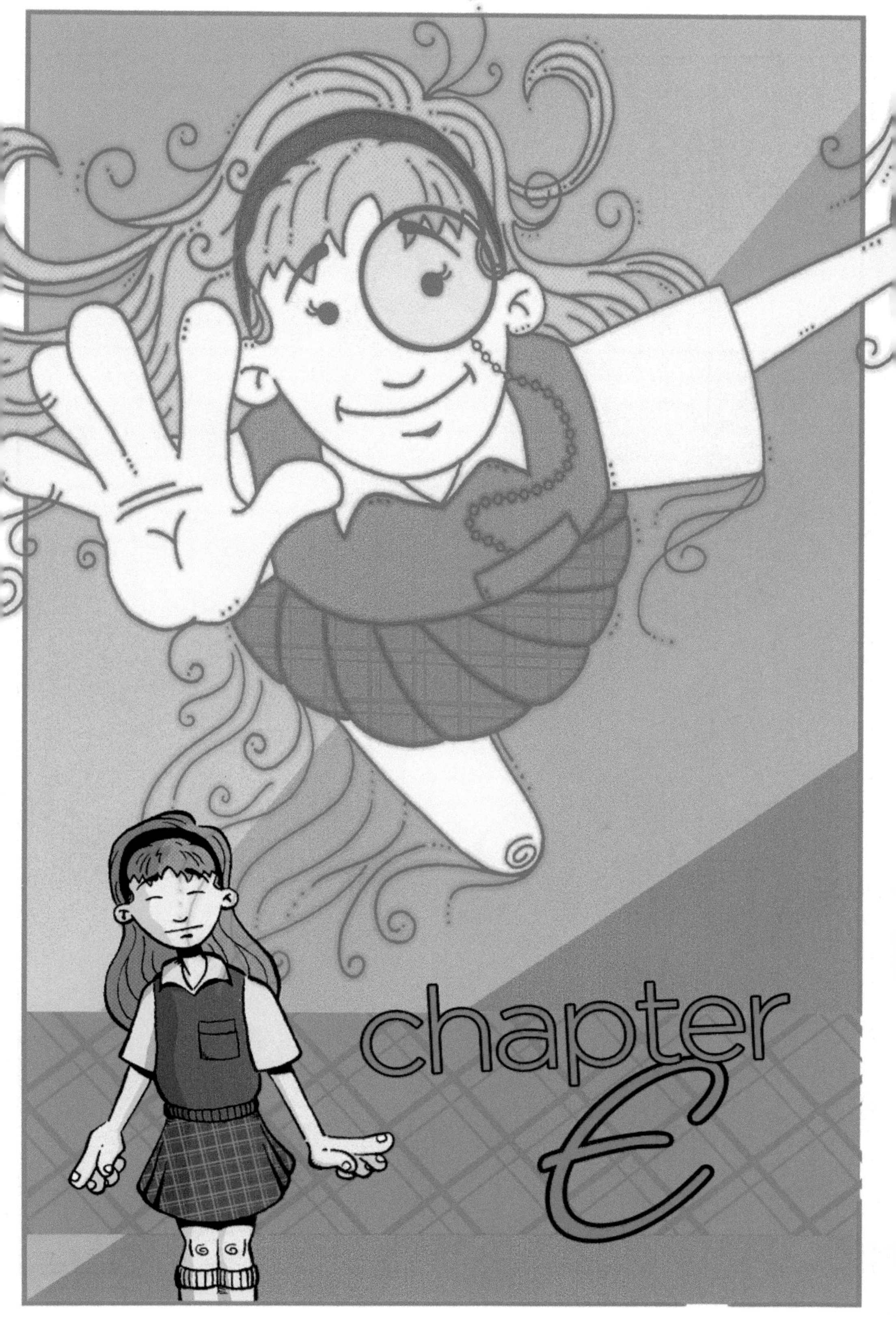
chapter
E

BLUE WATER presents

VIOLET ROSE

story by EMMA DAVIS
art by MIKEOART.COM
assists from ERIN O'SULLIVAN

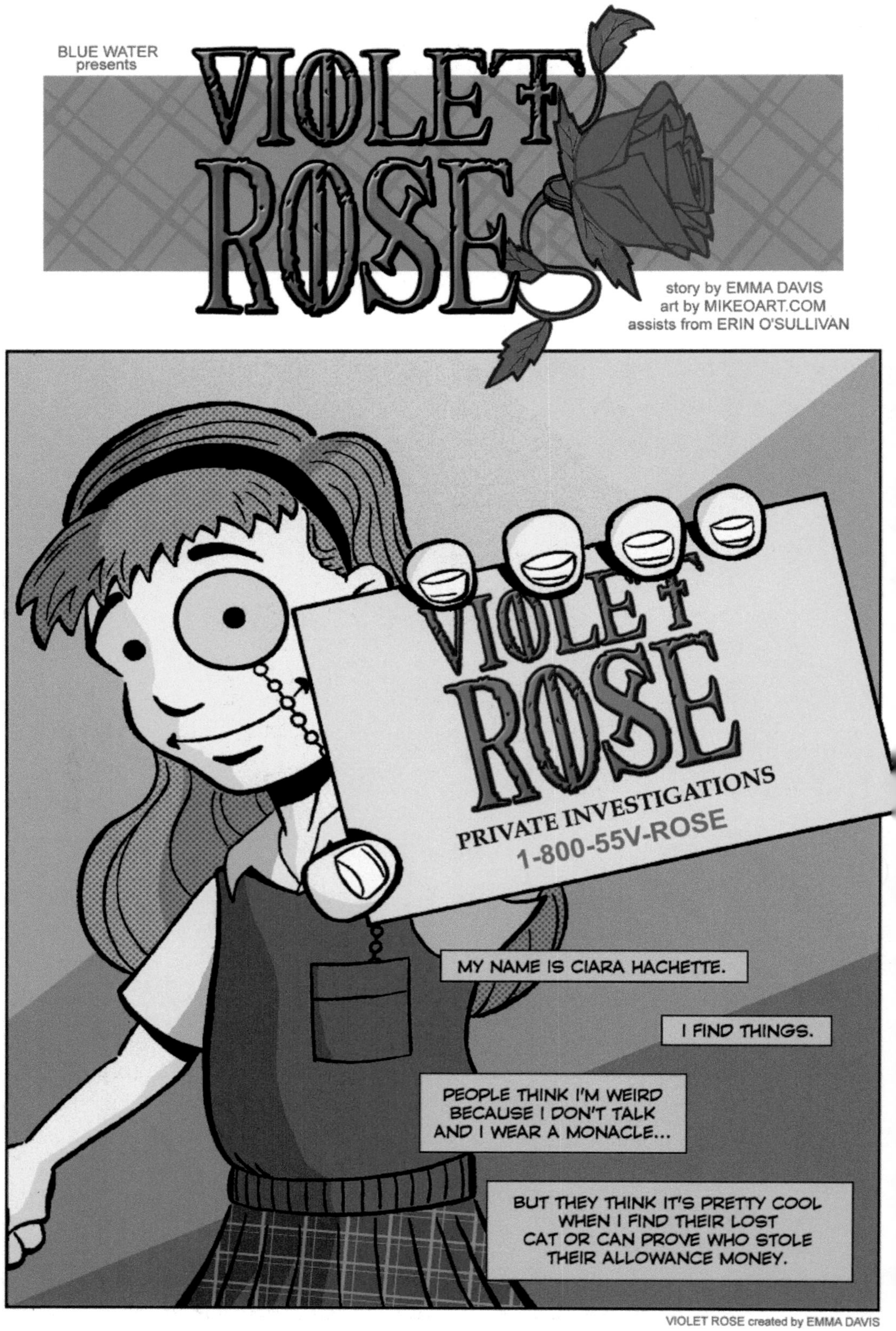
VIOLET ROSE
PRIVATE INVESTIGATIONS
1-800-55V-ROSE
MY NAME IS CIARA HACHETTE.
I FIND THINGS.
PEOPLE THINK I'M WEIRD BECAUSE I DON'T TALK AND I WEAR A MONACLE...
BUT THEY THINK IT'S PRETTY COOL WHEN I FIND THEIR LOST CAT OR CAN PROVE WHO STOLE THEIR ALLOWANCE MONEY.

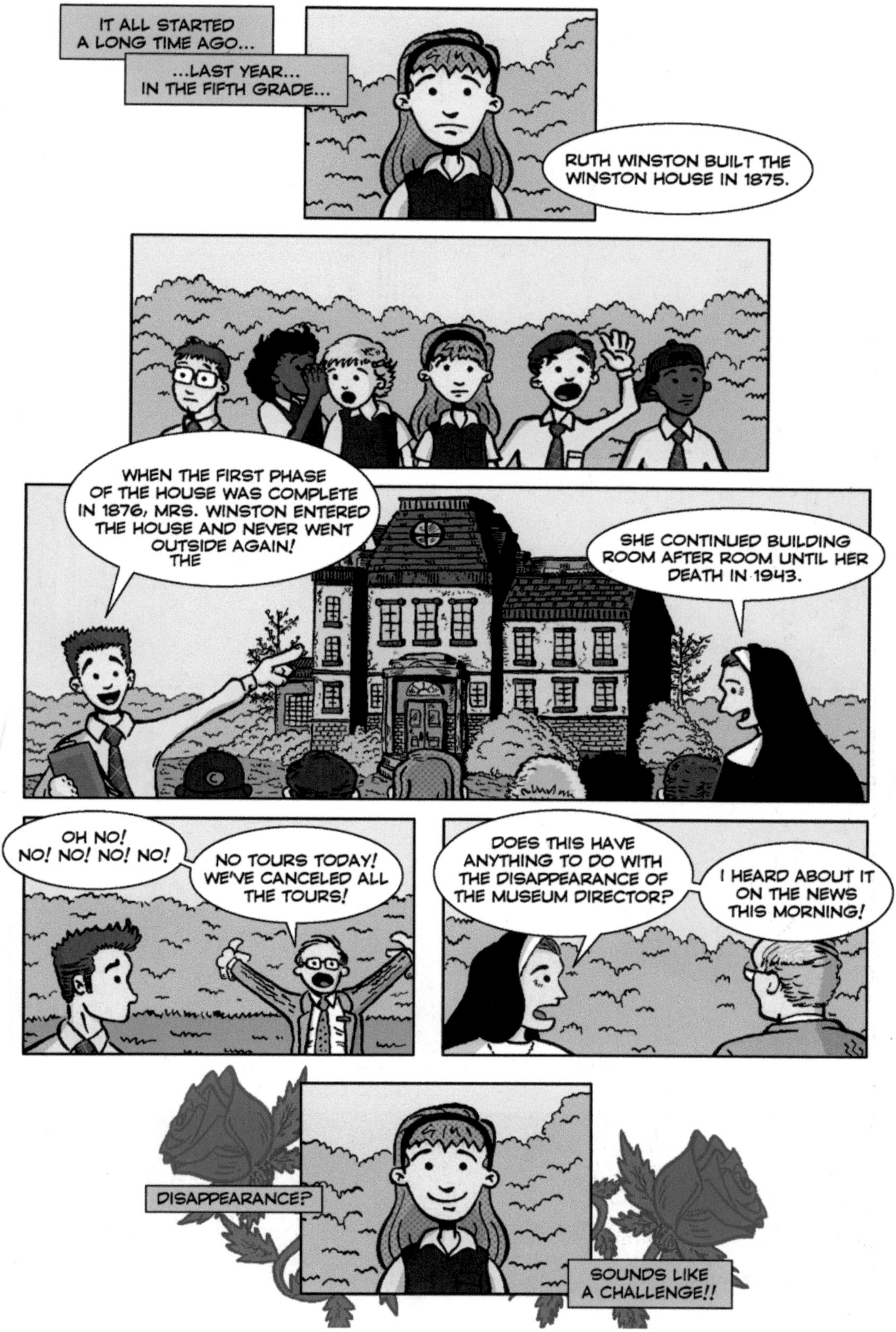
IT ALL STARTED A LONG TIME AGO...
...LAST YEAR... IN THE FIFTH GRADE...
RUTH WINSTON BUILT THE WINSTON HOUSE IN 1875.
WHEN THE FIRST PHASE OF THE HOUSE WAS COMPLETE IN 1876, MRS. WINSTON ENTERED THE HOUSE AND NEVER WENT OUTSIDE AGAIN! THE
SHE CONTINUED BUILDING ROOM AFTER ROOM UNTIL HER DEATH IN 1943.
OH NO! NO! NO! NO! NO!
NO TOURS TODAY! WE'VE CANCELED ALL THE TOURS!
DOES THIS HAVE ANYTHING TO DO WITH THE DISAPPEARANCE OF THE MUSEUM DIRECTOR?
I HEARD ABOUT IT ON THE NEWS THIS MORNING!
DISAPPEARANCE?
SOUNDS LIKE A CHALLENGE!!

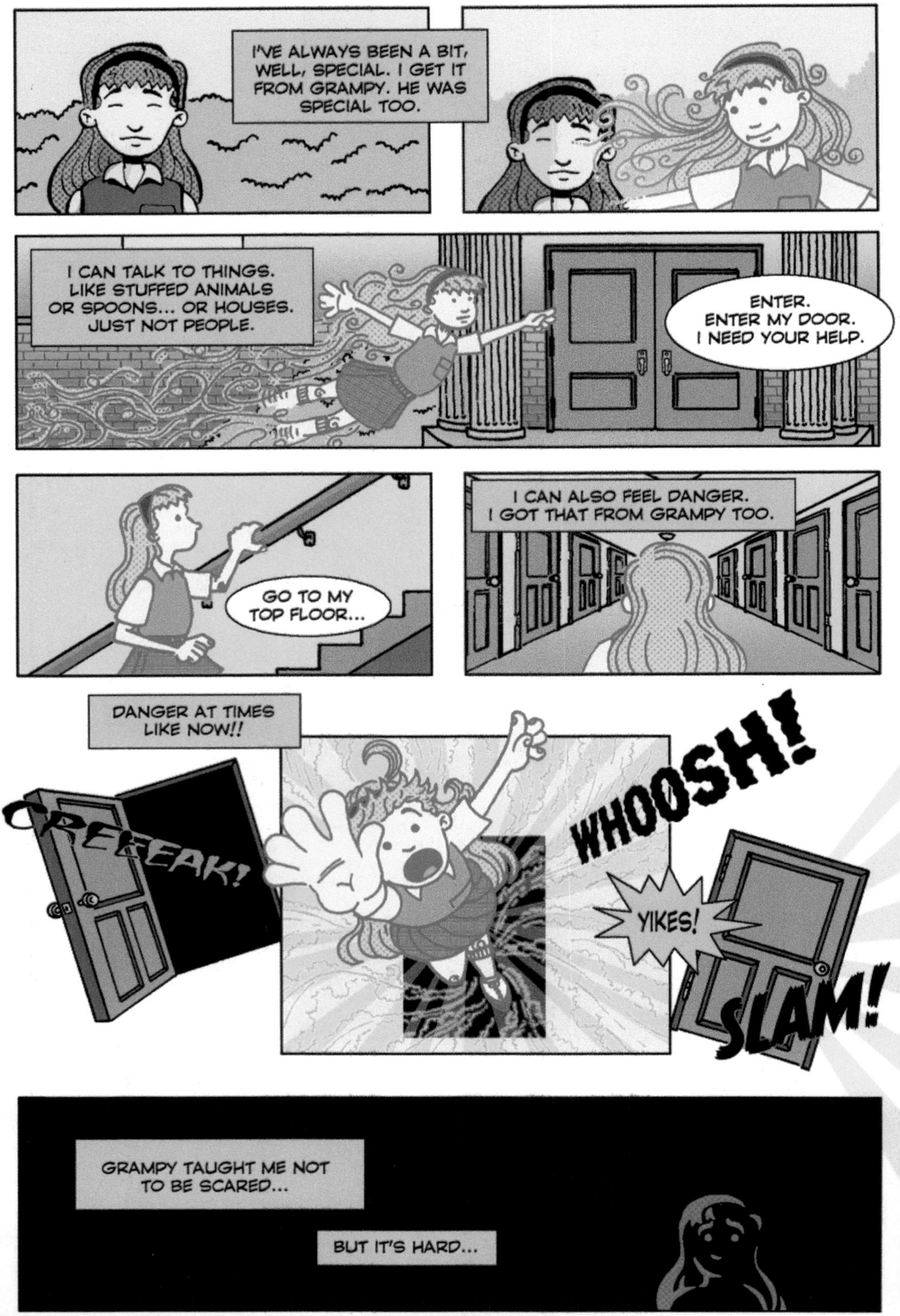

I'VE ALWAYS BEEN A BIT, WELL, SPECIAL. I GET IT FROM GRAMPY. HE WAS SPECIAL TOO.
I CAN TALK TO THINGS. LIKE STUFFED ANIMALS OR SPOONS... OR HOUSES. JUST NOT PEOPLE.
ENTER. ENTER MY DOOR. I NEED YOUR HELP.
GO TO MY TOP FLOOR...
I CAN ALSO FEEL DANGER. I GOT THAT FROM GRAMPY TOO.
DANGER AT TIMES LIKE NOW!!
CREEEAK!
WHOOSH!
YIKES!
SLAM!
GRAMPY TAUGHT ME NOT TO BE SCARED...
BUT IT'S HARD...

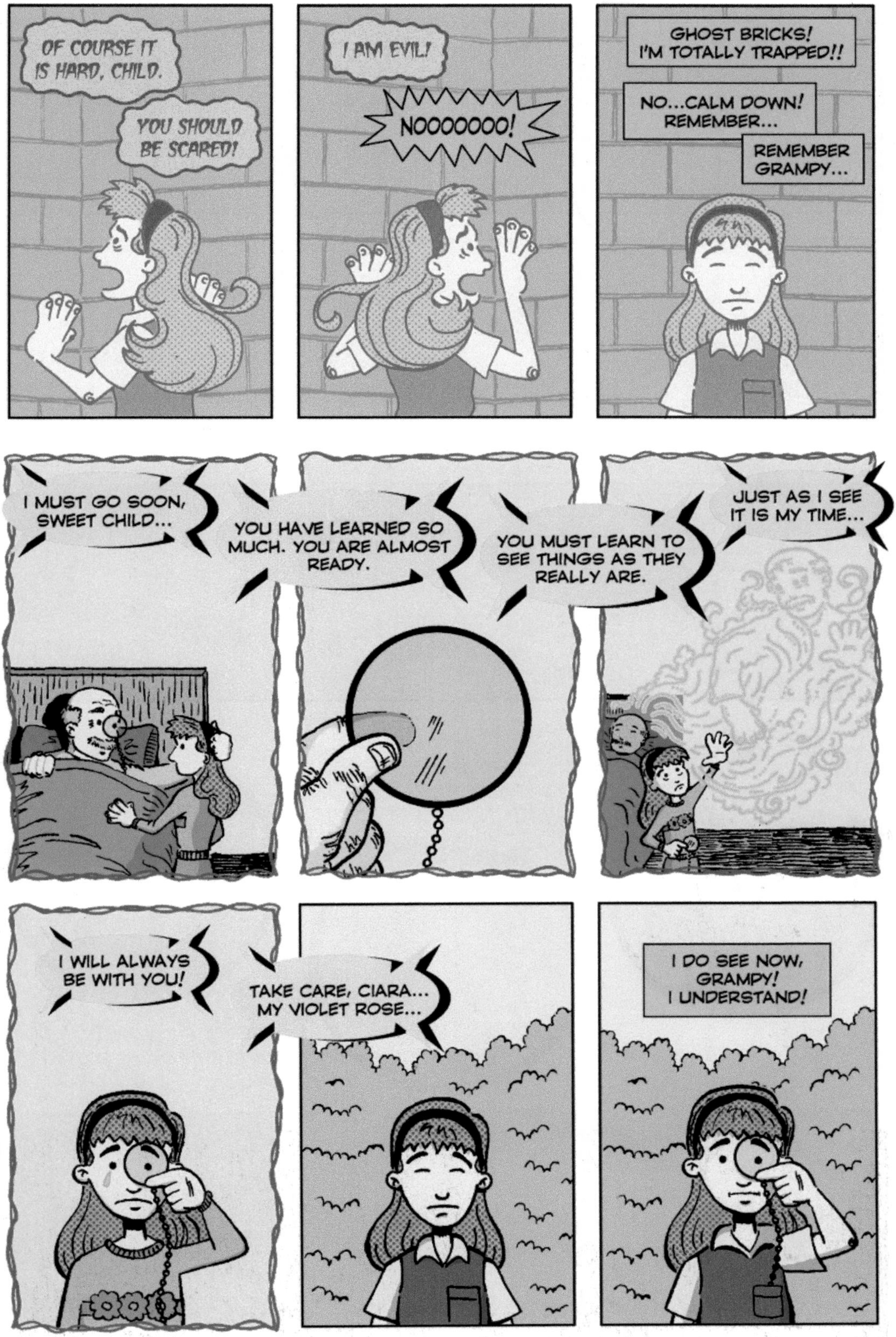
OF COURSE IT IS HARD, CHILD.
YOU SHOULD BE SCARED!
I AM EVIL!
NOOOOOOO!
GHOST BRICKS! I'M TOTALLY TRAPPED!!
NO...CALM DOWN! REMEMBER...
REMEMBER GRAMPY...
I MUST GO SOON, SWEET CHILD...
YOU HAVE LEARNED SO MUCH. YOU ARE ALMOST READY.
YOU MUST LEARN TO SEE THINGS AS THEY REALLY ARE.
JUST AS I SEE IT IS MY TIME...
I WILL ALWAYS BE WITH YOU!
TAKE CARE, CIARA... MY VIOLET ROSE...
I DO SEE NOW, GRAMPY! I UNDERSTAND!

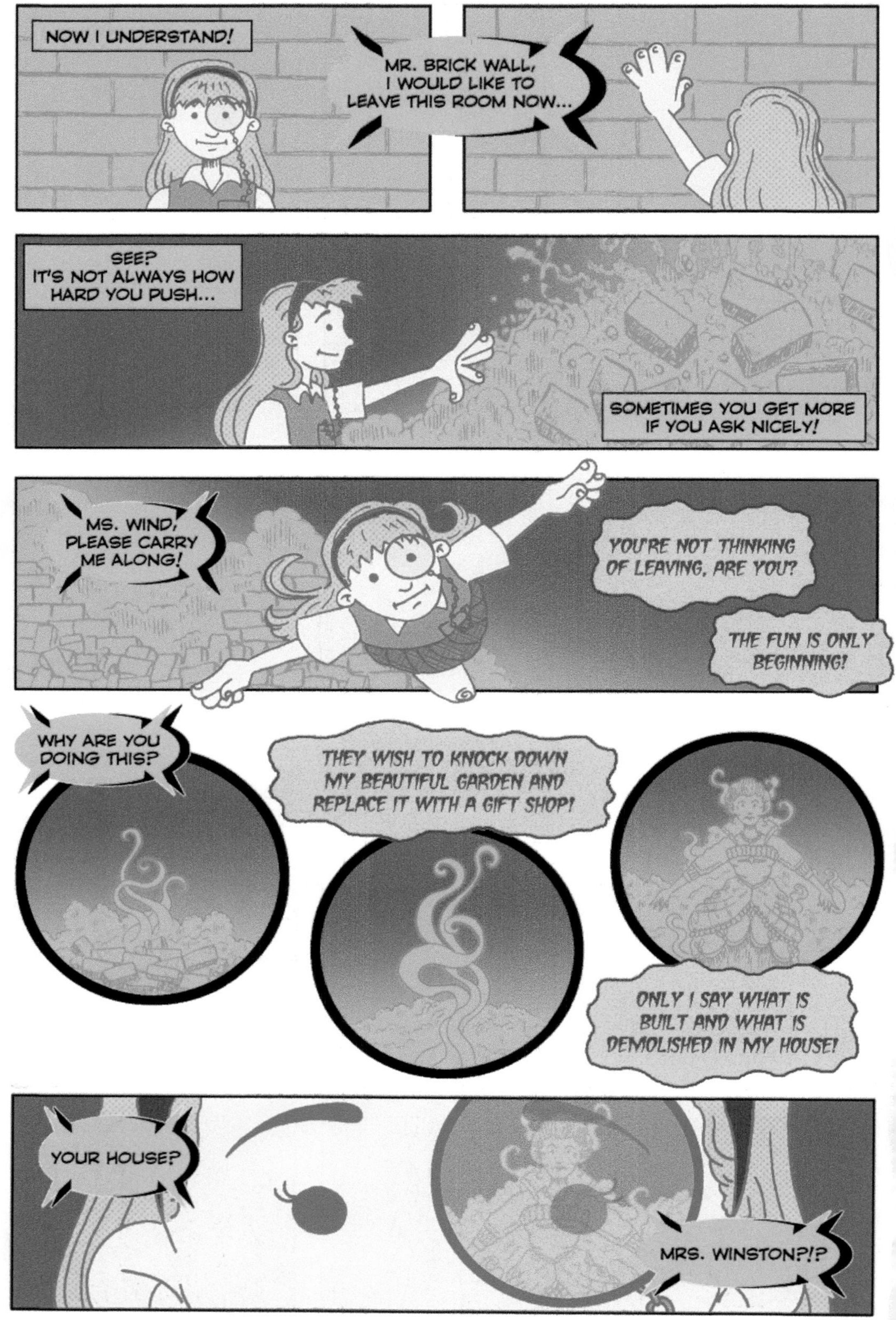
NOW I UNDERSTAND!
MR. BRICK WALL, I WOULD LIKE TO LEAVE THIS ROOM NOW...
SEE? IT'S NOT ALWAYS HOW HARD YOU PUSH...
SOMETIMES YOU GET MORE IF YOU ASK NICELY!
MS. WIND, PLEASE CARRY ME ALONG!
YOU'RE NOT THINKING OF LEAVING, ARE YOU?
THE FUN IS ONLY BEGINNING!
WHY ARE YOU DOING THIS?
THEY WISH TO KNOCK DOWN MY BEAUTIFUL GARDEN AND REPLACE IT WITH A GIFT SHOP!
ONLY I SAY WHAT IS BUILT AND WHAT IS DEMOLISHED IN MY HOUSE!
YOUR HOUSE?
MRS. WINSTON?!?

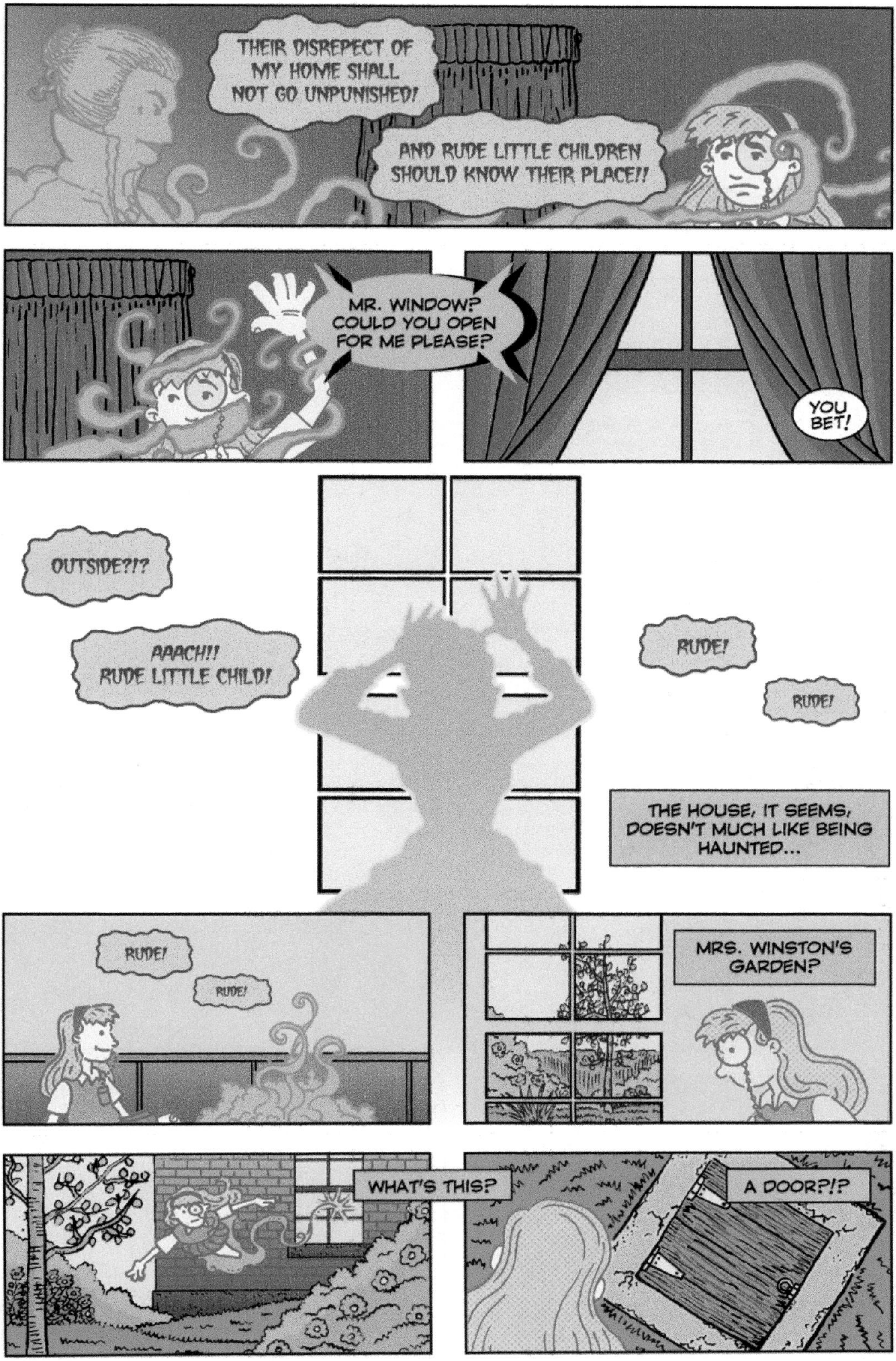
THEIR DISREPECT OF MY HOME SHALL NOT GO UNPUNISHED!
AND RUDE LITTLE CHILDREN SHOULD KNOW THEIR PLACE!!
MR. WINDOW? COULD YOU OPEN FOR ME PLEASE?
YOU BET!
OUTSIDE?!?
AAACH!! RUDE LITTLE CHILD!
RUDE!
RUDE!
THE HOUSE, IT SEEMS, DOESN'T MUCH LIKE BEING HAUNTED...
RUDE!
RUDE!
MRS. WINSTON'S GARDEN?
WHAT'S THIS?
A DOOR?!?

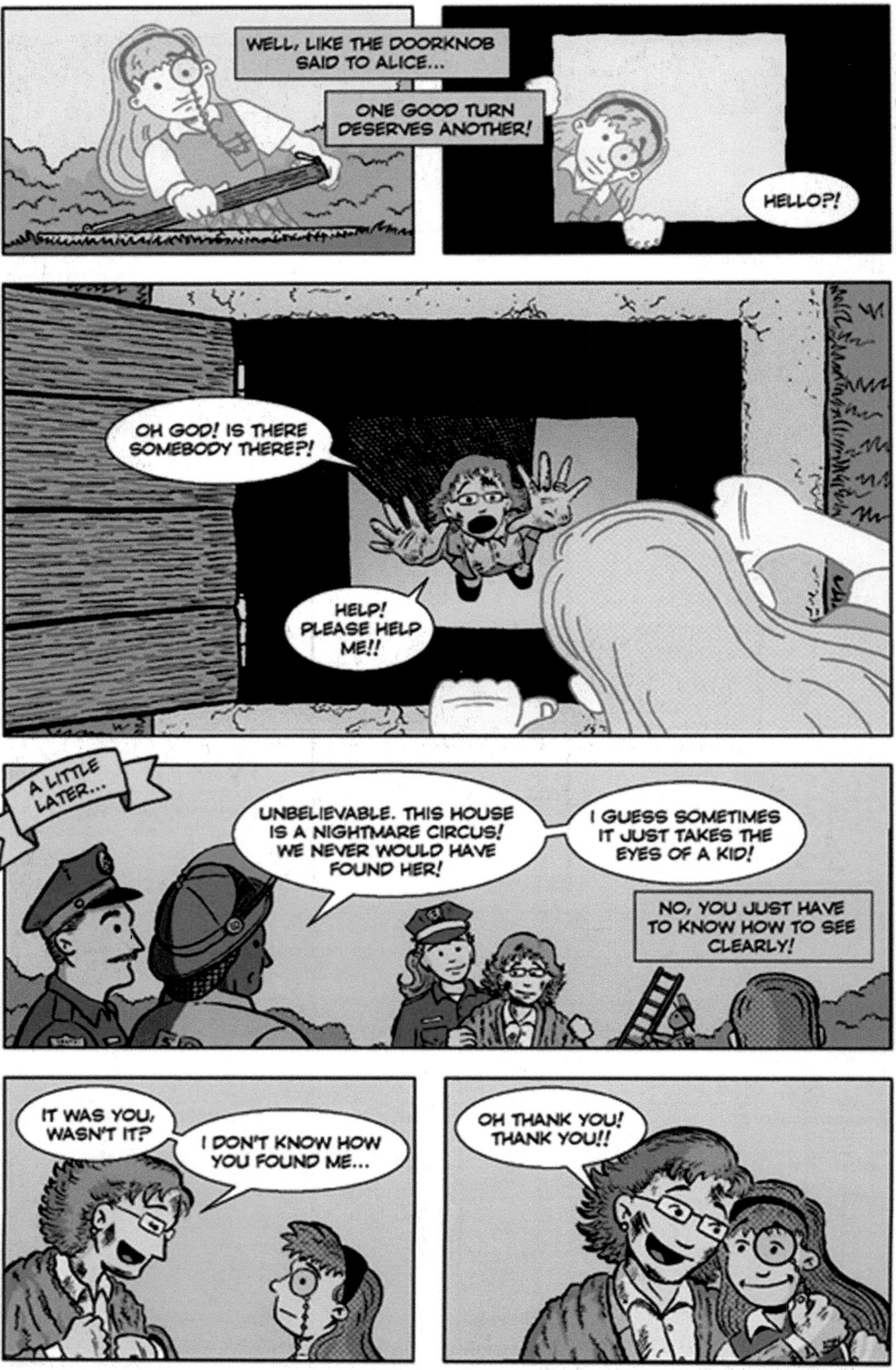
WELL, LIKE THE DOORKNOB SAID TO ALICE...
ONE GOOD TURN DESERVES ANOTHER!
HELLO?!
OH GOD! IS THERE SOMEBODY THERE?!
HELP! PLEASE HELP ME!!
A LITTLE LATER...
UNBELIEVABLE. THIS HOUSE IS A NIGHTMARE CIRCUS! WE NEVER WOULD HAVE FOUND HER!
I GUESS SOMETIMES IT JUST TAKES THE EYES OF A KID!
NO, YOU JUST HAVE TO KNOW HOW TO SEE CLEARLY!
IT WAS YOU, WASN'T IT?
I DON'T KNOW HOW YOU FOUND ME...
OH THANK YOU! THANK YOU!!

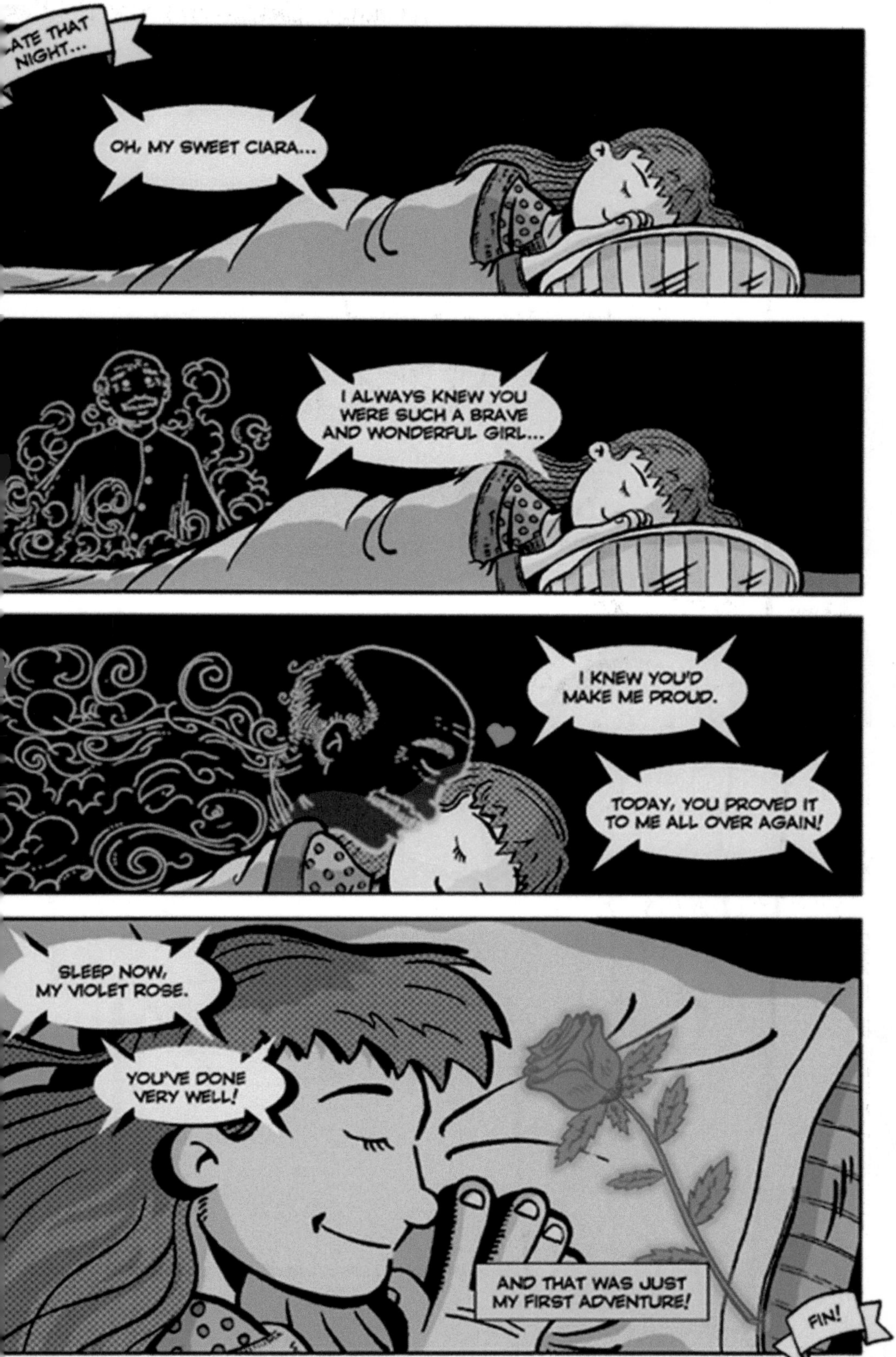

ATE THAT NIGHT...
OH, MY SWEET CIARA...
I ALWAYS KNEW YOU WERE SUCH A BRAVE AND WONDERFUL GIRL...
I KNEW YOU'D MAKE ME PROUD.
TODAY, YOU PROVED IT TO ME ALL OVER AGAIN!
SLEEP NOW, MY VIOLET ROSE.
YOU'VE DONE VERY WELL!
AND THAT WAS JUST MY FIRST ADVENTURE!
FIN!

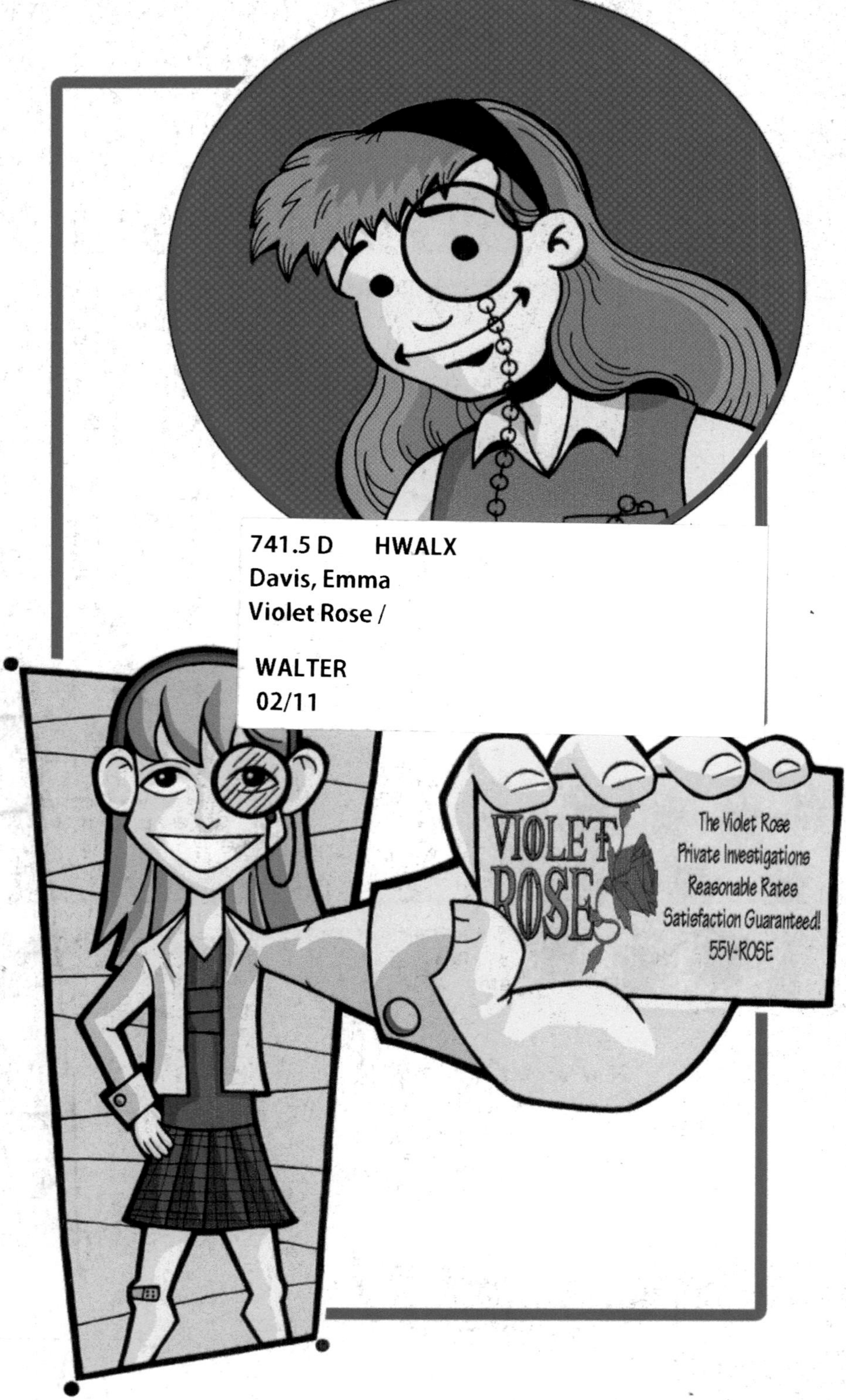
VIOLET ROSE
The Violet Rose
Private Investigations
Reasonable Rates
Satisfaction Guaranteed!
55V-ROSE